HER ONLY HOPE

THE FRANKIE BLACK FILES

J.D. WESTON

HER ONLY HOPE

To uncover the truth, she must bury her past...

PART I

CHAPTER ONE

"When the door slams, your world is damned."

The voice was whispered, haunting, and teasing.

"Who's there?"

Searching the darkness through the coarse fabric of the woven sack that had been pulled across her face, Hope Gilmour found no clue. The whispered voice of a child? A memory? Or the tarnished fruits of the dark, damp hole teasing Hope's imagination with its cruel tongue?

"Who's there?"

Her world was black, far darker than the darkest night, and the silence that ensued was the quietest Hope had ever known. The first tear rolled across her skin cutting a channel through the grime and angering the resilience she had worked so hard to build. Experience had taught her that the tears that broke her wall down would flood the gates of her mind.

She pushed back, fighting the urge to release the barriers that held the tears at bay.

The sweet songs of the birds that Hope had long enjoyed sang somewhere far away, bringing joy to some other place, where the light dared to spread its golden beams. She wondered if she would ever hear their song again with clarity, and not the muted, muffled tease that tickled her mind now with sounds of what could be.

"I asked who's there. I won't ask again."

But again, the sweet, feminine tone that had taunted her only moments before teased her now with silence, and she doubted if the words had ever been spoken.

Outside the hole, only the boughs of trees creaked, and the rustle of dead leaves added a layer of soft percussion with every breath of the wind. The sounds quelled the distant bird song as if they grew where two worlds met. One of natural beauty, light, and all things wild. The other of darkness, shadows, and the rotting smell of decay.

Footsteps approached and raised the tempo of Hope's heart bringing rhythm to the ensemble.

"With the falling sun, the footsteps come."

That voice.

"Who's there?" Hope hissed in the darkness. "Who are you?"

But no reply came. Only the steady drip of water into a nearby shallow pool. An image of her prison appeared in Hope's mind. Rock walls smoothed by years of moisture filtered through the earth leaving a damp sheen across the mildewed limestone. A sparse bed of leaves spread across the ground, blowing this way and that only when the door opened and a lick of wind found the corners of darkness that light dared not touch.

A heavy chain rattled on wood and a cool breeze scattered leaves across Hope's bare feet. The image in her mind grew and although the darkness deprived her of sight, with her eyes closed, she could see it all with such clarity.

Heavy breaths of a man. The soft touch of wood on stone as the door closed, ceasing the breeze and returning the hole to darkness. A shuffle of boots on the dry ground and the scrape of material like a waxed jacket.

Then silence.

Even the boughs of the trees outside ceased to creak, and the whistle of the wind faded away as if both worlds held their breath.

An anxious shiver ran through Hope's body from her bound hands held high above her head, across her naked flesh, and to her fingers and toes. A whimper escaped her lips, loud in the silence, and the image of her prison faded away as she sought to find his form in the grey beyond her mask.

From nowhere, a cold hand found her naked stomach. Her soft, young flesh was sensitive to his sharp, calloused skin and long fingernails that pressed as if feeling for something. It was as if, with just a little more pressure, the fingers would burst through her skin, reach inside, and tear her apart. But then the pressure subsided, leaving only tender fingertips that caressed the outline of her form and pressed against her beating heart.

An exhale, too long and slow to be anything but desire came from the man. The stench of his foul, stale breath clung to the material of her hood. But no matter how hard Hope tried to block his touch from her mind, her imagination teased her with wonders and possibilities. Her body tensed as if she might break free of her chains and overpower him. The fantastical scene played out in her mind. She would fight back at the earliest chance. He would have to untie her soon, and then she would take him by surprise. She would show him that she wasn't just an ordinary girl who might cry and let him have his way. Hope was stronger than most.

But her musings were futile.

The sour breath faded, leaving her to breathe the stale air of the hole. She waited for the touch, the first intrusive touch of a desperate man.

But there was nothing.

No calloused hands explored her body. No heavy lustful breaths on her skin. Just the silent lick of the cool breeze on her body, the creaking boughs of long-dead trees outside, and the decaying smell of the hole.

With her remaining senses heightened, Hope heard the sounds of heavy boots on dirt, a grunting of effort, masculine yet mature, and a wax jacket scraping against the bare walls.

He's leaving.

"Stop. You can't leave me here." Her voice was high and wavering. The wall that held back her tears started to crack. "You can't leave me here alone."

And then the wall broke, releasing the flood of emotion, and the once strong voice that people had stopped and listened to, her authoritative tone, split. A sob emerged, loud and sorrowful, and her voice lowered to a whisper of denial, resignation, and self-pity.

"No. You can't leave me."

The heavy door slammed into place with a boom that echoed off the hard, rock walls.

Be strong.

The image of Hope's incarceration returned. The cold and damp walls she felt with her hands chained above her head. The dirty floor that she felt beneath her bare feet.

Pushing the image to one side, Hope created her own place. A sanctuary. It was her bedroom. The room was large and furnished. A bed had been placed against the wall opposite where Hope now stood restrained. To her right, a fireplace took pride of place, simple but powerful in her mind's eye. As the image evolved, the dark, damp hole in the ground became a warm home to quell the truth outside of her Hessian mask.

Fear of the unknown weighed heavily, but Hope adorned the imaginary room with her family. Beside the bed was a small nightstand with a photo of her father. An old, wooden dressing table had been placed beside the fireplace. On it, beside her jewellery box and perfumes, was a photo of her as a child and her father. They were both smiling.

And Greg. Greg was there. He was lying asleep on the bed. His aftershave was strong. He always wore too much. But just knowing he was there, that he could see her and that she could feel him, warmed her for the tiniest of moments.

With her inner wall broken down, Hope let the tears roll. She issued no accompanying sobs or whimpers, finding solace only in the memories of the people she'd left behind.

"When the door slams, your world is damned."

Hope whispered the words aloud to herself as if, for the first time, she understood the sentence she'd heard just moments before when she'd awoken. Her words faded away, seemingly absorbed by the silent shadows.

And she stood, naked, bound, and afraid, but with a facade that was resolute, determined, and fierce.

For a short while.

"You're not alone," came the whispered reply.

CHAPTER TWO

A cold chill stung Frankie Black's feet. The kitchen tiles held onto the freezing night as a sponge retains water. With one hand on the coffee press and the other turning the pages of the previous day's Express, he neither thought about coffee nor the exaggerated and one-sided views of whatever stories were told in the paper. His mind was far away in a time when Jacqui would make the coffee and breakfast and get Jake ready for school, and Frankie would just admire her from afar.

The memories seemed warm and full of light. Always light. Golden sunshine, no matter the time of year, poured in through the kitchen window. But the stark reality was less romantic. The stark reality was cold with ominous, lurking shadows.

The French press touched the bottom of the jar and Frankie poured his first coffee of the day as he turned the final page of the paper. He hadn't read one story, hadn't taken in one article or advertisement, and he had even shunned the crossword page, a page that kept his mind working most days. He'd get back to it. Today his mind was busy enough.

The island in the centre of the kitchen in his four-bed, detached house in Upminster, Essex, a suburb of London, was where Frankie spent most of his mornings. Mostly staring into thin air. While the coffee press worked its magic, he often flicked through the pages of the newspaper in much the same way as he had that morning.

It was only on the bad days that he skipped the crossword.

The coffee poured black and aromatic, and the first taste felt like waking all over again. He folded the paper with one hand and set it down on the island on top of yesterday's unopened mail. The top letter, he knew, was from the bank, and ones from various other companies and utilities sat below in no particular order of urgency. He turned to stare out of the window into his garden where Jacqui used to kneel at the beds tending her plants as if they were her own flesh and blood, and Jake would be bringing his action figures to life in a forest of grass.

Warm hands slid across his sides and found his chest, and a face burrowed between his shoulder blades.

"It looks cold out."

He smiled at the voice. He relished the hidden meaning, the secret message that implied they should return to bed.

The image of Jacqui kneeling at her plants had vanished. There were no hands on his chest, no face was burrowed into his back. But her scent, or the memory of her scent, flavoured the coffee smell in the air.

And he dizzied with the plague of loss. It was a suffering that no individual should have to bear alone but one which any man or woman in love must be prepared to face.

"Not now," he whispered aloud as if the demons that taunted him would hear and take pity. "Please. Not now."

"Daddy, who are you talking to?"

Snap.

Gone were the visions of what once was.

Gone were the warm beams of light that filled Jacqui's kitchen. Because it had been Jacqui's domain. There had been no mistaking that.

And gone was the sweet, floral scent of her perfume that hung in the air with the coffee.

Only one thing remained.

The stark reality that his little boy needed his father to be strong.

"Nobody, Jake. I was muttering to myself." He cleared his throat and reopened the newspaper. "Did you sleep okay?"

"Like a frog."

Frankie smiled at the boy's use of language. His naivety and innocence had somehow softened the blow.

"You mean like a log?"

"No, like a frog. Like the ones in the garden."

"And how do frogs sleep?" Frankie sipped at his coffee and helped Jake into a tall breakfast stool.

"They sleep in their beds, of course." He spoke as if Frankie was somehow daft for not knowing that all frogs sleep in their beds.

Frankie felt the skin on his face grow taut as his smile broadened.

"And I suppose they wear pyjamas?"

"Of course they do or they'd get cold."

"And what do frogs have for breakfast?" Opening the fridge to find almost nothing at all, Frankie winced, hoping Jake wouldn't ask for much.

"Eggs."

"And what about when the frog doesn't have any eggs?" Closing the fridge and opening the cupboard, Frankie hoped frogs enjoyed cereal.

"Bacon?"

"I don't suppose frogs like cereal, do they? When there's no eggs or bacon?"

"I suppose." The boy had adopted a matter of fact tone conveying some kind of authority on the subject. "They especially like Coco Pops."

"Well, if the Coco Pops have all gone, I'd imagine that frogs would like Corn Flakes?"

"Not really. They prefer Coco Pops."

"Well, today this little frog is going to have Corn Flakes."

Frankie poured the cereal into a bowl and put the empty box in the recycling bin.

"Why don't we have Coco Pops?"

"Because Daddy needs to get some money for Coco Pops, Jake."

He slid the bowl in front of his son. The boy looked up at his father, smiled, and then picked up his special spoon.

"It's okay. Frogs like Corn Flakes too."

"Hey, Jake, I need to talk to you," said Frankie, as he leaned on the island to steady himself for what he was about to say. "Man to man."

"Is it about frogs, Dad?"

"Not quite. But we can talk about frogs all you like when we're done."

Jake considered it while he swallowed a spoonful of cereal then agreed as if he were a businessman giving permission for an employee to continue.

"You know I love you more than anything, right?"

Jake nodded.

"And there's nothing I wouldn't do to make sure you're safe."

Again, Jake nodded.

Frankie took a breath.

"How would you feel about staying with

Nanny and Granddad for a while? Just while I try and get some money together."

"No, Daddy."

Jake dropped his spoon into his cereal. His young face turned bright red in an instant.

But, sensing the outburst, Frankie continued, "Jake, listen. I need money. I need money to keep us safe and warm and to pay for eggs and bacon and all the things little frogs like."

"But, Daddy-"

"I need money to keep us together, Jake. Do you understand? I need you to be a grownup now. Just for a while. You're a big boy, right?"

"But I don't want-"

"I know all the things you don't want, Jake. And I promise you I've tried everything to make it work. But I have to get some money and, you know, Nanny and Granddad could use a big, strong man like you in their house."

"But I want to be with you, Daddy." His little boy's voice rose in pitch.

"I know you do, Son, and I want that too."

"So why are you sending me away?"

"Because I have to work. I have to find

something that will pay me enough to keep us going. I'll sell the house if I have to and we can move to someplace where we can be together. But I can't do any of that without money, Jake."

"Why can't you just get a job around here?"

It was the question Frankie had been dreading, and he exhaled as the words spilt out of Jake's mouth.

"Because I spent most of my life in the army. The only job I could get wouldn't pay me enough and would mean I'd be away from you. So I stay. I choose to stay to be with you. But, for just a little while, I need you to go and look after Nanny and Grandad so I can get out there and find some work. Will you do that for me? If it means we can be together when I get back?"

"How long will you be gone for? The last time you went away, it was only for a few days."

"Nothing is confirmed yet. I might not even get the job."

"How long, Dad?"

"Three months." He said it straight. He couldn't paint a pretty picture. He couldn't soften it with cotton wool. Not the way Jacqui could have.

Jake shoved his bowl away, spilling milk on the table. But as much as the urge to wipe the mess up teased at Frankie's peripheral, he stayed put. It was happening now. The conversation he'd been dreading for too long had finally come out of nowhere.

"I won't see you for three months? What will you be doing? Is it army stuff? Why can't I come?"

He never enjoyed discussing his previous career with his son. Jake only knew a fraction of the truth. There was no way Jake could ever know what Frankie had done. There was no way anybody could ever know.

"Sort of. It's a job for some old army mates."

"Where? Is it close? I could come to visit. Grandad would take me if I asked him. I'm sure he would."

"I don't know where it is. But it'll be somewhere far away."

The boy's stare grabbed onto Frankie's stomach and twisted it. He coughed away the tightness in his throat and looked away, giving him time to blink and clear his eyes.

"So do you think you could go and look after Nanny and Grandad for a while?" Then the shrill tone of his mobile phone sounded from Frankie's office. "I'll be one minute. Let me answer that. Okay?"

He left the boy staring at his cereal and walked along the hallway to his office feeling Jacqui's stare from every picture that hung on every wall.

In the dark office, Frankie's mobile phone lit a small portion of his immaculate desk. The number was showing as unknown. Frankie hit the connect button but said nothing, still reeling from the conversation with Jake.

"Is that Frankie Black?"

The voice was serious and deep, but the call was too early to be the bank. Frankie imagined the man who belonged to the voice. He was taller than average. He sounded confident and sure of himself, a trait that was ingrained from wealth. But he didn't have the accent of the well-to-do or middle-class society. Therefore, Frankie deemed him to be self-made. A successful business owner maybe.

Frankie knew the next line. It was a call he'd been both hoping for and dreading. It was a call they needed to receive. Frankie and Jake. A call that would bring distraction along with daily reminders of who he once was and who he was now.

A father.

A widow.

Alone.

He stepped from his office and peered along the hallway, but Jake had left the table, leaving his cereal bowl and an atmosphere so thick Frankie could almost taste it.

The bedroom door slammed at the top of the stairs and Frankie winced.

"Is anybody there? Is that Frankie Black?"

He hit the red button to end the call.

CHAPTER THREE

"Who are you?" Hope's voice, more like a breath than speech, was tense and demanding.

Footsteps faded through long grass like a dying wind in the bristling treetops.

"I'm like you."

"Can you see?" With hope in her heart for the first time, Hope pulled at her restraints. "Are you chained too?"

"I can see what little there is to see."

"But are you chained? Can you move?"

"I can move. But there is nowhere for me to go."

"Who are you? What's your name?"

"Does it matter anymore? Does it matter

what I used to be called when there's nobody to call me by my name? In time, you'll see that it's better to forget who you were and embrace who you will become."

"Of course it matters. What do I call you? Is there a way out? Can we escape?"

No reply came.

"Answer me." But the anger in Hope's voice was clear. Fuelled by frustration and fear, and outraged by the audacity of the man and the girl, whoever she was, Hope pulled at her chains again. "I said answer me. You can't let them do this to us. We have to escape. If you can see and move then release me. Or at least take off my mask."

"It doesn't matter what my name is. Or yours, for that matter. When the door slams, your world is damned."

The words came at Hope like a hammer blow to her chest, pummelling any glimmer of hope into submission.

"What is that nonsense? Just help me remove my mask so I can see."

"You're not ready."

"Not ready? Not ready for what?"

"For your transformation."

"For what?"

Silence returned like an unwanted friend. It was as if a third person was there with them, sharing Hope's fears and frustration and filling in the gaps when the other girl had nothing to say.

"Answer me."

The silence spoke once more, clear and articulate above the creaking bows and muffled birdsong.

Until Hope's resolve crumbled for the first time.

"I'm sorry."

"Are you?"

Her voice. Hope closed her eyes. Her voice felt so good. So calming and tranquil, like some kind of angel leading Hope through a dark and evil forest.

"Yes, I am. I shouldn't have snapped. I just-"

"You're frustrated. You don't understand what's happening. It's okay. It's just the first phase of your transformation."

"Stop speaking in riddles. Talk to me properly. We're not transforming. We're trapped."

It was the unwanted third person's turn to talk. And Hope heard all it had to say.

"I can't help it," said Hope eventually. "I'm sorry. Please, tell me who you are."

"Who I am? Or who I was?"

"What? Who you are, of course. What's your name?" She softened her voice, hearing her own bitterness sour the flow of conversation. "Please. Tell me your name. Even a simple thing like your name would help. It would help me picture you."

"Don't picture me. Picture your world instead. Picture who you are and who you might be."

"I don't understand. Who I might be?"

"Start from the beginning," said the girl. "I can help you understand."

"From the beginning?"

"Tell me why you're here. Or at least why you think you're here."

"We're here because that sick, old man is a creep. He needs to be locked up."

"You're wrong."

"He's sick," said Hope. "Why else would he do this? He's going to kill us. You know that, right? He killed my boyfriend."

Hysteria broke free of its shell. Its ugly head rose and thickened Hope's throat. It filled her eyes with the tears that were now free to run with no dam to hold them back. The moments replayed in her mind, and she was no longer chained to a wall in a black hole with a lunatic. She was lying breathless in a field with Greg. Two empty beer bottles were lying beside them in the long grass, and Greg's lean body was entwined with her own. The heat from their sweaty skin combined, forming a fire like radiance where they connected. And Greg's hardness waned against her leg. She remembered thinking that she would never forget that time. The sun, the blue sky, and tall grass around them, mute spectators to the passion they had shared.

Teasing at Hope's hard chest with his forefinger, Greg mouthed silent words as if the dream itself sought no substance in the words he had spoken, but knew that the image of him would suffice.

"You're wrong." The girl sounded defensive, deflecting any slander against the man. "He's not what you think."

"How can you say that?"

The memory faded to a haze. Although no clouds passed below the sun, a shadow cooled the skin on Hope's legs. She pulled Greg closer until he rolled on top of her.

Those moments, Hope had enjoyed the most. When the rampant and furious lovemaking was over, when the throes of orgasm had drained her of energy, and her body called for tenderness. Greg had always been good at tenderness. Previous lovers had rarely stayed to enjoy it, dressing and leaving as if a contractual obligation had been fulfilled. But Greg always had time for tenderness.

Hearing her voice rising in emotion, flavoured with spite and hate, Hope calmed herself, trying to shun the images of Greg's body to one side. It was the only way the girl would continue to talk. And hearing her was the only way Hope would survive.

"How can you defend him? Look at what he's done."

"In time, you will understand."

"I'd understand if you just told me what's happening. Please. I need to know. I'm going insane."

"Start from the beginning. Tell me who you are."

"I'm Hope."

"And why are you here?"

"Because he took me. Because he killed Greg. I saw it."

The shadow on Hope's legs grew to cover her body and the breeze was cool on their combined sweat. She saw the look on Greg's face, a fraction of a second of confusion and twisted doubt as the silhouetted man stood over him, his arms raised high in a pose of death.

"There was blood. So much blood." The urge to wipe her face was strong, but the chains sank their teeth into Hope's wrists when she tried. "He's a killer. He's going to kill us."

"You're not answering the question."

"What question? What else do you need to know? He killed Greg and he'll kill us too."

"He saved us."

"Saved us? Saved us from what? From happiness? From life?"

"From hell. Tell me who you are."

"You're crazy."

"Who are you?"

"I'm Hope. I told you."

"And who is Hope?" The girl's voice became monotone, trance-like as if she could see deep into what Hope was saying. Or maybe she had always spoken that way and Hope just hadn't heard it before.

"What? I'm just a girl. A student. I don't understand."

"You will. What does Hope like to do?"

"I like to walk free. I like to breathe the fresh air and enjoy time with my friends. I don't like to be locked in a hole and chained to a wall with a hood over my face."

"Friends? Are they really Hope's friends?"

"My friends, you mean? Stop talking as if Hope is someone else. I'm Hope. Me. Hope Gilmour."

"You'll see in time."

"See what? What will I see? Please. I don't understand. I'm..."

"Scared?"

It was the truth. As much as Hope tried to ignore it, she couldn't deny it. She could hear it in her voice, in her breathing. The girl would hear it too.

"Yes."

"Are you scared of the past or of the future?"

"The future, of course. What's going to happen? Who are you?"

"Before you can deal with the future, you must understand your past. You must understand why you are here."

"But that's just it. I don't understand why I'm here."

"Who is Hope Gilmour?"

"I told you. I'm just a girl."

"Is Hope loved?"

"Of course."

"By who?"

"My dad. He loves me. And-"

"Greg? Did he love you?"

"I think so. He said he did once. But only after we-"

"Your mother? Does she love you?"

The mention of Hope's mother dulled the emotions that were running riot. It had always been the same. There was no love lost, no regret, no maternal pang. It was a conversation her father had always avoided, which had left a hole in Hope's world.

"I have no mother."

"Oh. Did she die?"

"No. I've just never known her. I don't understand. Tell me what this has to do with why I'm here."

The girl left a space for their quiet friend to voice her opinion. She spoke, loud and clear, weaving a web of wondering in Hope's chaotic mind. Images of Hope's past flashed once then faded to nothing, only for the next image to flash past.

Images of boyfriends. The silhouetted man with his arms raised. The final look on Greg's face. Mental images Hope had created of the mother that never was. The look of realisation and fear as Greg saw the horror in Hope's eyes. A little girl on a swing.

But before she had time to see if the girl was Hope as a child, Greg was back, his face contorted and his blood spattering across Hope's face.

Breathing with force, Hope tried to shake the images from her mind. Unwanted memories prodded at her conscience with bony, taunting fingers of guilt.

Until the girl's voice came. She was standing before Hope, unseen but close.

"Tell me, Hope. What's the worst thing you have ever done?"

CHAPTER FOUR

They drove in silence.

Frankie's several futile attempts at making conversation had done no more than push Jake further into himself. The boy was a young reflection of his mother in nearly every way. There was nothing the boy could do that wasn't a reminder of Jacqui. Frankie felt the sharp stab of painful memories, and the further into himself the boy retreated, the harder the knife was twisted.

A school teacher waited at the gates with a clipboard and a pen marking off the names of the young students as they filtered into the school grounds.

"That's Miss Dilworth, isn't it, Jake?"

But Jake didn't even look up. He waited for the car to come to a stop with one hand on the handle and the other on the seat belt release.

"Jake, wait."

A sideways glance was all Jake could manage. Maybe it was because he was ashamed of the tear in his eye. Maybe it was because he just didn't understand why Frankie had to leave. But hanging in the shadows of both possibilities was the truth. Frankie was alienating his son. The time they spent arguing or wallowing in silence was time that should have been spent reconnecting.

The car door slammed shut.

Mrs Dilworth looked up from her clipboard, greeted Jake, and peered over her spectacles as Frankie put the car into drive and joined the queue of parents waiting to leave the side street. All around him, on the footpaths and in the other cars, parents laughed with their children. And if they weren't laughing, they were at the very least smiling. It was as if they knew something that Frankie did not like they understood and were close to their children. Whereas the void between

Frankie and Jake seemed to grow larger every time Frankie disappointed his son.

And then it came.

The first tear. Like a scout sent to gather intelligence, it raised its ugly head, took a tentative step on Frankie's cheek, and then rolled to freedom, calling out to the army that followed that the coast was clear.

And they came.

It wasn't the first time Frankie had cried. He was a long way past the shame and embarrassment of a grown man showing his emotions. But he'd learned to repress them. He'd learned how to hold them back.

Like a drill sergeant, the tiny part of his mind that controlled his thoughts banished the memories of Jacqui when Frankie was low or missing her. It redirected the thoughts of the times they had shared. Each time Jake reminded Frankie of Jacqui and a pang of emotion threatened to show itself, the drill sergeant stepped in, keeping Frankie on track.

It wasn't healthy. He knew it wasn't. But it had gone on for far too long.

He just missed her.

Sitting in traffic waiting for the road to clear, Frankie knew it wasn't a pang of emotion that had shown itself, and it wasn't that he just missed her.

It was because he felt so alone.

A sob rose up from his gullet, so powerful it forced its way through Frankie's barriers and emerged loudly as if it was borne of the pressure inside his body, a pressure that had built up from repressed emotions.

The army of tears marched onward.

No longer restrained by his mental control, the thoughts followed. Jacqui smiling at Frankie from the balcony of their Parisian hotel room. Jacqui rolling over in her sleep and pulling herself closer to Frankie. Her smell, her hair, her voice. It was all Jacqui.

And still, the tears rolled. They were beyond stopping. He could feel them drip from his chin. He could feel their warm dampness on his shirt.

And he was powerless to wipe them away. Each tear was a memory. Each tear was running free and, for the first time in as long as he could remember, he could think of Jacqui with joy.

A car horn honked behind him, rousing Frankie from his dreams. The road ahead was clear, and behind him, in his mirror, a line of cars was waiting. He raised his hand to apologise, wiping the tears from his eyes and crept forward onto the main road.

It was as he was pulling out that his phone rang over the car's system. The screen announced the caller as Tom. Frankie inhaled, long and hard. His finger poised above the green answer icon, he readied himself and hit the button.

"Tom?"

"Hi, Frankie. How are you?"

"Let me guess. Jake called you?"

"He did. Is everything okay, son?"

Calling him son was Tom's way of reaching out to Frankie. It reminded Frankie of the old-school army officers he had known during basic who would use the word to maintain some kind of pecking order, while they offered a subliminal hand of assistance.

Diverting the conversation, Frankie sought the upper ground.

"What did he say, Tom?"

"That he's coming to stay for a while."

"Is that okay with you?"

"Of course it's okay. I'm not calling to complain. We've been through that before. Whatever you need from us, it's yours."

Kindness, when Frankie was down, was one of the hardest things he could deal with. When the emotions were high and his control had faltered, kindness just seemed to tip the balance. He pulled onto his driveway as the urge to sob built to a crescendo, but he silenced it with a deep breath, exhaling quietly so that Tom wouldn't hear.

"You sound upset, Frankie. Is there something we can do?"

He switched off the engine, closed his eyes, and cleared his throat.

"Frankie?"

"I'm here. What did he say, Tom?"

"Just that he's coming to stay." Knowing the intonations of Tom's voice, Frankie waited for the second part of his sentence. Tom always paused on the things he didn't understand. It was a good thing, as far as Frankie was concerned. It made the man less likely to react with emotions and make a rash decision. "He said he was coming for three months. Is that right, Frankie? It's not a problem, but three months?"

Tom deserved an explanation. Frankie searched for the words. Or a cover story.

"I need some time, Tom."

He couldn't lie.

"I see, Frankie."

"Do you?"

It was too harsh and Frankie knew it.

"Just as you lost your wife, we lost our daughter, Frankie."

But how then were Tom and Mary able to function?

"She was our only child."

"I know."

"She was everything to us, Frankie. But by God's good grace, at least she left us with you and Jake."

"Everything he does, Tom. Jake. Everything he does reminds me of her."

"We notice it every time he comes. The way he sleeps, the way he eats, the way he answers back. It's all Jacqui, Frankie. She lives and breathes through him."

"I need some time to get over her."

"You'll need longer than three months, son."

"I didn't mean that. I'll never get over her. I'm sorry. I just-"

"It's okay. You need some time to come to terms with it. That's how I think about it."

Picturing Jacqui's father in his slippers

and cardigan, Frankie listened as the wind caught the telephone handset. He'd stepped outside to be out of earshot of Mary, his wife. Tom was good like that. He was a man's man and respected other people's privacy. Mary was not so empathetic.

"So how are you going to do it?"

"Do what?"

"Come to terms with it. How are you going to adjust?"

"I don't know, Tom." It was the truth, and hearing it out loud made it sound as stupid as it was.

"You told Jake you have a job to do. A three-month contract. Do we need to back that story up? Are you really going away to work?"

"I can't work, Tom. I can't do what I do."

"Wouldn't a bit of work take your mind off things? Help you find a new routine? Routine always helps."

"I can't work, Tom. I..."

"It's okay."

"What I do takes me close to people. I have to be close to their loss, to their suffering, and all it does is remind me of my own. How can I help other people if all they do is remind me of my own suffering? I can't do it. It's been more than a year and I don't know why I feel like this now. I don't know how I've functioned for this long. But I'm struggling. I need time."

"That's okay, Frankie. Calm down, son. I'm here to help."

"I'm sorry. I'm a wreck. I don't want Jake to see me like this. I don't want him to resent me. I need time to get through it so I can be a father to him."

"So you're going to take three months off to sit and look at photos of Jacqui?" asked Tom.

"If that's what it takes."

"It'll take more than that, son. If you want my advice..."

Frankie opened his mouth to tell him his advice was not wanted, but caught himself, a sign he was regaining control of his emotions.

"Go back to work, Frankie."

"I turned a job down this morning."

"A job you can't tell me about?"

Words defied Frankie.

"It's okay," said Tom. "You don't have to tell me about it. As long as it's legal and above board."

"It is. But I can't have everyone knowing."

"That's not a problem. But if you need me to help, if you need a pair of ears, call me. Contrary to what you might think, I have a few secrets myself. Mary doesn't have to know the ins and outs of everything, and sometimes that's for the best."

"Thanks, Tom."

"It's fine. You don't need to thank me. Just take some time to get your head around Jacqui's death. It's a shift in your mindset. That's all. You can do it. God knows you've got yourself through far worse than most of us will ever have to face. You're strong, Frankie."

He laughed. Once. It was more like an exhale but felt good nonetheless.

"I don't feel strong, Tom. Not right now."

"It'll come back. And, as I said, I'm here to help. But if you're going to sit there and wallow in self-pity for three months, I'll be sending Jake home and you can get through it the hard way. But if you want my help, you have to help yourself."

"Tough love?"

"Something like that, Frankie."

There was a pause where Frankie was sure he should be thanking his father-in-law, where he was certain he should be explaining the job, for the conversation's sake if nothing else.

"Is the job still open, Frankie?"

"I don't know."

"Well, check." Tom's assertive tone shook Frankie from where he'd mentally curled up in a ball. "If I don't hear back from you by three o'clock, I'll assume you've taken the job. I'll take care of Jake and Mary. You just get yourself on your feet."

"I don't know what to say."

"Nothing, Frankie. You don't have to say anything. Just buy me a beer. As I said, I lost a daughter too. We need to share our grief."

Frankie disconnected the call. He wiped his eyes on his shirt sleeve and switched off the car.

Inside his house, he closed the door and stared at the empty hallway. Jake's cereal bowl was still on the kitchen island. From above the fireplace in the lounge to Frankie's right, Jacqui smiled down at him. It was his favourite photo of her. He'd taken it in London on a day out. It had been raining and they were soaked from the deluge. Jacqui was standing among a river of umbrellas and city suits, facing the flow of commuters. She was smiling. Even in black and white, her smile was radiant, infectious, and even though they had been soaked to the skin, her smile warmed the memory. The photo reminded him of a river parting around a rock. That's what she had been.

A rock.

A rock amongst the chaotic life of Frankie Black. She was a rock that had supported him. She was the hard thing that he had when he felt soft and weak.

"What do I do, girl?"

As nice as it was to look at, her smile offered no response. But still, Frankie admired it.

"What would it be like if you were still here?"

Just a smile.

"I could stay here and look at you for three months and more."

He could smell her. Sweet and floral. Her perfume was there in the room as if she stood only a few feet away.

"God I miss you."

The grip of a thick hand on his throat preceded another wave of emotion. But his inner drill sergeant stepped in, barring the way for any bursts of tears, sobs, and self-pity. It was as if it held up a hand, holding everything back and pairing with Jacqui to team up against Frankie's urges.

And then they spoke.

It was only Jacqui's voice, and it was as sweet as her scent, bringing with it a calm ease that cooled Frankie's sweaty hands and cleared the fog in his mind.

She smiled down from that street in London. A rock among the river of umbrellas and suits. A picture of strength.

But in the reflection of the glass, Frankie saw himself. A picture of hurt.

CHAPTER FIVE

"I don't understand."

"You will."

"You're talking in riddles. It's not fair."

Above the thumping of Hope's heart, she could hear the girl moving away and the warmth of her body and breath, which Hope hadn't felt before, left her skin naked to the cool air.

"Don't go. I'm sorry."

"So tell me."

"The worst thing?"

"You must have something," said the girl. "Something you are deeply ashamed of. Something that keeps you awake at night with the hard bite of guilt. You cannot transform unless you are willing to recognise the bad things you have done."

"But I don't want to transform. I don't want to think about the things I've done. I want to get out. Is this a game? Because it's not funny."

"Then you will stay chained and hooded. The only way out of here is through transformation. The only way you will ever breathe the fresh air again is by repenting your sins. You do want to breathe the air again, don't you, Hope? You do want to be free?"

"Of course I do. Please at least take off my hood."

"The first stage of your transformation is to recognise your sins."

The girl backed away. Hope heard it in her voice.

"Stop. Don't go. Stay close." The silence spoke, urging Hope to reveal her darkest memories. "There was a girl. At my school. She was poor..."

"Go on."

"I made her cry. I made her sad. I regret that."

"What did you do?"

"Is it not enough that I made her cry?"

"It's a start. But not nearly enough. I know there's more."

"How do you know?" said Hope. "What do you know about me?"

"About you? All I know is that you're bitter, you're angry, you're confused, and unless you listen to what I say, unless you try to understand, you'll die in here."

"I'll die?"

"Look inside yourself, Hope. Search through all that darkness, find those terrible things, and bring them into the light. Free your body of the terrible memories so they may remain here in the hole."

"I stole money. From my father." Her words came in bursts with the flurries of her sins that presented themselves for Hope to verbalise. "I used to creep downstairs at night and find his wallet. I'd take money so I could buy cigarettes and..."

She stopped.

"What else did you buy?"

"Drugs. But not for me. For Greg. It was only some weed. Well, mostly anyway. But I didn't have any. Not all the time. Only sometimes."

Coaxed on by the silence, Hope remembered the nights that she and Greg had spent either in his bedsit or in his car-sharing a joint. He had a small mirror that he kept beneath his bed, and sometimes he would arrange lines of that soft, white powder on it. She could see it clearly as if the moment was re-lived and she was a third person, silent, un-heard, and unseen. Hope was lying naked on the bed and with the powers of that soft, white substance that flowed through her veins, she could do anything. All her inhibi-tions were cast off. There had been a camera. Greg's camera. He took photos of her between the sniffing of lines.

Sometimes he would join in but he kept his face out of the shots. Never his face.

It was always about her. She was always the focus.

"I let Greg take photos of me and videos. Only once though. Maybe more. But I did bad things. Things that would embarrass my dad. Things that would bring shame to the family. I did it to spite him. I did it because..."

"Go on."

"Because I hated him. Although I didn't. I just thought I did. You know what it's like. When you're young and there are rules."

"You felt constrained?"

"Yes. I felt like I couldn't be myself. I know my dad loves me. I know he was only protecting me, but..." Searching for the words, a flicker of clarity shone once in Hope's mind then evaporated, taking with it her trail of thought. "It felt like I needed air. It felt like I was being held down while all my friends were free to do what they wanted."

"And so you rebelled with drugs?"

"Yes. Well, no. I rebelled with Greg. Dad doesn't approve of him. So I did everything Greg wanted me to do."

"Everything?"

"Everything. Because I knew it would hurt Dad. It was the only way to get back at him."

"And does he deserve to be treated like that?"

"All he had to do was relax. All he had to do was let me be a woman. Let me wear what I wanted to wear. Go where I wanted to go. But no. He always had to intervene. He always had to make it hard."

"He was being a father," said the girl. "You told me that he loved you. Do you love him?

Do you love him as a doting daughter? Do you look to him for strength?"

"No."

"So what is he to you?"

"He's my father. He..."

Hope paused, wondering what it was she sought from the man.

"Tell me, Hope. Does your father provide for you? Does he provide a home and food?"

"Yes. Of course. That's what fathers do."

"And when you're upset, does he try and console you? Does he make you laugh and cheer you up?"

"He tries. I don't let him get close enough."

"But he still tries?"

"Yes."

"And right now, do you think he's wondering where you are?"

"Probably."

"Do you think he's worried?"

"No. Well, yes. Probably. But I'm always out. I can't stand to be at home."

"Do you think he will call the police?"

"Yes. He's done it before. More than once. He tries to control me. He thinks I'll run away."

"And would you?"

"If I could."

"If you could find a fresh source of money, you mean?"

It was true. No matter how Hope tried to twist the facts, there was no escaping it.

"Yes."

"And do you still think he deserved to be treated like that?"

It was painful to hear. It was painful to think. But voicing her answer tightened her throat once more and that hard grip of guilt clung to her gullet.

"No."

"He's probably at home right now wondering where you are, hoping for the front door to open, but really waiting to find two policemen ready to deliver the news he's been expecting."

"Stop it."

"Can you imagine how that feels, Hope?"

"I said stop it."

"Can you imagine what it must be like to pour all your love into your child, only to have her rebuke you, to shun you, and to not let you in?"

"You don't know what he's like."

But as much as Hope tried to find reason in her actions, there was none.

"Tell me, Hope. What would you say if your father opened that door now? What would you say if he pulled off that hood, unlocked your chains, and held you? If he said nothing, as there would be nothing to say, but he held you tight?"

Hope stayed silent. None of the words she could think of gave justice to the weight of what the girl had said. The scenario she had described. She could imagine the scene. She could picture her father's strong hands ripping off the hood and clearing her snotty face of hair. She could feel his hands as he cupped her cheeks and his warm breath as he kissed the top of her head. And she could envisage the anger with which he would rip out the chains from the wall. The lengths he would go to free her.

"Would you hold him too?"

"Yes."

"Would you kiss him? Would you tell him how sorry you are?"

"Yes."

"And would you promise to go with him to your home? Would you explain all the terrible things you have done so that you can start over? So he can have the daughter he always wanted and you can have the father you need?"

"Yes. Yes, I would. I would do that and more."

"And would you love him, Hope? Would you love him as if there was no other man? As every daughter should."

"Yes. Yes, I would."

"What would you say to him? What would you say when you feel his tears of joy on your face?"

The scene in Hope's mind was real. Masked from reality by the hood she wore, her mind carved images, so vivid and clear, but cruel by design. She tried to hold it back. She tried to stop it coming. But she couldn't. She had no strength. Her weak and trembling legs gave under her weight and the bite of the chains once more sank their teeth into her skin.

And she sobbed.

There it was.

It came again, louder, as if her body needed to release the anguish. Breathless with emotion, she cried. Hope cried harder than she could ever remember crying. These were not just the tears that had flowed earlier, which had been the result of her loneliness. She cried now, wailing in shame. Wailing for the grief of her father.

"I'm sorry. I would tell him I'm sorry. I would tell him I've never been so sorry and so ashamed of myself."

Hope gasped for breath. She sniffed away the snot from her nose and felt the warmth of the girl's breath on the side of her face.

"Please. Untie me. I know now that I've been bad. I know I've done wrong and I understand. I'm sorry."

"Do you love your father?"

"Yes."

"Good."

"Please. At least remove the hood. I need the bathroom."

"Shhh."

The girl's breath was cool but sour like unwashed feet. But Hope didn't mind. Her proximity offered companionship. A sense that she wasn't alone.

"You've taken the first step, Hope. How do you feel?"

A thousand words sprang to Hope's mind.

Angry, despicable, furious, shallow, fuming, raging.

"Rotten."

"And?"

"It's like a weight has been lifted. I can see life now. I can see what's out there."

"Good."

The girl's hand touched Hope's arm. The feeling startled her for a moment and the girl withdrew. But Hope found herself wanting more. She offered her arm again, blind save for the environment her remaining senses helped her mind to create. The girl's fingers touched Hope's arm once more. They were soft and cool. No, they were cold. Like ice. The sensation was alien but welcome.

She felt the girl smile somehow.

"Because we've only just begun."

CHAPTER SIX

Beside the log burner in Frankie's lounge was his favourite chair. It was a Queen Anne armchair in oxblood red, and its leather was as soft as the day he'd bought it. The winged back, designed to keep the occupant from a cool breeze, offered both security, like a cave or a hole, and focus, like the blinkers that prevent a horse from distraction.

But nothing could distract Frankie from the torment. He would welcome a distraction if one came along. He even searched for a diversion in the newspaper crossword, but he found only memories, heartache, and questions amidst the checkered boxes and clues.

On the coffee table in front of him was an

old biscuit tin that had been re-purposed to store photographs. It had been there for months, since Jacqui had died, waiting like an obedient puppy for some attention. But Frankie knew the puppy would bite. It offered the promise of comfort, of memories and the chance to glimpse Jacqui in all her wondrous glory once more. But its teeth would be sharp.

To his right was a cabinet. It was where he and Jacqui had stored the alcohol, and as he touched the handle, Frankie was reminded of the day they moved in.

Jacqui closed the door on the removal men and leaned against it with fatigue. Her head had dropped back to rest on the wood, but her eyes had glanced into the lounge and she voiced her vision with creative authority and love.

"That goes there."

"What goes where?"

Frankie had fallen into his favourite chair and was resting his aching feet on a box, hoping for a reprise. They had been on the move all day and the house was strewn with furniture and boxes, all of which, in Frankie's mind, could wait until morning.

"That cabinet goes there in the corner beside the fireplace, and your chair can sit next to it. That way, when you come home and you're tired, you can sit in your favourite chair and pour yourself a brandy. Besides, I like the red with the wooden fireplace. It's kind of a classic look."

"Timeless, you mean?"

"Yes. There's something about it that conjures up images of an old gentleman's study."

"And would this old gentleman have his doting wife come and perch herself on the arm of his chair?"

Jacqui smiled. Frankie heard her walk through the room. He heard her open a box. Then he heard the unmistakable sound of glass kissing glass and a drink being poured. She joined him. But instead of perching on the arm, she slid into the chair beside him, hooking one of her slender legs over his and passing him his drink. Her hand pulled at his shirt and found the skin beneath. And then it tugged at his belt.

"This old gentleman agrees with that idea."

But the moment was cut short by the slamming of car doors outside and Jake's excited voice as he ran to the door.

Jacqui rested her forehead on Frankie's in disappointment and smiled.

"Hold that thought," she whispered, eye to eye with Frankie, and then kissed him hard until the front door opened.

She pulled away just as Jake ran into the room, and the memory faded, leaving Frankie alone in the lounge with the cabinet in its place and the ghosts of the memory lingering in his mind.

Once more, there were the sounds of a bottle kissing a glass and a drink being poured. But it was by Frankie's own hand. He set the bottle down on the coffee table, leaving the lid off, and raised the cut-glass tumbler to his nose to savour the rich, fruity flavour. It smelled of the old gentleman's study that Jacqui had envisaged. Wood-panelled walls, bookshelves adorned with deep red and green leather spines, and the hide of an aged animal that covered the hardwood floor.

He sipped.

He felt the burn.

And he felt the stab of memory.

The lid of the tin came off with ease and fell to the floor with a metallic crash.

Frankie sipped his drink again and scattered a handful of photos across the table, staring and numbed, as memories flashed through his mind. The majority of the photos were of Jake, just as many family albums or archived biscuit tins held memories of children. Jacqui and Frankie played the supporting cast. The doting mother with adoration in her eyes. The hero father painting a nursery, building a cot, and later a treehouse.

But interlaced within the family shots were tales of love. Holidays that he and Jacqui had taken before Jake had been born. Photos of Paris, Mumbai, Dubai, and the Maldives showing the young couple finding themselves and building the relationship they thought would last a lifetime.

Wherever they were, Frankie had always been able to capture Jacqui's personality as she embraced the local culture. She wore an abaya in one photo, which was taken at the Grand Mosque in Abu Dhabi. It had been twilight, and her reflection on the marble floor with the ambient lighting framed her between two minarets.

In Mumbai, she had worn a simple dress. It was knee-length, respectable, and conservative, and she was smiling as she haggled with a street vendor over the price of a used book. Frankie remembered the book and found it remarkable how the little details remained. For Whom the Bell Tolls was on a shelf in Frankie's office. It had been a gift for Frankie. It was, in essence, about the cold brutality of war, and was now laced with the romantic smells of spices and the sounds of that Indian street.

He flicked through more of the photos and paused at an enlarged five-by-eight print of Jacqui on their private beach in the Maldives. She was wearing her favourite wide-brimmed hat, and the sun cast the hat's texture onto her face as it found the tiny gaps between the weave. She was sitting with her arms stretched back facing the calm Indian Ocean with hues of the green, tropical trees behind her, blurred but present.

Frankie sipped once more, savoured the taste and the smell of the drink, then took a larger mouthful, wincing as the burn flowed along his throat, and enjoying the cool that followed with his next breath.

"Oh, Jacqui."

He wondered if things would be different

if Jake had not been born. He wondered if Jacqui would still be around. But the trade was ill-conceived. The thought of parting with Jake or having never even held him, seen him, or known him was, at its best, un-thinkable.

As if by chance, the corner of a particular photo revealed itself below the one of the Maldives. It showed a flash of colour that Frankie recognised without a shadow of a doubt. It was one of the more recent photos, perhaps the last he had ever taken of Jacqui, and with the memory, she returned once more. She perched on the arm of the chair and Frankie could smell her.

She leaned forward to reach for the photo and Frankie could feel the breeze of her movement.

She laughed out loud, that soft, girlish laugh.

And Frankie could hear her.

He reached for her. He longed to touch her soft, smooth leg.

But felt nothing.

And she was gone.

Sliding the photo out, Frankie admired her. She wore a short summer dress. It was the type she had often worn with a floral pattern and low V-neck. She was leaning over Jake, her face a picture of compassion as she tended to a wasp sting. Jake's face was contorted with childish agony, his eyes squinted, his head tilted back, and his hand raised for Jacqui to inspect the wound. At the time, Frankie hadn't understood why he'd taken the photo. He'd considered it afterwards and deemed it inappropriate. Where most fathers would have been consoling the boy, Frankie had snapped the shot.

Maybe it was for this very moment when he would be sitting alone, reminiscing, mourning, and savouring the memories.

The memory came alive once more, the colours desaturated but the details clear and prominent.

Above the sound of Jake's screams and Jacqui's calming voice, the phone rang. It had been a call they had been expecting but dreading. Jacqui glanced up from beside Jake and caught Frankie's stare. She had known then. She had known that it was the call that would send him back into action. She had known that no matter what information was divulged on the call, he would not be able to tell her where he would be going or how long for.

But he hadn't known that it would be the last time he would see her beautiful smile.

Jake had stopped crying by the time the call had finished. And, as if to add weight to the mood, the sun slid behind a cloud when Frankie stepped into the garden.

He stooped to pick up Jake and sat him on his hip then reached for his wife to offer a silent goodbye. There had been no exchange of words. No cherished phrases of comfort. Just a knowing look, a kiss, and then, before emotion showed itself, he'd left.

Frankie dropped the photo to the table, but he missed and it fell to the floor. He sank the remainder of his brandy and collected the photo. As he sat up, as if chorusing the memory, his phone began to ring.

The number was withheld, as it had been earlier that morning.

He answered the call and listened. It was what he always did. Listened. He listened to the intonations of the voice, and he listened to the strength of it, the anguish, the suffering.

"Hello?"

Mild suffering. Scared and panicked. But

in control. It was a man's voice. A man who had no place left to turn. It was the same reason they all called. There was nowhere left to turn.

"Hello? Is this Frankie Black?"

"Yes."

There it was. The initial transaction. He knew what the next line would be. He knew what it would mean. Frankie considered the photo. His boy in pain. The man's child in pain. The compassion in Jacqui's face. The compassion in the man's voice. The phone calls both then and now. He considered how long the man must have stared at the phone before daring to dial Frankie's number. The sacrifice he must have made.

And the sacrifice that Frankie would make. The journey he must take to get through this.

"I hear you're a man who knows how to find people."

CHAPTER SEVEN

"No. I've told you everything. Let me out. You can't do this."

Silence announced the girl's displeasure and the teeth of Hope's restraints found the abrasions on her wrists. A warm trickle of sticky blood collected in the palm of her hand and her inability to tend her wounds increased her mounting frustration.

"Let me out. Just untie me. Help me for God's sake. What's the matter with you?"

Hope's growing emotion barred her sense of place. She could no longer feel the girl's presence beside her and could not hear her feet in the dirt.

"Where are you? Tell me where you are."

Realising that her temper had driven the girl away again, Hope attempted to soften her voice. Three deep breaths were enough to calm her.

But with the calm and quiet came the fear. When her anger had reigned, the terror of her situation had been quelled. But in the silence, her fear grew. She imagined a shadow rising up the damp walls behind her like the birth of a beast, flexing and finding its strength and clenching its sharp talons.

There was no sound save for the dripping of water into a pool like the second hand of a numberless antique clock. The incessant beating of her heartfelt like the distant drum of an Amazon tribe preparing to go to war, building the tension among the masses who danced with flailing limbs and sharpened spears, each of them wearing nothing but the skins and feathers of their first kill.

"I'm sorry."

Her words escaped with sincerity, slipping through her defences before she had time to react. She marvelled at the darkness, and terror provoked her imagination. With the words, the fear grew taller, hunching against the roof of the hole and drawing out the darkest thoughts from Hope's darkest places.

"I just sometimes..."

Should she say it?

She'd started now and not to finish would leave the sentence open to the girl's interpretation.

And Hope needed the girl.

She hated the thought of needing her, but it was true. She did. She needed her hands to remove the hood. She needed her heart to release the chains. But, above all, she needed her voice to keep the growing shadow of fear at bay. A distraction from her vivid imaginings.

"Sometimes I get scared. I get scared and I'm rude. I can't help it. I don't mean anything by it. Honest, I don't. You must understand."

"Sometimes we all need a little fear to help us along."

There it was. The voice. She was further away than before in a new corner of the room. The corner where Hope had envisaged her bed might be. She pictured her there. Her voice was hard and cold as if in her short life, she had been hardened to whatever came her way. She had long, dark hair, which was matted, in Hope's mind. But through the grime on her pale skin, green eyes, piercing like beacons, shone with life.

"You're there. I thought you'd left me. Please." Speaking words of weakness came easier than before. Showing weakness was difficult. She usually had a barrier to block it.

But the barrier was a pile of crumbled tears.

"Please don't leave me."

"I will. One day."

"Why?"

"Because my time will come. Soon, in fact. And it will be your turn to lead."

"I don't understand."

"We're here because we need to transform, Hope. We're here because of the things we have done. And only when we have fully transformed will we be released."

"How do you know all this? Are you one of them?"

"No, Hope. I'm like you. At least, I was like you. But now-"

"You're transformed. Yeah, I get it. You talk in riddles."

"Would you prefer I didn't speak at all?"

"No. No, please. I didn't mean that." Considering what the girl had said, Hope searched for a way to prolong the interaction. Anything to mask the pain in her wrists and her need for the bathroom. "Tell me your name. Please tell me. I can see you in my mind's eye but the details aren't clear. A name might help me see you as I hear you."

"Out there, my name was Beth."

"It's a nice name. Is it short for Bethany?"

"No. Just Beth. It was the name I knew anyway."

"And you transformed?"

"I'm close."

"And did you have to talk about the bad things you did?"

"The bad things that Beth did? Yes." Beth spoke quietly as if she was remembering the time when she too had opened herself up and revealed those dark places to a stranger.

"Tell me. Please, tell me."

"No, it's forbidden."

"Just a little."

"I can't."

"If you do, I'll tell you mine."

The pause came with a sense of persuasion. Blind to the words and with her freedom in chains, Hope felt the balance shift. She imagined Beth. Her hair hung across her face and she wore a tattered dress. Those green eyes peered out, but they were moist now. Being provoked by memories of what she had done had invoked shame and, for Hope, shame meant there was a story to be told. A story she might relish. If Beth told her tale and, somehow, if her sins were darker than Hope's then maybe, just maybe, she could reveal her own dark past.

"Have you ever felt shame, Hope?"

"Once."

"I have too," said Beth. "Have you ever wished that you had been somebody else? Had some other fortune and been given some other path to take?"

"Haven't we all?"

But it was as if Hope's responses went unheard. Beth had dipped a tentative toe into a world she had long left behind and seemed to find a fleeting pleasure there. Pleasure in the memories maybe. Or pleasure in the knowledge that a new world awaited her. A new life.

"I have," continued Beth. "I was like you in a way. In many ways, in fact. But I didn't have the fortune of a father to guide me. Whoever it was who fathered me somehow escaped the torturous parenthood of raising Beth."

"You didn't know your father?"

"No. I was fostered. My foster mother tried to steer me towards God from a young age. But the harder she pushed, the more I rejected, and, like you, I sought a means to do the things that would bring shame. Not with any purpose in mind and with very little deliberation. But something inside me, some dark hand, controlled me. I don't think I was bad. But something inside me was. There was something rotten inside me and the further into the darkness I sank, that evil flourished."

"I know what you mean." Her words rang true in Hope's heart. It was as if she'd found somebody that understood her. Finally. "I have that same feeling."

"Then there's hope for you yet."

There was a smile. Unseen and lost to the darkness, it spoke to Hope in silence, in warmth, and with a tenderness that can only be felt.

"I ran with the boys," said Beth. "They were older and they too had shunned our surrogate mother's words of God. Together we ran, we laughed, and we felt the freedom of parentless children. The world was our play-ground and the boundaries of society were removed. If we wanted something, we took it. We were unstoppable. Four insuppressible children on the road to nowhere. We were bubbling with enthusiasm. Each of us, a team. For a while at least."

"What happened?"

A new world showed itself in Hope's mind, blurred and pale like the water-coloured tones of a memory where four children, a girl and three boys, screamed and laughed. They ran from angered adults with no faces, just pounding feet that failed at every turn, leaving the children to wreak some new havoc in some new adventure in some new place.

"We grew older, the four of us. It was a time of discovery. Other children came and went, and each new child who arrived in the big house, beneath the inductions and the charade of love our foster mother had created, faced a choice. At the time, it hadn't seemed so. But when I look back now, I see it. It was a choice. Simple and in its purest form. Follow God and our foster mother, serve and obey. Or take the low road with the four of us, where fun and excitement ruled and adventure was always waiting. But few ever joined us. Most chose the path of least resistance and came to look down on us from the lofty heights of obedience."

"And those that joined you?"

"They didn't last. Either they didn't fit or they couldn't handle the banter. We fought like dogs among ourselves, but the fights were forgotten moments after they had finished. So most newcomers strayed. They were tempted by the fruits of our foster mother. I'm glad now. I'm glad for each of them."

The dark, sinister side of Hope listened with glee. It wanted more. The story was vivid in her mind, and with each spoken word, Beth's face became clearer.

"What happened? Where are they now?"

"We grew older, Hope. It's as simple as that. I wish I could say that we were finally caught and our posse was broken apart because that's what we needed, but I can't. We grew older and our bodies changed. And with the alterations, our curiosities grew. At first, they laughed, as young boys do, when I ran and my swollen chest bounced. But as time went by, each of them laughed less and, one by one, they moved closer. Closer until they came to protect me. They were like three brothers to me, but to them, I was different. Not a sister but something far more cherished. We were in the woods once behind our house. There was a clearing in the trees where we sat and smoked the cigarettes we had stolen. On occasion, one of us would steal some whiskey or whatever we could find in the house. We rolled in the grass and bathed in the sun, untouchable, free, and wild. But the sun and the drink increased their bravado. We were no longer children, carefree and equal. I could feel their eyes on me as we soaked up the sun. I longed for us to be equal again. I felt different. So I let them touch me so we could get back to being equal. They touched me with the curiosity of children and I touched them. Each of them in turn. I thought that if we had seen each other and touched each other, there would be no more curiosity left to distance us."

"But?"

"But the opposite happened. Our curiosities turned to desires. And my three brothers became my lovers. We frolicked in the sun that day, exploring and answering the questions that each of us had. And after that, each night, one of them would sneak into my room. I loved them. I loved them all and they loved me in return."

"You make it sound like a movie."

"Life was a movie for us. Back then. We still ran riot. We laughed, stole, and demolished the fruits of other people's lives. We were still bad, although between us all there was love, kindness and a tenderness that was pure and somehow didn't belong in the hearts of four evil children. But all things must end. And the choices we make at those times are the choices we live with and die with."

"Why? Why did it end?"

An unease grew in the pit of Hope's stomach. It was a movie she didn't want to end. She envisaged four young lives that Hope didn't want to change. She didn't want them to grow.

"Our foster mother. It had to be her. The fight between us had to end sometime. She opened the door to my room one night and she didn't like what she saw."

Grinning, Hope gave off a laugh. The images in her mind were clearly conjuring the scene with vivid detail.

"She unleashed the powers of God on me. She acted as if I was the devil and shied when I stood up and met her face to face. She told me I would burn in hell, and that I was nothing more than a demon in her home. Then she cast me away in the night."

"But what about the boys? Didn't they stand up for you?"

"Shamed. All three of them. She dragged me from my room. I was pleading with them to say something, to admit that it wasn't just me. But they looked down at me like I was nothing. She stopped me beside them and asked them if they had anything to say. But like the cowards they were, each one of them turned their heads and shrank back into their rooms. And she took delight in their actions. Her grin grew wide and smug. And she cast me out."

"That's terrible. They were your brothers."

"I'll never forget her last words to me. She said that if I returned she would call the police and that I would rot in a cold, damp prison for all my sins." Beth paused to remember the story the way she had lived it, and Hope wondered if her own imaginings were accurate. "That night, standing alone in the dark, I realised that it was over. My life. My time with my brothers. It was all over."

"Then what happened? Did you ever see her again? Did you ever see your brothers?"

The eloquence with which Beth had spoken was lost with the story. Her voice returned to its monotone narration of a long, distant memory.

And in the darkness, Hope felt the smile she had sensed earlier fade to a blank stare.

"Yes. Yes, I saw them all again. One more time. Each of them was standing at their bedroom windows like dolls in a playhouse. They were looking down on me in the darkness, condemned. She stood there too at her window at the top of the house with her bible in her hand. And, one by one, the fire that was borne of my own young hand and my own sweet revenge consumed them all."

CHAPTER EIGHT

A 1951 Aston Martin DB3 cruised through the winding Lincolnshire country lanes. On both sides of the road, sprawling fields of maize, barley, and potatoes spread for miles, interlaced with villages marked by church spires that reached out of the green, defiant of time, as they had done for centuries.

Had the weather been nice, Frankie might have had the roof down. But the low, brooding clouds threatened rain and the movement in the trees suggested that a fair wind was blowing.

The Silversmith Pub stood on the edge of Lincoln city to the north-west of the ancient medieval cathedral and castle that attracted thousands of tourists each year.

The car park had been empty save for a few cars of various ages and two work vans, which Frankie assumed belonged to workmen who were likely washing the dust from their throats after a hard day. He parked the car in full view of the pub's rear doors, where sufficient windows would allow him to keep an eye on the Aston.

At a corner table with a view of the entire pub, Frankie waited with a bottle of beer, trying to match the voice on the phone to the faces at the bar and those who entered through the doors.

In his mind, the man would be middle-aged, a smoker, and heavy-set with a shaved head to conceal his baldness, a symbol of vanity for men who rebelled against the signs of age. A shaved head is a choice. Clinging to a diminishing head of hair is a fight.

An old man sat at one end of the bar, turned sideways to interact with whoever would offer him a chance at conversation. But few did.

A group of men close to him, dressed as tradesmen and ready to wash away a week of hard graft with another cold pint, talked with little regard to eavesdroppers about customers. One man, whose friends called him Del and who Frankie established to be a plumber, told an anecdote about his apprentice, who was standing beside him glowing with embarrassment, about how he'd jumped out at his boss from one customer's bedroom with a pair of women's underwear on his head. The lady of the house, who had arrived home unexpectedly early, had screamed with fright, which turned to rage when she realised who the underwear belonged to and told them both to leave with the job half-finished. The young apprentice glowed once more. But he smiled when the other men all laughed. Even Del, who had very likely lost money on the job, saw the funny side, and he ordered a round of drinks from the boy's salary.

Beyond the tradesmen, a couple in office clothes huddled close. Perhaps they were a couple enjoying a quick drink before a night on the town. But the body language told Frankie otherwise. Only the man wore a wedding ring, and he inched closer to the woman as they spoke. It was the look on his face as he headed to the door to answer his phone that told Frankie the drinks were not wholly above board. The meeting was not a precursor to a show or a dinner but a stolen hour or two before he headed home to his wife.

A group of youths occupied the far end of the pub. Only one of them appeared to be above the legal drinking age and it was his job to visit the bar to order drinks.

All in all, Frankie placed the pub as a working man's drinking hole. The type of place where locals knew everyone and outsiders were noticed, acknowledged, and monitored. The analysis was confirmed when Frankie locked stares with one of the tradesmen, who simply nodded, took a mouthful of his beer, and re-joined his conversation.

The girl behind the bar, a young brunette wearing a tank top and jeans, and with a tribal tattoo on her shoulder, hovered close to the group of men, interacting on occasion. She had adopted a defensive approach, teasing the older men with her youth. But when the apprentice spoke, her eyes softened. She flicked her hair across her shoulder and leaned on the bar, hanging on every word he said, skilfully maintaining the barrier between her and the older men but dropping clues that the younger man should talk to her.

The door opened and a suit walked into the pub. The man who had locked eyes with Frankie found the newcomer in the mirror, assessed him, and then continued talking, leading the conversation. The apprentice turned to see who had entered, nodded, and then turned back to his colleagues with a sneaky flick of his eyes to the bar girl. She reached for a pint glass and began pouring a Guinness for the man, who dropped his laptop bag beside the bar, found his wallet, and paid for the drink while it was settling.

As if feeling Frankie's stare, the man's head snatched to the right, finding Frankie looking back at him. Then, taking his drink and telling the girl to keep the change, he collected his bag and made his way towards Frankie's corner.

"Are you...?"

Frankie nodded before he could finish. They were far enough away for nobody to hear their hushed conversation, but there was still no need to announce Frankie's name.

"You found the place okay then?"

"It's a long way. Let's get to the point."

The man turned his glass so the tiny Guinness emblem faced him then squared the beer mat with the edge of the table.

"I understand you're a man who might be able to help me."

The voice matched, but the man himself didn't live up to Frankie's imagination.

"I might." Frankie continued his mental judgment of the man while he spoke. "It depends on what you need help with."

"My daughter's missing."

"How long?"

"A few days now. The police aren't helping. I don't know who else to turn to."

Frankie nodded. "And who are you?"

"Jeremy Gilmour. My daughter is Hope Gilmour. She's eighteen. About five foot six."

"Do you have a photo?" Reaching across the table, Frankie waited for the photo. There was always a photo. "Save the description. They're usually biased anyway."

As if pre-empting the question, Jeremy Gilmour produced a four-by-six-inch photo from the inside pocket of his jacket. He passed it across the table then took a nervous drink, replacing the pint onto the mat, turning the glass, and then squaring the mat once more.

Frankie studied the photo for a few seconds, committed the image to memory, and then pocketed it.

"And you live around here?" Frankie eyed the man's clothing. He wore a suit, tailored, judging by the cut and the lining. His shirts were monogrammed and he wore no wedding ring. "Somewhere within walking distance, but not too close that you might be recognised. A nice house. Four bed. Detached with a driveway and a double garage in a prominent part of the city."

"Almost exactly." Jeremy frowned at Frankie's analysis. "Save for the double garage."

Frankie raised his brow in silent question.

"It's a three-berth garage."

"The first is for your daily car, a saloon, I'm guessing. Something tasteful but not extravagant. The second is kept free. And the third is for your weekend car. A little Porsche or a classic British sports car."

"Again, almost exactly correct. But how do you know my wife doesn't use the second garage?"

"Because you're not married."

"How do you know? Have you researched me?"

"Yes," Frankie told him straight. Then surprised him. "I began when you stepped through the door. Although I was expecting a larger man with less hair, I can't be right all the time. But you're not wearing a wedding ring and you haven't checked your phone since you arrived. A married man would check his phone at this hour. A married man would have a wife wondering where he was, especially when his wife has a missing daughter."

"Do you think you can find Hope?"

There it was. Frankie had demonstrated all he needed to.

"How long has she been missing?"

"Three days."

"And when did you last see her?"

"Tuesday evening. I arrived home from work. She was in her room. She was supposed to be studying, but I know for a fact that she skipped college."

"And it wasn't the first time, was it?"

Jeremy's eyes narrowed at Frankie's insight.

"No. No, it wasn't. She's been missing college with increasing regularity apparently."

"And you say the police won't help?"

"They say they're looking." Jeremy looked away, a sign of guilt or that there was more to come. "But it's half-hearted."

Frankie waited. His fingers interlaced, elbows resting on the table and eyes fixed on Jeremy's.

"It's not the first time I've reported her missing."

Again, Frankie left a space for Jeremy to fill. He needed details. There was no room for vague half-responses.

Jeremy closed his eyes, summoning the strength and will to tell the story.

It would come. Frankie knew it would come. It always did.

"We haven't been getting on. Well, to be a little more accurate, we haven't seen eye to eye in years. She's wild, you see. It's like she does everything to oppose me because she knows it'll upset me."

"Give me an example."

"The clothes she wears. She's barely a woman, damn it, and she walks around with her..." He checked behind him to make sure the locals weren't listening. "With her back-side hanging out and her..." He looked down at his own chest but was unable to use the words a man might use to describe a woman's chest about his own daughter. It was as if the idea repulsed him. "It all hangs out, Mr Black. No father wants their daughter to go out looking like that. There are all sorts of men out there. Men that have far fewer scruples than you or I."

Jeremy sipped at his drink and sat back as if he and Frankie had somehow formed a bond as gentlemen. But he knew nothing of Frankie. For all he knew, Frankie could have been one of the men he was referring to.

"So she wears short skirts and tight tops? Show me a teenager that doesn't."

"It's not just that. It's everything. I ask her to be home at ten and she comes home in the middle of the night. She doesn't even hide it, you know? Do you remember sneaking home late and trying not to wake your parents when you were that age?"

Frankie nodded. It was slight but it was a confirmation.

"Well, she doesn't. She makes every effort to make sure I know what time she gets home, banging doors, talking on her phone. She doesn't care. I ask her to clean the house, and when I come home, it's even messier. It's everything, Mr Black. The list goes on and you might think these are minor things, but they grate on me. She's insubordinate, and she does it to see how far she can go before I break. And when I do break, she just laughs and disappears for days on end."

"Hence the police reports?"

Jeremy nodded.

"I'm not a bad father, Mr Black. I'm trying to raise her alone and I feel like I've got to the final stages before she can meet someone nice and grow up. But there is only so much a man can take."

"Do you hit her, Jeremy?"

The question was designed to turn the man around. A full five-minute rant about his daughter had taken him further from her than he realised. What he needed was to be re-minded that he loved her.

"No. No, of course not. Why would you say such a thing?"

"I know what men can be like when they reach their breaking point. I am one, after all."

"Do you have a child? Do you..." He chose

his words carefully then continued despite Frankie's cold stare. "Raise your hand?"

"Yes and no. Yes, I have a son. And no, I've never raised my hand."

"But you know what it's like."

"So do you think she has run away?"

Jeremy nodded. "Yes. Well, I hope she has."

A questioning eyebrow coaxed him on.

"The only other possibility I can think of is that one of those men I described earlier..." He stopped to clear his throat.

"It's okay," said Frankie. "Does she have anywhere else to go? A family member? A family friend?"

"No. She has an aunt nearby, but Hope managed to alienate her a long time ago. The two don't get on."

"Can I ask about her mother?"

If Jeremy's face had been recorded from the beginning of the interview and played back in silence, Frankie mused that he would have passed through nearly every emotion a human could express. Love, sadness, loss, anger, and frustration. But at the mention of Hope Gilmour's mother, a bitter resent formed on his face. There were no words needed to substantiate his expression, but Frankie allowed him to continue to get the full picture.

Jeremy lowered his voice and stared at the floor as if recalling the events in his mind.

"Her mother was rotten. Bad to the core. Do you know what I mean, Mr Black?"

Nodding, Frankie waited for the follow-up.

"It was a very short relationship. You can hardly call it a relationship, it was so brief."

"You had a one night stand?"

Jeremy ignored the comment.

"I knew her through a friend of a friend. She was beautiful, Mr Black. A real catch. But our lives just weren't in sync. She was wild and free, and I was on a path to success. But this one night..." Jeremy mused and stared at the flock wallpaper conjuring the memory. "I still can't remember how it happened exactly. How I let it happen that is. I was with some friends at somebody's house. We were drunk, and by the end of the night, only she and I were left. The others had either partnered up and found a bedroom or were passed out in various parts of the house. I wasn't ready to go home. At that point, I was living in a flat still working my way up the ladder. You know?"

Frankie nodded, although he could only guess at what working your way up the ladder might mean or entail.

"The house was nice. It was comfortable. So I stayed. And so did she."

He sipped at his drink as if the memory called for it.

"She watched me from the opposite sofa. I wasn't interested. I just smiled and tried to make pleasant conversation. I never was great with the ladies, Mr Black, and I can assure you if I had been, she would have been way off-limits. But I wasn't. And well, she began to tease me. She didn't talk, you understand? She just began to reveal more of herself. Toying with me. You know? To see what I would do. A raise of her leg. The sly unbuttoning of her top button."

"She seduced you?"

Again, Jeremy Gilmour ignored Frankie's comment.

"I think she expected me to jump on her. But I didn't, of course. I think I'd seen almost every inch of her by the time she realised I wasn't going to take the lead."

He took another sip of his drink.

"So she did."

Inside, Frankie was smiling. It was the type of story that, had it been told by any of the men at the bar, would have been embellished with small details and crude gestures. But from the mouth of Jeremy Gilmour, it sounded innocent and naive.

"She said she wanted to know what going with a nerd was like. She called me a square and a fuddy-duddy. She said she wanted to see if there was a real man beneath my shirt and tie."

A tiny laugh emerged from Jeremy. It was a laugh of regret. The type of regret that comes with life's tiny mistakes that, in hindsight, seem ridiculous.

"And that was that. I'll spare you the details. I'm sorry. I've already said too much."

"Not at all."

"Needless to say that she didn't find the type of man she was looking for beneath my shirt and tie, Mr Black."

"And she came knocking on your door a few weeks later with the news?"

A slight nod of Jeremy's head confirmed it, and he lowered his head in shame.

"She had no intention of keeping the baby. She only came to vent some kind of anger. Of course, it was my fault. I should have used protection. I should have been more careful. I shouldn't have damn well done it. But I did." He lowered his voice again as the final details emerged. "And I would have to pay for the termination. She was bad, Mr Black. Poisonous." His upper lip curled as he spat the words and shook his head to rid himself of the memory. "She took my money and I can't tell you how many sleepless nights I had thinking about that poor life that didn't stand a chance. I'm not ashamed to tell you that I cried, Mr Black. It all felt so cold."

"And nine months later?"

"Nine months later, I received a phone call. It was from the hospital. I wasn't allowed to witness the birth. But I heard it. She screamed like the devil, cursing and..." He shook his head again as the memory of it all played out. "Such vulgarity. Such a vulgar girl. Bad to the bone. I was allowed in when the child was born. I'll never forget the look on her face. It wasn't hatred or bitterness I saw. That, I was used to from her. It was shame. Shame, Mr Black. Can you fathom that?"

Remaining impartial, Frankie said nothing, leaving Jeremy to finish the story.

"The nurse cradled the baby in her arms. She was wrapped in a white blanket and I can remember it with such clarity. I wondered how such a peaceful, beautiful wonder such as her could come from such an evil person." His voice softened as he reminisced. "The nurse passed her to her mother, smiling her way through her cold stares. But she refused her. Her mother, I mean. She wouldn't take her. The nurse said it was common for mothers to reject their child at first. So she passed her to me. I was the first to hold her. I stood by the window with my child in my arms, and I prayed that by some will of God I could pass her some of my kindness. Some of my heart. If I could, then there was a chance the girl might grow up to be good. She might grow up to have some kind of decency."

A glistening appeared in Jeremy's eyes. But he was unashamed of his reaction. He made no attempt to wipe his eyes.

"And it was then that her name came to me. There was a chance that the good inside me could overcome the bad her mother had passed on. There was, Mr Black, Hope."

CHAPTER NINE

"You killed them?"

"I don't know. I ran. As I always had. I ran until I could run no more. I ran until my lungs felt they would burst and the sound of the sirens had faded."

"But where did you go? Did they find you?"

"I disappeared into the only place I knew. The streets. Where girls like you and I can thrive. For a few lewd moments with a desperate man, you can survive for a day. Maybe more. That all depends on how drunk they are."

Taken back by the news that Beth was a killer, a self-proclaimed killer, Hope felt uneasy. Blind to the world and chained to the wall, she searched the room for her voice. The danger was high now. No longer was Beth an equal prisoner in a dark room. She was a killer.

"Now it's your turn."

Warm, stale breath on Hope's chest. She struggled against the chains but found only teeth. She fought for distance but found only the cold, hard wall.

And the warm trickle of her own urine on her legs and feet.

"I'm sorry. I couldn't help it."

Shame and embarrassment pushed Hope into herself. The bond they had shared, which Hope had felt as Beth had told her story, seemed to be gone, leaving only the shadow of fear looming above her and around her in the very air she breathed.

"Tell me your story. I know there's one in there."

She was close.

"Tell me what you did, Hope."

"Nothing like that."

"So then it should be easy."

"It's too bad. I can't."

"Then you keep the hood on. Once you

start it'll be easy. Like rolling down a hill. Once you start, you just can't stop."

It came to her, sharp and prominent among the whirlwind of thoughts, of times and of regrets. It stood out like a green tree in a desert, full of life. A story begging to be told.

And Hope knew it was one she must tell.

"Go on, Hope. I'm listening."

"Don't rush me. I'm thinking."

"Where did it happen?"

"It was a squat. A rundown, old house in town. There were people in every room. The corners were the most sought after. It was safer in the corners. You could see who was coming, and you could sleep."

"Were you homeless? You don't look like the type of girl who would survive."

"I wasn't homeless. I was with Greg. He wanted to buy something."

"Some drugs?"

"Yeah. But I was just with him. They weren't for me."

"I won't judge."

There was humour in Beth's tone as if she knew and had been there.

"The air was pungent. I can remember it like it was yesterday. The warm smell of heated spoons like warm hot cross buns mixed with vomit and urine. It was a terrible place."

"So why did you stay?"

"For Greg. He wanted to get high. He wasn't an addict."

"Of course."

"He wasn't. He just enjoyed the buzz. He told me it was like floating away."

"And you never tried it?"

"Not that, no. I did other things but I never injected anything. That was too far. It seemed like a step further than I was willing to take. But Greg enjoyed it so I never stopped him. He always made sure I was okay before he did it. He made sure I was safe before the drug took him. He was good like that. He was so gentle. I watched as he heated the spoon and saw the flame of the candle in his eyes. I was fascinated at how careful he was when he loaded the syringe. He wasn't stupid. He was always careful and always used a new syringe. I remember how his vein stood out from his arm as if it longed for the needle as much as his mind did."

Hope stopped, remembering the scene. The dirty floorboards. The figures cloaked in blankets around the room. The graffitied walls. And Greg, holding her gaze as the drug took him.

"It was like he was falling. Or dying. I hated that part the most. His eyes kind of slipped away. They grew distant like they were sinking. Until there was nothing left of him but a vacant look on his face. And he was gone."

Sensing Beth walking away, Hope imagined her sitting down in the far corner of the room, where her imagination had placed her bed. With the freedom of movement, she lounged, leaning on one arm while Hope, bound and hooded, told her story, listening with intent. Hope wondered if she was as fascinated as she had been when Beth had told her story. If she wasn't, she would be. It would be the first time Hope had told anyone what she had done. But it felt good so far. To peel away a layer of defence and reveal the Hope beneath would be to run naked in the fields with the wind in her hair and grass beneath her bare feet.

"I held him. I covered him with a blanket and I held him. I thought that, by touching him, he would know I was there. Maybe I would be in the atrocious dreams he would find. Maybe I would keep him from slipping too far. But once he'd gone, once he'd slipped into the abyss, another man came around. One of the blankets stirred. A face I hadn't seen before roused from this drug-induced slumber and he found me alone. He stared at first as reality drifted back to him. And then the questions came. Who was I? What was I doing there? Did I have anything? I ignored him at first. But he was relentless. I guess a girl like me in a place like that was rare. He could see I had money. My father's money. I remember the way his eyes danced across the room, never settling on one thing for longer than a second. He checked Greg wasn't awake. And he looked at me. He looked at my legs. Then he looked back at me. I knew something would happen. I could see it in his eyes. There was a hunger. That's the only way I can describe it. He can't have been older than thirty. He had thick hair, matted and ru-ined, and a ginger beard. He drooled as he watched me. I don't know if he was aware of it, but the way it hung from his mouth made him look like a rabid dog."

"Did you speak to him?"

"I said nothing. I was too scared to in case

I woke the others. I covered myself with Greg's jacket and tried not to make eye contact. But I could feel him staring. Each time I glanced back, he would be looking. As time went by and Greg slipped further away from me, the man edged closer. His eyes, always his eyes, flicking over me like I was a piece of meat. Before long, he was just a few feet away. If he had reached out, he could have touched me. So I rummaged through Greg's jacket and found his stash. I waved the little bag at him the way you'd wave a bone or a toy at a puppy."

"And was that what he wanted?"

"I don't know. But that's what I gave him. I did exactly as I'd seen Greg do. I mixed the powder with water and heated it. I waited for that warm smell like baking, only more chemical. I even gave him a new syringe from Greg's bag."

"You gave him a fix?"

"I did more than that. I gave him everything I could get on the spoon. I don't know how much it was but it was far more than Greg ever used. I filled the syringe with all of it while he pulled off his sock. Then he snatched it from me. Before I could even doubt what I had done, the needle was in his toe. Part of me wanted to stop him. But that was the weak part. Most of me wanted to watch him. And I did."

"He overdosed?"

"Right in front of me. I was expecting him to convulse, you know? Like they do in films. But he didn't. He just lay there with white foam spewing from his mouth and matting his ginger beard."

"You watched him die?"

Verbalising it that way softened the guilt. There was no mention of the word kill. There was no mention of Hope. Only death. And it had come to a man who had walked the line for too long.

"Yes. I watched him. Expecting him to jump up. Expecting him to know what I had done. A dark patch formed on his pants and the smell of urine was even stronger. I dropped the bag beside him, covered Greg with his jacket, and I left him there. I ran until I could run no more. It was raining. I remember being soaked to the skin. But I didn't care. And each time I saw his face in my mind, my weakness pushed him away, trying to forget."

"And your darkness?"

"Smiled."

In the blackness that was Hope's world, she saw Beth smiling. She felt the bond return once more. They were equal again. Although Hope had not killed by her own hand, she had done little to prevent the death.

They were equal.

The dirt on the ground crunched beneath Beth's feet. It was a faint sound perceptible only in the absence of sight. Her warm breath graced the skin on Hope's bare chest, and there was peace.

A soft finger traced the outline of Hope's stomach, and there was tenderness.

A strong hand tore the hood from her head.

CHAPTER TEN

"Tell me about her boyfriend, Jeremy. I'm assuming an eighteen-year-old wild child has a boyfriend?"

"Yes. Yes, she does."

Hardening his appearance to that of a protective father once more, Jeremy pictured the boyfriend. Or perhaps he was remembering a particular moment. Whichever it was, Frankie was sure he would vocalise his thoughts soon enough.

"Greg. That's his name."

"Does he have a surname?"

"I don't know it." A hissing sound followed as Jeremy cursed himself for not knowing. "I should have asked. That's what a father does, isn't it? I should know the name of the boy that..."

He stopped as if he was unable to speak the words aloud and admit that his little girl did the things that every father dreads.

"He's just as bad as her. God help his parents. I mean, she's always been bad, but when she met him, she took it to a whole new level. Now she drinks, she smokes, and not just cigarettes. I found things. Paraphernalia..."

"So you searched her room?"

"I was worried about her. She wouldn't talk. What else could I do?"

Ever impartial, Frankie offered no response in defence or argument. He took a mouthful of his beer, set the glass down, and interlaced his fingers, a sign he was ready for Jeremy to continue.

"It wasn't just drugs either." Checking behind him once more to make sure nobody had moved close enough to hear them, Jeremy moved his glass to one side and leaned in. He wore a look of disgust, of shame and embarrassment. "I'm a senior partner in a law firm, Mr Black. I've spent my life working my way up the ladder. I'm well respected for my knowledge and experience, you understand?"

Frankie nodded his confirmation but said nothing.

"A few months ago, I noticed people in my office were behaving differently. They were off with me as if they couldn't bear to be in the same room as me. I thought nothing of it. I hold a position of power and people are often careful about what they say. I was the same when I was younger. I didn't want an off-hand comment to taint the hard work I was putting in. But it went on. The weirdness. Then I noticed the legal secretaries childishly giggling together whenever I walked past. At first, I thought it was my hair or my appearance. But the behaviour continued. The smirks, the distancing, it went on."

He sat up, proud of his intelligence and achievements.

"So I played a trick. I feigned entering my office and when I was sure they weren't looking, I stepped into the fire escape. From there, I doubled back and sneaked up on them and listened to them gaggling like crows. I peered through the little window from behind them. I was there an hour listening to them harp on about nails and husbands and boyfriends and..." His brow furrowed and his voice deepened. "Certain things that should not be divulged to anybody, and certainly not in the workplace, Mr Black. Do you understand?"

"I do." He couldn't help but give a little laugh as he spoke. He'd been shocked when he'd learned that Jacqui used to do the exact same thing with her friends. "They tell each other everything, Jeremy. It's a shock to us all when we find out."

"Well, I had reason to reprimand them all. It was shocking behaviour. And I might have if..."

It was coming. Frankie prepared himself to keep a straight face.

"If one of them hadn't opened an email and clicked on something."

"What was it?"

"The girl in question called the other three over to her desk and they all huddled around. Conspiratorial little so-and-sos. I couldn't see what they were looking at, but somehow I knew it was related to their recent behaviour." He raised his head and dug his index finger into his collar to loosen it. "So I sneaked in. They were deep in laughter and didn't hear me. So I crept up on them as they all jostled to see the screen."

Frankie knew what was coming. He didn't know how but he sensed the story's direction.

"They were startled when I asked what they were looking at. The look on their faces was priceless. The other girls ran back to their desks and the girl whose computer they were looking at tried to close the Internet browser. But I stopped her. She tried to argue with me, saying it was nothing and that I shouldn't sneak up on them like that. But I knew it was about me somehow. I knew the contriving little bitches were laughing at me."

His face soured, offering little more than pride in his successful mission.

"Porn, Mr Black. That's what it's called, isn't it? Lewd, salacious, indecent, filthy videos of girls doing disgusting things. And men too. I'm not a complete prude, Mr Black. I know what goes on this world, but..." He stiffened as if somehow his posture would allow him to finish. "My little girl, Mr Black. They were looking at my little girl baring all to the world and sundry." Turning away, as if lost in the horrific memory, he growled, "And with that boy."

"Greg?"

"I've never been so embarrassed, Mr Black."

"Call me Frankie." Enough of Jeremy's history had been aired that formalities were no longer required. A trust had developed. A trust between two men of unspoken confidentiality.

"I've never been so ashamed, Frankie. I knew it was him. I couldn't see his face. But I knew. I was angry like never before, Frankie. I was angered to the fullest. I returned to my office and found the website myself. And she was there on the front page. With him." A helpless tone and demeanour came over the man as he narrated the story as if the memories had exhausted him. "The things they did, Frankie. The things they were doing for all the world to see. My little girl."

"It's okay. You don't have to go into detail."

"But you don't understand. Somebody had sent the website link to the secretaries. Somebody had managed to get into my email. They sent the links to my entire email address book, Frankie. Everyone I know. All of my clients, colleagues, and friends. All of them. All of them have seen her and the things they were doing."

"Do you think Hope sent them? I imagine she would have access to your laptop?"

"I can't think of anyone else who might do it. It sickens me that she would do such a thing in the first place. But to send it to everyone I know? It would destroy me and she knew it."

"And has it destroyed you?"

"My reputation carried me through, barely. You can imagine the apologetic emails I had to send and the sudden decline in social invitations. But I'm recovering from it. It's a slow endeavour and thankfully many of my clients are adult enough to see through it. Some are even compassionate. Imagine that."

"So, do you think she's with this Greg, then?"

"Yes. Well, I did. But..." He stopped and finished his pint. "I'm sorry. Do you mind if I get another?"

"Go ahead. I'd say you've earned it."

"Can I get you...?"

Pre-empting the offer, Frankie raised his hand palm out. Although a brandy would go down well, he thought. A brandy might pro-vide distraction between Jeremy's words to avoid him finding similarities in the struggles of fatherhood.

"No. Thanks anyway."

But the reprise offered time for thought. The offer of a brandy, regardless of his decline, returned the memory of his chair, of the photos, and of the rock in the river of umbrellas and suits.

And he was there.

Jacqui peered down at him, smiling, soaked to the skin but smiling. And in the river that flowed by, a head now turned. It was Jeremy. As if to say that amid happiness, there is suffering. You only have to look.

"Are you okay, Frankie?"

Jeremy was at his chair wiping the froth of Guinness from his upper lip.

The rock in the river faded.

"I haven't bored you to death yet, have I?"

The feeble attempt at humour was Jeremy's own way of providing a distraction, which meant that what he had to say would not come with ease.

"You were telling me about where you think Hope is."

His face straightening at Frankie's dismissal of his humour, Jeremy returned to his theory.

"He wasn't a good lad. I've told you once already. He was older and he was violent. I had some friends run some checks on him. It's one of the perks of being in my position. I have, or should I say, had friends in high places."

"So he has previous?"

Nodding, Jeremy took another sip of his pint and wiped his mouth.

"Drugs and violence mainly. Add to that some car thefts, robberies, and assaulting a police officer and you have yourself a prime candidate for a lifetime behind bars."

"Has Hope been in trouble?"

"I'm worried that she's done something bad, Frankie. I'm worried that she's gone too far."

It was a twist in the tale that defied the possibilities that Frankie was building in his mind. Then he considered Jeremy's choice of words as if he hadn't heard them the first time around.

"You said Greg was violent. You said Greg wasn't a good lad."

Nodding, Jeremy pulled his gaze from a

blank space on the wall as if his next sentence demanded conviction and sincerity. He looked Frankie in the eye, imploring him to find the bond that fathers share.

"The police found his body yesterday."

PART II

CHAPTER ELEVEN

The air was dank and stale but, to Hope, she could have been breathing the fine mist that rolls off the barley fields with her feet dampened by the early morning dew.

"Thank you."

But even with the hood removed, the pleasure and security of sight evaded her. Only the sound of her own voice offered any indication of the size of the room. There was no echo, but somehow the volume and depth at which her voice sounded to her brought with it the detail her remaining senses used to form a picture. It was an image of security. The one place in her world where she had always felt safe.

In the corner was her bed with her desk to one side, her chair, and the photographs of her father and Greg along with the rest of her bedroom furniture. She imagined it all there, laid out as Hope liked it.

"Your eyes will adjust in time."

Beth's words came from that place in Hope's imaginary room. She stood beside Hope's bed.

"And the chains? What about the chains? I'm tired. I can't sleep like this."

"You have to earn freedom, Hope. It's the next phase of your transformation."

"The next phase? I just opened myself up to you. I told you everything I could about me. And for what? You removed the hood and I still can't see anything. That's not fair."

"No. No, none of this is fair. I wish I could tell you that things will get better, that it'll get easier. But the truth is, Hope, if you want to leave this hole, you're going to have to do things you don't enjoy. You're going to hate it. You'll wish you were dead. You'll wish I was dead. You'll cry, you'll suffer, and you'll expose every weakness you have. And then one day, one day when you just can't take any more, when you feel like giving up and your mind tells you that this place is okay, you can live here, you can survive, then you'll see the light."

"What do I have to do?"

"Suffer, Hope. You have to suffer."

There was no dressing of the words. They were harsh but they were spoken with truth.

"When the door slams, Hope, your world is damned. The world as you know it is gone and the choices you make now will decide if you ever leave this place."

The tirade of curses building inside Hope quelled. There was a new sound. Footsteps approached through long grass then stopped.

"Is it him?"

Hope's whisper cut through the darkness. But she found no reply. The sense that Beth was close by was gone, replaced by an over-whelming feeling of loneliness.

The padlock and chains rattled against the wooden door.

Daring not to breathe and aware of her nakedness, Hope stood helplessly. She tried to back away but found only the cold wall be-hind her, and she worried the chinking of her chains alerted the man to her fear.

Bright light poured in from the doorway,

blinding Hope as if the heavens had opened and only the worthy could see beyond. She turned away and found the darkness even darker. Where the light should have shone to reveal Beth as she pictured her waiting beside Hope's bed, she saw only the inky black of the blind. The large shape of the man, blurred and vague, filled the void as he ducked into the entrance, his breathing laboured and hoarse like a smoker's as he struggled through what appeared to be a tunnel. His waxed coat scraped the walls and his heavy boots touched the earth floor inside.

As Hope's vision returned, squinting, she saw the man for the first time, lit from behind like an angel but with the sour features of evil etched into the deep lines on his shadowy forehead.

He studied Hope with eyes hidden in deep, dark sockets in the shadow of a single, heavy eyebrow. His head cocked to one side and the glints of his eyes rose as he took in every feature of her body. But with her wrists bound, no matter which way Hope turned, she could not escape his gaze.

He grunted. It was a deep sound from way down in the pit of his stomach. But it was when he stepped closer that the real fear be-gan. Quivering legs and a fluttering heart gave in to the man's presence and Hope's weight fell onto her chains. Iron teeth found her soft flesh with a renewed appetite.

Turning away, she dared not to look at him. She dared not to meet his eyes and cow-ered to protect the parts of her that she feared might entice the man.

Then, without warning, she felt the warmth of her bladder spread across her legs.

The shame was too much. The fear was too strong.

She cried, silently but heartfelt.

And a shape, small and light, came to stand beside the man.

She wore a white gown or a sheet but re-mained barefoot. She had long, dark hair that could have been red in the light and her face was gaunt, giving prominence to cheekbones that seemed to dominate her pale skin.

"She confessed her sins."

Beth spoke without asking and with what appeared to be very little fear of the man. As she stood beside him, they both peered at Hope as farmers might value livestock.

He grunted in reply and reached into his

pocket to produce what looked like a small bag or a bundle of cloth.

"Thank you."

For a moment, Hope could have sworn that the two exchanged a look that conveyed an understanding, a silent partnership or agreement.

But the man grunted for the third time. Then he turned with one final glance at Hope as she cowered in the new light. He made his way back into the tunnel. His breathing once more became laboured and raspy as he heaved his huge mass through the door.

Chancing one last look, hoping to find the clarity hidden by shadows, Hope glanced at him. He seemed to linger, loitering outside while she sought detail from his silhouette.

Then the door slammed. Once more, Hope's world became damned.

Chains rattled and a heavy padlock banged on the wood before his heavy boots kicked at the long grass, fading until they were no more than a whisper like the leaves in the trees.

Then nothing.

Hope wondered what was outside, where she was and what it looked like. Scant details sought only from the hard wind and the man's footsteps summoned an image of long grass and dead leaves. Branches rocked in the breeze. But was there one, or two, or many? Was it a forest? A field? Or maybe it was his own garden and the reality was that there were more houses close by. Places she could run to perhaps and people who might help.

What if she screamed?

What if she shouted?

Would she be heard?

"There's nowhere to run to." It was as if Beth could read her thoughts and Hope found herself gazing at the source of the sound. A door maybe? It was hard to say. The girl stepped closer. "Even if you could break through the chains and the wood, where would you go?"

"Anywhere. Anywhere but here."

"There's nothing out there. In here, you're safe, Hope. In here, you have a chance at purity. Out there..." Beth shook her head and followed Hope's stare. "Out there, you will die, sullied, impure, and brandished by shame."

"I'm thirsty. I need some water. And food. I've never felt such hunger."

"There's water waiting for you." Beth

found Hope's bloodied hand and splayed her fingers against the damp wall. "As much as you can drink."

"That's filthy. I can't drink that."

The thought of licking the seeping moisture from the dirty wall repulsed Hope. Her stomach rolled at the thought and she dry heaved. A burning combination of acid and saliva collected at the back of her mouth and she spat, letting the drool hang there until she recovered and straightened.

"You will. In time."

"I'm not an animal."

"The water is as pure as the earth can give you. That's what this hole does. Haven't you worked it out yet, Hope? The hole cleanses you. It takes all the evil, all the filth, and-"

"Spits us out?"

"Returns us, Hope. It returns us as pure as the day we were born."

Her last sentence hung in the air, but any thoughts of response were muted by the questions in Hope's mind.

"You're free," said Hope. "You spoke to him like you were an equal. Why aren't you chained up like me? Why didn't you run when you had the chance? You even have clothes. Why am I naked? It's humiliating."

"It's simple, Hope. I'm cleansed."

"Cleansed? What does that even mean? You told me what you did. You're worse than me."

"I was bad. And yes, the things I did were truly awful. But that was the old me, Hope. The hole has cleansed me." She stopped, and Hope found two glistening eyes in the darkness. "I'm ready."

"And how do I get these chains off? What do I need to do to move my arms and lay down? How do I become ready? I'm so tired, Beth. I'm scared and I-"

"Be patient, Hope. I was the same. But I promise you, listen to me, do as I say, and you'll be like me."

"And clothes? It's cold in here. How do I get-"

"Be patient, Hope. Do as I say. The next step is hard but not as hard as the first."

"What do I need to do? God, this is frustrating." She kicked out behind her, hurting her foot, but she bit her tongue, closed her eyes, and felt the pain abate like the ebbing wave of a freezing ocean.

Breath, warm again, on Hope's chest.

She was close. Closer than before.

A hand, soft and calm, alien yet reassuring, found Hope's cheek. She startled then settled, allowing the girl to navigate her way as the blind navigate through life.

"Tell me, Hope."

"Tell you what?"

"Will you tell me anything I ask?"

"If it means getting these chains off then yes."

"Will you tell me anything I ask because you want to be cleansed? Or because you want to be rid of the chains?"

"Both. I want to be like you. I want clothes and freedom and..."

"And?"

"You have peace about you. Despite everything you've done. All the bad things, the lies and the stealing. You're at peace. I want that."

"So there's good inside you?"

"I wasn't always bad. Please tell me how."

Beth spoke in a whisper as if the knowledge was secret, sacred, and not to be heard by the undeserved. Her words accompanied the breeze of breath that found the soft down on Hope's skin and woke the goosebumps on her back.

"Tell me the kindest thing you have ever done."

CHAPTER TWELVE

Lincoln city centre was small in comparison to London. But, in Frankie's experience, every city in Britain shared certain traits: a pedestrianised shopping centre, an area of history, an industrial area, and, bordering the city and the suburbs, areas of affluence where the likes of Jeremy and Hope Gilmour lived.

After his chat with Jeremy, it had taken a few hours for Frankie to walk around Lincoln, understand the layout, and get a feel for the city life at its most basic level. Students, drunk on cheap alcohol and high on a life of irresponsibility, staggered with linked arms, bracing against the night's chill. Some sang and some shared a bottle of wine as they walked, and Frankie couldn't help but picture Jake one day doing the very same thing in a similar city, free for the first time with new friends and no cares in the world save for passing his exams.

Sitting on a park bench out of the wind, Frankie whiled away the night hours considering his son. He was estranged by Jacqui's death when the tragedy should have brought them closer. Frankie wondered how long it would be before the time came for Jake to go to university. Every part of Frankie's imagination saw Jake as a strong, young man, determined like Frankie yet gentle like his mother. There was no doubt the boy would do well. He was intelligent and quick. But he was still a child. Just as Hope Gilmour had ventured down the wrong path, Frankie feared that Jake might do the same.

A scatter of heels on the cobbled street and a hushed giggle of two girls in tiny dresses echoed through the street. The sight of a man sitting alone on a bench at night didn't shock them or change their behaviour in any way, except only to increase their volume and boldness.

"Alright, mate." The girl had a London

accent. The parent in Frankie wondered if she often called out to strange men. He nodded and watched them walk away, considering the interaction with vague interest.

Twilight crept up. Like the opening of the world's eyes, it announced a new day. It was day one of Frankie's hunt for Hope Gilmour and he had almost no place to start. He pushed himself up as the first of the morning delivery vans trundled by at the far end of the road.

The south side of the city was marked by the River Witham. Frankie had passed it the previous evening and had seen a riverside walkway just a few minutes from where he was sitting. He found the bridge again and stood on it as the morning sky began to light the commanding Lincoln cathedral that towered over the city.

On one side of the bridge was an industrial area. It consisted of large units with builder's merchants and wholesale markets of meat and fruit and veg, and the obligatory dog van that was just opening, preparing for the morning rush of bacon rolls and polystyrene cups of bad coffee.

On the other side of the bridge was the

train station and the high street. It was clear that money had been spent on the area. The pavements were newly laid and the stylised, newer buildings were sympathetic to the traditional look of the older buildings.

He continued over the bridge then circled back to find the waterside. A bundle of clothes and blankets on top of a pile of flattened cardboard boxes was the first sign he was on the right path. Then, a little further along, he found the underside of the bridge. A small service road ran beneath it and beside the river, but there was very little traffic and the only sounds Frankie heard were the squabbling ducks on the water and the foraging pigeons.

A single pair of eyes stared at him from the back of the bridge twenty metres away. A single bundle of blankets. A single pile of flattened cardboard boxes. The girl was sheltered from the wind and rain by the huge, concrete structure and the small thickets of trees on either side. It was the perfect spot to sleep rough.

She eyed him as he approached.

"I'm looking for a friend of mine. A girl."

The girl didn't reply, but her eyes followed him as he moved closer. He stepped off the path onto the poured concrete, walking slowly to assure her that he meant no harm.

"Can you help me?" Raising his voice in case the wind had carried his initial question away, Frankie watched her eyes flick from side to side. A sign of nervousness.

Lank, dirty hair hung over the girl's forehead. Her eyes peered over her knees, which were drawn up to her chest and wrapped in an old sleeping bag.

"I'm not going to hurt you. I'm looking for a friend. She goes by the name of Hope."

"We're all looking for a friend, mister."

She had a northern accent and her voice was rough to match the texture of her skin. But before he could respond, to Frankie's left, a man wearing too many jackets, a woollen hat, and fingerless gloves stood from his hiding place, letting his blankets fall to the ground. He stepped from the copse of trees.

"Why don't you leave the girl alone?"

"I'm not looking to hurt her. My friend is missing."

"You're looking in the wrong place." He stepped closer to Frankie, closing the distance to just a few metres. Frankie raised his hands in the international gesture of surrender and backed away from the man to find another approaching him from the other side.

It was a trap.

"Listen, guys." Frankie searched for an exit but found none. "All I'm doing is looking for a friend. A girl."

The first punch connected with Frankie's jaw but wasn't followed up in time, giving Frankie time to recover, find space, and then size the two men up as each of them closed in. The girl, who was the bait in their trap, stood up and walked towards them.

"I'm not looking for trouble. You don't want to do this."

But Frankie's words fell short as the first man to Frankie's left grinned a yellow smile through a thick salt and pepper beard and moved closer. His bright, red nose seemed to stick out from his face as if it had been stuck on as part of a prank or costume.

Frankie flattened it with a lightning-fast jab. But he felt the immediate thump of the other man's fist against his ribs knocking the wind from his follow-up hook. Both men rushed in, knocked him off his feet, and then piled on top of him as he kicked and punched at whatever he could. With one man pinning each shoulder down and weeks of alcohol on their breaths, Frankie searched for clean air to one side and saw the girl walking towards them.

"Nice work, boys." There was just enough time for Frankie to place the girl's accent as Newcastle before she delivered a kick to his side. "I told you we'd find him."

She pulled a fingerless glove from one hand, folded it, and stuffed it into one of her pockets. Then she bent and began to pat Frankie's jeans down, feeling for the contents. He writhed on the ground, twisting as far as the hold the two men had on him would allow. But the girl moved with him and found the envelope of cash Jeremy Gilmour had handed over only a few hours before.

"We hit the jackpot."

Her attention shifted to the wad of folded notes. She ran a grubby finger over the edges in awe of the sum of money. But the promise of funds for more alcohol proved to be their undoing. Both men turned to see inside the envelope, allowing Frankie his first chance of retaliation. He raised one leg up, hooked the man to his right around the neck, and dragged him down. The movement stunned the man with the red nose who was too slow to react. Frankie's hand found the soft flesh of his neck, squeezing and pushing the man to the ground. Frankie rolled with him and, just as the girl began to run, he reached out, grabbed her ankle, and pulled her to the ground. The two men scurried away before standing. But as they both came at Frankie for another attack, Frankie tore the envelope from the girl's hand and pushed her away.

"I didn't come looking for trouble. Trust me when I say I'm not the man to pick a fight with. I'm just looking for a friend of mine. That's all."

He backed away, raising his hands to calm the situation.

"If you haven't seen her, I'll just move on."

It was clear how much the money meant to the girl and the two men, and they watched the envelope disappear into Frankie's pocket with expressions of lost opportunity.

"How often do you pull this scam?"

Neither of them replied.

"Okay. I'll ask you all one more time. I'm looking for my friend. Hope Gilmour." Pulling the four-by-six-inch photo from his pocket, Frankie held it up, waving it around for all of them to see. "Have you seen her?"

The girl shook her head. The men followed suit.

"So we'll leave it there. I'm sorry to have disturbed your morning."

Eying them all one last time to register their faces, Frankie nodded and turned to walk away. But as he did, a harsh Newcastle accent called out in a voice that betrayed her youth.

"Wait."

Frankie stopped.

"You're really not him, are you?"

Turning, he found the girl relaxed and with an almost bemused expression on her face.

"I'm not who?"

The three friends glanced at each other once as if confirming her statement among themselves before the girl continued.

"You're not him." She stepped closer. "You're really not the killer, are you?"

CHAPTER THIRTEEN

"Another story? This is ridiculous."

"Not a story, Hope. A truth. But this time it'll be easier. You won't need to scour your darkest memories. If there is any good inside you, this memory will be sitting on top like a cherry on a cake."

There had been times in Hope's life when the light had shone and banished the darkness. They had been brief, but they had been the closest moments between her and her father. And it was those memories that showed themselves to Hope as if they were submerged in swirling waters.

The waters ceased to swirl and one memory stood clearly above the rest. She could see her face and that of her father, but when she tried to speak, her throat closed, her chest tightened, and her eyes burned the now-familiar sting of emotion.

"I can't."

"You can't think of a time or-"

"I can't seem to find the words. Why can't I? Am I really that bad? Am I so evil that my mind refuses to speak the few good things I've done?"

"It's not as easy as it sounds, is it? But it'll come with time. I struggled too."

"You did?"

"Of course. When you're in a dark place with dark thoughts, the good often eludes you."

"But I can see it. I can remember the times." She stopped and the waters began to swirl, blurring the images she had seen with such clarity. "Or can I? Was I dreaming?" Unable to remember the moment, as fleeting as it was, all Hope could think of was her father. "I was with my father. We were..."

But the good was gone. Lost to the swirls.

"It's okay. It'll come. Take your time."

"But I can't. I want to say it. I want to tell you so you know I'm not all bad."

"When I lived on the streets," said Beth, "I met all kinds of people." If Hope could have seen Beth, she imagined her eyes would be staring into the black so the memories her mind conjured could show. Her voice softened, seeming to lose its authoritative tone and adopt a tenderness as if the memories were stored in her heart for safekeeping. "I met a man once who, like me, had been born with nothing, fostered, and lost to the working class world until he lost his little job as an apprentice and had to sleep on the streets. He would eke out a living selling anything he could find. Small things. Clothes, bags, and anything he could carry in his cart. Anything other people discarded."

"One man's trash is another man's treasure. I've heard that saying before."

"And it was true. He found things, cleaned them, and sold them. He did this while all around him junkies were getting high and drunks like me were drinking themselves to death. He stashed his money in a hole in the ground so when the news spread of what he did and jealousy found him curled in a ball on the ground, kicked and beaten, he lost nothing but pride."

"In the face of adversity?"

"Exactly. He did this until he could afford to rent a small room above one of the local shops, where he cleaned the items and sold them until he had enough money for a small house with a garage as well. Then he upped his game. He took home large pieces of unwanted furniture, cleaned them and fixed them up, then sold them. It took years but, eventually, he bought a van so he could collect the items. Then he moved to a house. His own house. He built such a name for himself that he had to hire a helper, a man he'd met during his time on the streets, and he bought another van. His little business grew and grew. He had a shop with more workers, more vans, and his little house with a garage became a big house. Then, one day, he found himself a girl. Over time, she became his wife and she blessed him with a wonderful child. A girl."

"But hang on. How did you know him? Did you meet him on the streets?"

"Eventually. It took years for him to build his little empire. He employed people from the street to give them a start in life. He was a good man. But one day it all came crashing down. He never told me why. He never spoke of it and if I asked, he would close off. He'd withdraw within himself. I guess we all have things that we wished we could forget."

"Or that are too painful to remember. That's so sad."

"All I know is that the world he had built came tumbling down. He walked away from his life and gave up. The house went. He could no longer afford to pay his staff, leaving them no option but to go back to the streets and to the lives they had left behind. The banks took everything from him. Everything he'd built up was gone in the blink of an eye. Then, with nothing to his name and with just a photo of the family he'd lost, he made his way into town."

"To sleep on the streets?"

"No. I wish he did. I wish I could say that. But he didn't."

"I don't understand. What did he do?"

"I found him on the railway bridge that I used to sleep under. It was out of town and a long walk from anywhere, but I liked it. I didn't have to fight for space there. Beneath the bridge was the warmest and safest place I could find. I'd been out, eating berries from bushes and whatever I could scavenge. I was just getting back when I saw him and I knew something wasn't right. I stopped beside the hole in the hedge I used to climb down to the railway, and I watched him. His face was blank, staring into the distance. There was no-one around and the traffic was light. He didn't move. Whatever was going through his head had him pinned down."

"Did you know what he was going to do?"

"I had an idea. But when I heard the rumbling of an approaching train, I knew. I have no idea how long he'd been standing there, but he only moved when he heard the train. I walked faster. I didn't want to spook him by running. The train grew closer. It was out of the city and was moving at full speed, getting louder and louder. He put one foot on the wall and I began to run. Out of the corner of my eye, I could see the train tearing through the countryside. It was unstoppable. He stood up on the wall, raising his arms like a high diver, outstretched, you know? Like Jesus on the cross. He flinched though when the train sounded its horn. I think the driver had seen him. There was a squeal of brakes and sparks, but there was no way the train would stop in time. I dropped my bags and began to run as fast as I could, but it felt like I was running through tar or syrup. No matter how hard I ran, it felt as if something was holding me back. I was ten metres away when he closed his eyes. The train was braking hard but still going fast."

Beth paused for a breath as if reliving the moment. The hole was silent, as if before there had been some unregistered sound, some ambient noise, that had now quietened. But there was nothing.

"He leaned forward, letting gravity pull him down. I remember the driver's face. I can still hear the squeal of the brakes and the sparks. And I can remember the weightlessness of him as I shouldered him to the ground."

"Oh my God, you saved him?"

"Some might say I saved him. Some might say I was a hero. But as time passed and I grew to know him, the notion of the phrase meant nothing. I'd condemned him to a life of misery. In the moments that followed, we lay there. A car passed but did not stop. The train stopped and was silent. And in the distance, police sirens approached. I knew I'd saved him. But I also knew that because of me he would be arrested. What else could I have done?"

"Nothing. You saved him. He should be grateful."

"I took him to my little space below the bridge and we listened as the police arrived. It seemed like hours. I said nothing. He said nothing. He just stared at me and all I could do was look away, busying myself with making sure nobody found us until the police left and the train rolled on, fading into the distance with its heavy rumbling shaking the earth. We sat on. I longed for the rumbling to continue. I didn't want it to stop. I knew that as soon as silence returned we would have to speak. And that would be the hardest. But it did stop. It was silent until the birds began to sing and we heard the wind in the trees once more."

"Who spoke first?"

"It was him that spoke. I had nothing to say."

"What did he say? Was he angry? Was he upset still?"

"There was no emotion. Not really anyway. I boiled water on a little gas stove I had and made him tea in an old polystyrene cup

I'd found. He took the tea and held it in his trembling hands. I watched as he looked around my little space, my little sanctuary. He was the only person to ever see it and by letting him in I'd somehow lost all my security. I think he knew that. I think he saw that place and knew it was all I had and he surprised me when he spoke. Two glistening eyes in the half-light and a blank face that seemed to be void of life."

"What did he say?"

"Two words." Beth's voice trailed away and she paused while Hope imagined the scene and what he might have said. "Thank you."

CHAPTER FOURTEEN

The Morning Glory cafe stood two streets from the riverside. It contained twelve tables each covered in red and white checkered table cloths with a container of cutlery and condiments as a centrepiece. The tables were arranged in three neat rows of four. Frankie chose the seat closest to the door, where a slice of fresh air breathed through the tiny gap in the doorway, cooling the musty aroma of his three companions.

Noticing the objective look from the cafe owner, Frankie called out to him, "They're with me." The man was standing behind the counter, half in and half out of the kitchen, and reddened at Frankie vocalising his thoughts. "Four coffees and four bacon rolls please."

"To go?" The owner had an Eastern European accent that Frankie tried to place.

He stared at Frankie, daring him to argue. Frankie rarely backed down from a dare but was in no mood for an argument with the man who would cook his breakfast.

"We'll eat in, thanks." Frankie pulled out his chair and sat down.

"I can't allow it, sir. You can stay but I'm afraid your friends will have to go. I have other customers to think about."

"I'm sure you can find it in your heart, sir. It's just coffee and breakfast. It's cold out."

"That's not my problem."

Offering a smile to the three ashamed human beings at the table, Frankie pushed his chair back and approached the counter. He gestured with a flick of his head for the owner to come closer for a discreet chat.

The man obliged and leaned on the counter as if protecting his property.

"They're not welcome. I don't care what you say. I'm sorry. That's the way it is."

"What about the waitress?" Frankie peered through to the kitchen behind. "Is she supposed to be working here? My guess is that if she's serving and you're manning the till yourself then the other kitchen staff probably have questionable passports. My guess is that you somehow managed to get into the country legally and set up a business. Well done. I'm all for enterprise. But your staff don't have that luxury, do they? You're keeping them going until their papers come through. I'm right, aren't I?"

The man-sized Frankie up in a single glance.

"Everyone has a right to work."

"And everyone has a right to a cup of coffee and a bacon roll. So you've got three options." Frankie mirrored the man's stance by leaning on the counter. "One. You try and throw them out. But, let me tell you, you'd better be quick because I've fought them and they're not as slow as they look. The one with the red nose has a great right hook. Two. You throw my friends out and I report your questionable employees to the authorities. You'll lose your license and we won't get our breakfast. Or three. You bring us our food with a smile and we both never mention any of this again. We get fed. You don't go to prison."

The owner of the café held Frankie's stare for a moment. Then broke it off.

"Good choice. Now please bring me and my friends our breakfast."

"You shouldn't have done that." The embarrassed looks on the two men's faces mirrored the girl's words as Frankie sat back down. "We're used to it."

"You're right. I don't have to do anything. But I want to. I believe in paying my way."

"We can't tell you much." The man with the red nose leaned in and spoke in a hush. "There's not much to tell."

"Tell me what you know."

Frankie reached for the bundle of notes in his pocket, peeled off fifteen twenty-pound notes, and divided the smaller pile into three. He slid each of the even piles toward each of the three people with whom he shared his table.

"Before you pick up those banknotes, let me tell you something. Out there somewhere is a friend of mine. Her name is Hope Gilmour. She's eighteen years old. She's been missing since Wednesday morning and her boyfriend was found with his head caved in on Thursday morning. That means she's been alone for two days with no money, no food or water, and no phone to call for help."

The girl's face lit up as Frankie spoke.

"I saw that." Lowering her voice to a whisper to match the conversation, her eyes widened. "I read it in the paper. Not the girl, Hope, but the boy. The police said he was wanted. Is that right?"

"That's right."

"Do you think she was killed too?" asked the man beside Frankie with the hard punch and foulest breath.

"I don't know. That's what I need to find out. Nobody knows if she was actually with him. As far as the police are concerned, he was alone. The relationship wasn't exactly approved of by the girl's father."

The three friends glanced at each other then lowered their gazes to the table and the tantalising three piles of money. Sensing that information was coming, Frankie sat back and waited. In his experience silence was the best method to get someone to talk, and it was the girl who broke the silence.

"She could have been taken."

"Taken? Why would she be taken?"

"That's who we thought you were."

"I don't understand."

"Well..." The girl's eyes flicked between her two friends as if she sought permission to share a secret. They nodded. "That's why we were waiting for you. That's who we thought you were."

"You weren't robbing me? You thought I was a kidnapper?"

"He took our friend last week. Beth. And before that, I heard that another girl was taken. Both were in the early hours of the morning. We aren't the only ones fighting back. Everyone on the street is looking for him."

"He's taking girls off the street?"

"One every week. Maybe if he has your friend Hope, he didn't need to get a street girl. Or maybe he's getting braver."

"Have any of the girls been found?"

The girl shook her head.

"Your friend. Beth. Where did you see her last?"

"By the river under the bridge. It's our spot."

"And the police?"

Both men offered a single laugh in unison and the man with the nose pulled out of the huddle.

"Don't be daft, mate. We don't exist. Why would they put effort into looking for a person that doesn't belong anywhere?"

"Because you're human beings?"

"Thanks, but you're wrong. You've seen how people react. We're outcasts. A reporter came around from the local rag. He did a little article. But it was more of a page filler than a plea for any type of information."

"You." Frankie stared at the girl. "How did you-"

"Mona," she cut in. "Mona is my name."

"How did you come to be homeless, Mona?"

"I ran away. Same old sob story. You must have heard it a thousand times before."

"Abusive stepfather? Alcoholic mother?"

"Something like that."

Frankie nodded. "And Beth? She's definitely been taken? She hasn't just caught a lucky break or, I don't know, met someone?"

"No. I saw it happen. But I was too slow to react. I saw her being bundled into a car, blankets and everything. Then she was gone. I chased after the car as soon as I realised what was happening. But we weren't expecting it. I mean, you don't, do you? It's like an illness. You never think it's going to happen to you or someone you love until it does."

The words stung.

They drove a nail deep into Frankie's chest and cast images of Jacqui's face contorted with pain and agony as her body fought the disease.

"Are you okay?"

"Can you tell me anything else? The car? The man?"

All three shook their heads as four bacon rolls arrived with four coffees on a tray held by a tight-lipped, dark-haired girl who could have been on the front page of a glamour magazine given the right opportunity. The bacon rolls and coffees were delivered with little grace, effort, or manners, and she turned with a flourish to leave as fast as she could. On any other occasion, Frankie might have said something about her ability to waitress. But the news he'd heard, the car and the man they had spoken of, weighed heavily on his mind. He turned his attention back to his new friends, catching each of them with a look of sincerity.

"Thank you. All of you. Thank you.

You've been very helpful." Pushing his chair out, Frankie slid another twenty onto the table to cover the bill. "Enjoy your breakfasts."

He reached for the door, but as he did, a voice called out to him.

"There is one more thing."

The man who had said the least paused as if he was surprised by the volume of his own voice. He quietened when the sullen waitress looked up from the counter. Then he turned to Frankie.

"If you find Beth..."

His voice trailed off, and his eyes fell to his lap where his fingers fumbled at nothing.

Frankie nodded.

"You'll be the first to know."

CHAPTER FIFTEEN

"The point is, Hope, that regardless of how bad you think you are, there is good inside you. It's hard to say it out loud. It's hard to talk about the things that show kindness because that's not who you think you are. You think you're bad. You think that by speaking out loud about the good things you've done, that somehow I'll see a weakness. It's not true. By vocalising those good things, you're telling the world how good you can be given the chance. You're telling this place that you're ready to move forward."

"But am I really ready?"

"I think you are. But you have to want to move forward."

In the silence and darkness, Hope could hear the crisp puckering of Beth's lips as she spoke and she lost herself in the girl's articulate speech. She spoke with confidence yet reserved enough volume to maintain innocence. Her whisper-like voice was alluring, addictive yet somehow commanding.

"I want to. I do want to move forward. I want to be better. I want to do all the things you said. I want to leave this hole cleansed."

Beth emitted an exhale through her nose. Hope heard the relief, although it was slight, she was sure she heard it.

"Good. So take your time. Tell me the kindest thing you ever did."

The waters swirled once more and, from the melee of faces, places, and times that rose to the surface then sank back down, only one memory, the same memory as before, emerged with superior clarity. And while the memory hung there, teasing Hope, she sought the words to begin before it sank once more.

"I was younger. Fourteen or fifteen, I think. And, like you, I had never known my mother. My father avoided the subject, and each time I questioned him, he somehow manipulated the conversation onto something else. I think that's half our problem, my father and me. There's a whole raft of knowledge that we don't share, and that knowledge is my history. I told him it's my right to know. I told him that I needed to know and that I wouldn't go looking for her if only I knew. But each time, he said that it's his job to protect me and that keeping my mother away was the best way he could do that."

"But you went looking for her anyway?"

"Not at first. I had an image of my mother but it was mostly a caricature of the impression my father had given me of her. She was an older version of myself with similar but more mature features and evil eyes. I remember evil eyes. It was about the time when I had one foot in the light and one foot in the darkness. Some days I would be good and others I would do anything I could to push my dad to his breaking point. So he used to take me for drives. *Us time,* he called it. Time when there were no distractions and we could talk. He has a little classic car so, if the weather was nice he would take the roof down, and I'm sure that in his mind we were the picture of perfection. The idyllic father and daughter combo. I also knew that, during these drives on the long and winding country lanes, he couldn't escape my questions about my mother. So I asked him again and waited for the flash of red in his eyes and the little pulse that beat on the side of his head. One day, he pulled the car over into a lay-by and turned off the engine."

Hope was there. Gone were the swirling waters of memories. In her mind, a desaturated scene played out. Her father gripped the steering wheel, fighting the urge to ruin the father and daughter drive with an outburst and seeming to battle with a knowledge that he was reluctant to voice. Overhead, birds sang, and bees and butterflies danced their daily routine.

"I have to tell you something." He spoke with a reluctant yet empowering tone as if what he was about to say was the key to Hope's questions. It would be the deciding factor in whichever path Hope was to take. And he knew it. He stared straight ahead through the tiny windscreen and let his hands fall to his lap. "I believe that your mother is evil. I believe that good and evil exist not just as descriptions but as entities, as substance. And I believe that we are hosts. We are guided by whichever entity we host. I'm not a scientist or a doctor, but I've met enough people, both good and bad, in my life to have formed a reasonable conclusion. Your mother, Hope, was host to an evil beyond which I have ever seen."

"Is that the only reason you don't want me to see her? Surely I can make my own mind up. I'm nearly an adult-"

"I also believe," he cut in, furthering his explanation, "I also believe that there are things called biomes. It's a theory that scientists believe in, which somehow fits my concept of good and evil."

"What's a biome?"

"Scientists called them bacteria. But I think of them as energy. They are all around us. Even now, they are in the air and they guide who we are. When a mother gives birth to a child, she passes on her own biomes to that baby. They are the first biomes that baby ever has. They are the first influence of that child's personality except for the genetic patterns that come from DNA."

"Oh, come on, Dad. Is this a science lesson or a dad trying to get out of telling his daughter who her mum is?"

"I'm keeping it as simple as I can. I believe that when your mother gave birth to you, she passed her own biomes onto you. Her own evil biomes. I was there, Hope. She didn't hold you. She didn't kiss you. She could barely look at you. It was me who took you from the nurse."

A shiny glaze appeared over her father's eyes and his mouth tightened as he swallowed hard.

"Since the day I took you from that room until this very day, I've tried everything I can to rid you of your mother's evil. Most days, I look at you with pride, Hope. The way a father should dote upon his daughter. But there are times when..."

"When what, Dad?"

"When I look at you and all I can see is your mother's evil eyes staring back at me and her evil grin as if she's inside you, in your heart, somewhere I have never been able to reach."

"So he believes you truly are evil?"

Roused from the conversation in the car by Beth's voice, Hope blinked away the memory. But the tale she was telling was still clear.

It had a direction now and she knew what she had to say.

"Yes and no. He believes my mother passed onto me her own evil, but that the love and kindness he has shown me since the day I was born can somehow overcome that."

"He believes in you. He sounds like a good father."

"Yes, he does. And yes I guess he is. He deserves far better than me."

"It sounds like you don't believe in yourself."

"I believe there's good in me. I didn't then. I didn't think of good and evil as anything of substance until that day. I didn't think of my-self as either. Until that day."

She stopped, knowing the next few words would lead her into the tale she had been un-willing to tell.

"But I just had to know if what my father had said was true."

CHAPTER SIXTEEN

Frankie emerged from a shop with the previous day's local newspaper. The shopkeeper had been confused as to why Frankie hadn't wanted the up-to-date news but had eventually obliged.

Keeping the paper folded, Frankie took the long walk back to his car, which was parked in the car park of the Silversmith Pub where he'd spoken to Jeremy. The morning sun cast long shadows, the cool night gave way to the rising heat, and, as the city awoke to a new, blue sky, the buzz of activity grew. By the time Frankie reached his car, the roads were busy with students, parents, and workers beginning their day. But for Frankie, it was the beginning of an investigation. And while he enjoyed the smug thrill of not being tied to a chair or reporting to a boss for eight hours a day, he knew the next few days would be heavy on his mind, his body, and, most of all, as he still felt the gut-wrenching pang of loss, it would be heavy on his heart.

The front page of the Lincolnshire Post headlined with a report of a local parade. Two photos depicted a carnival with banks of smiling spectators as groups of people from all walks of life marched by. It was a piece designed to invoke a sense of community within Lincolnshire.

Page two offered a very different mood.

The headline read *Wanted Lincoln Man Found Dead*. The first photo was taken from the edge of a field, presumably where the photographer had parked his car and where the police had erected barriers. It showed a crop of barley with a white tent on the left side. Several investigators wearing white forensic suits were standing outside and two uniformed officers guarded the gate to the farmer's field. In the distance, a church spire, silhouetted by the waking sun, rose up from the tree line reminding Frankie of his journey into Lincoln. He'd seen the view before on the main A-road he'd used on the way into the city, a north-to-south artery with villages on either side.

Frankie started the car and cracked the window open to let in the last of the morning's cool air while he read the report. There was no mention of where the incident had taken place, only that it was twenty-five minutes south of the city. He checked his watch then drove out of the car park.

The morning traffic was heavy, and while he waited on a steep hill for it to amble along, he admired the view across the surrounding countryside. The city had been built around a medieval castle and cathedral that both sat on the highest hill offering spectacular views for miles in every direction. Ancient buildings, stone walls, and cobbled streets were all time-less memorials to a thousand years of good times and bad, suffering and joy, life and death.

The surroundings invoked imagination. Frankie wondered what the reaction would have been if a young man had been found bludgeoned to death a thousand years ago. He wondered what the reaction would have been if the man in question had been an up-standing member of society. He wondered if the story would have made the front page of the Lincolnshire Post.

The road passed over the river via a bridge. He looked but saw no sign of Mona and her friends on the pathway below. The city faded away in his rear-view mirror and he settled in for the ride, checking his watch to mark the twenty-five-minute point. The photo had been taken in the early morning and the sun had been low in the sky, which meant that if the road continued north-to-south, the field in question would be on his left-hand side, eliminating fifty per cent of the villages and fifty per cent of the church spires he would see along his journey. He opened the news-paper on his lap and studied the photo of the field, the tent, and the distant church.

At twenty minutes, Frankie slowed the car to forty miles per hour, ten slower than the limit, and waited for the next village to show. A sign on the side of the road told him that Sleaford, the next large town, was thirty miles away and the village of Shelton was one mile away.

Shelton would be coming up on his left. A

line of thick trees separated two fields and, as the landscape rolled by, the village began to emerge. It was small, even by Lincolnshire standards. It had a church to the north of the village but its steeple had a belfry and a spire. The photo in the image had only a tall, pointed spire. He passed the trees and found no farmer's gate. It was enough for him to pass by and mentally cross Shelton off his list.

The next sign informed Frankie that Sleaford was now twenty-seven miles away and that the village of Addleton was only two miles away. Beside the name of the village was a small sign in the shape of a flower. Once more, he slowed to forty miles per hour as he approached Addleton. Checking his rear-view mirror, he pulled into a lay-by. Beside the road into the village was a farmer's gate. With the newspaper in his hand, Frankie left the engine running and ran back to the gate. He peered down the lane named Addleton Road where he saw a sign that read *Welcome to Addleton*. Below it, written in fading, white paint but with the love and pride of the local villagers, was that same small flower symbol and the words *Winner of the Best Kept Village*

Award 2009. Then, below that, Please Drive Carefully Through Our Village.

The village itself was a further mile along the winding lane. Frankie pictured well-kept lawns and cottages built from picturesque Lincolnshire stone adorned with ivy. There would be a village green where locals would meet on dog walks and a local pub. There was always a local pub. Huge chain stores had been the infamous ruin of small British shops in villages such as Addleton. It was far more convenient for locals to procure their groceries in one trip rather than visit various different stores.

But the pub could never be replaced.

The farmer's gate appeared to be the same as the one in the photo. It was made of steel with six rungs and was held up by two wooden posts. But when Frankie looked across the fields at the distant rooftops of Addleton, he saw no church. It was only when he stood on the second rung of the gate that he saw it hiding behind a line of oak trees. Once again, it was at the north end of the village, but it couldn't have been the church in the photo.

With Addleton crossed off his list, Frankie climbed back into his car.

The next road sign told Frankie that Sleaford was now only twenty-five miles away and that the next village on his left would be Grafton, another two miles away. There was no small flower symbol beside the village's name.

As Frankie pulled onto the road, far off in the distance, grey, finger-like clouds reached toward him. Behind them, a bank of thunderheads loomed, dark and brooding, ready and waiting.

CHAPTER SEVENTEEN

"It was near Christmas time when I saw my own mother for the first time. I can remember the cold and the lights and the people in the streets all laden with shopping and bursting with smiles. The windows of the pubs were fogged with the warm breath of the early evening punters. From every doorway came a blend of carols, laughter, and sickening Christmas spirit. I was still mad at my father for what he'd said and how he'd been withholding information. I'd been through every piece of paper in the house, through his filing cabinets, through diaries, through address books and phone bills, matching every number to one of his contacts and calling the numbers I didn't know."

"But?"

"But I found nothing. There wasn't a shred of information anywhere that would help me find my mother. So I stole his office keys one night. I sneaked past security and unlocked his office when nobody was there. In there, I found his safe. The code was easy. It was my birthday. I don't know what I expected to find. Maybe a photo. Or a letter. But there was nothing out of the ordinary except for an old file with a sealed envelope inside. It was the letter-sized type with bubble wrap inside, you know? It felt important."

She didn't hear a sound but somehow Hope knew that Beth was following her every word. She felt the connection.

"On the back of the envelope was the stamp of the law firm Dad works for. I could have just tossed it back. I should have tossed it back. But I didn't. I was sure it was important. So I opened it. I was so intent on finding out who my mum was that I just opened a random envelope that wasn't addressed to me. It could have been anything. But, somehow, some part of me knew."

"'The evil biomes?'"

Hope laughed once. A nasal breath, singular and short-lived.

"No. But there was a connection. Inside was another envelope but this one was half-size, flat, and brown. Again, it was marked with the stamp of my dad's law firm on the back." She swallowed hard and cleared her throat as the girl she saw in her memory retrieved the smaller envelope and held it in her hands staring at the markings on the front. "It was his last will and testament."

"You found his will?"

"I opened it too. I didn't even open it carefully. I tore the thing open and emptied the contents onto the floor."

"And what did you find? What did it say? Did it mention your mother?"

"Yes. On the last line above his signature. Below the passing of his assets and below the mentions of relatives I hardly knew. It was there. It was as if it was only there to appease me, to allow me closure once he's gone. When he wouldn't be there to pick up the pieces or when he wouldn't be around to care."

"What was her name?"

"Jane. Her name is Jane Osborne."

"Did you find her? Did you track her down?"

"I searched everywhere. It was a mission. I had to find her before my father realised I'd opened his will in case he contacted her. In case he did something. But there was no record of Jane Osborne anywhere. So I went to the town hall. I went alone and I spent days looking until, just when I was ready to give up, I struck gold."

"You found her?"

"I found the marriage certificates. The records for marriages are kept on file for anyone to see. And there she was. Jane Osborne."

A cool breeze somehow found the tiny hairs on Hope's skin as she spoke the name of her estranged mother.

"Jane. That's a nice name."

"Yes. She was studying at the university. You're the first person I've ever spoken to about her. All these years, she was nothing. Then there was a chance she could be something to me. A real person. And now she is real, now I actually have a mum, talking about her seems so weird."

"Was she as evil as your dad thought?"

Another laugh. Singular and brief.

"I think I saw her through different eyes. At first anyway. I stood there on that street on Christmas Eve surrounded by joy and happiness, and all I saw was a downtrodden woman. A woman who was struggling to get through life like she carried a burden, or a weight, or something."

"And did you speak to her?"

"No. I watched from a distance. I followed her through the town and watched her as she waited outside a school. She looked like all the other mums there. And then I saw her daughter."

"She had another daughter?"

"Yes. She was much younger than me but she was beautiful, Beth. The softest and sweetest thing you could imagine. But something was missing from her. No, sorry, not missing, but present. There was something present. A sadness. The other children ran from the school and held their mum's hands. But this girl didn't. She walked as if she shared her mother's burden. She walked slowly and with trepidation. I followed them again. They walked back through the town, the girl carrying her own school bag. I tried to get close so I could listen to their voices. I imagined myself with them. I imagined that we walked as a family to our home, no matter how small or ill-equipped it might be. I imagined it. I imagined the joy of my mother calling me down for dinner. I imagined having a little sister who I could share the excitement of Christmas with. I wanted to hear them speak. I wanted to hear my mother's voice. My family. But when I did get close enough, what I heard were not the words of a loving mother. It was the bitter tongue of evil. The girl cried and still the woman, my mother, snapped and snarled at her. It was resentful. It was angry."

"Do you think that was why the little girl was sad?"

"Yes. Yes, I do. And when the little girl's pleas had pushed her over the limit, my mother raised her little skirt and slapped her bare legs. I could feel it, Beth. I could feel the sting on her cold skin. I was hiding behind a street corner. It was dark and I was lost in the maze of back streets. I peered around the corner as she slapped the girl again. The whack of her hand against the girl's backside was loud above the screams. But I think, somehow, she felt me. My mother. She felt me watching. Because she stopped and looked my way. I ducked around the corner, fearful that she might come at me. And what could I have done? She was raging. She was evil. And she was my mother."

"Did you look back?"

Smiling as she relived that moment, standing in the darkness, the waters swirled once like something inside her was trying to hide what she had done or forgotten the moment. Hope clawed at the memory, narrating it as fragments showed through the water.

"No. Part of me wanted to. Part of me enjoyed the voyeuristic pleasures of stalking my own flesh and blood. Part of me wanted to stay where it was safe. It was the part that my father spoke to. I thought of him then. How kind he is. How soft, thoughtful, and gentle he can be. But I couldn't picture them together. In the end, I didn't need to look back. My mother's voice screamed along the street echoing off the houses. And the tiny footsteps of a child's buckled school shoes clattered along the road. I froze. The footsteps grew closer and there was nowhere for me to hide. But before I could even think about what I did, I was opening my arms in welcome and, as the little girl ran around the corner, she ran straight into my arms. I hushed her. I stroked her hair and felt her hot tears on my face. And still, my mother screamed at her to come back."

"You get back here right now, you little monster."

It was her mother's voice, loud, harsh, and cruel in the empty street.

And Hope was back there. Back in that street with the cold wind burning her ears and her heart thumping as it had done at the time. Hope held her little sister with only seconds until the moment would come crashing to a halt.

"What's your name, little girl?"

But the girl just sobbed. Her face was burning hot with emotion and she trembled in Hope's arms.

"Polly? Where are you?"

"Polly? Is that your name? It's okay. I'm not going to hurt you." Whispering in the child's ear, Hope tried to hold her away so she could look into her eyes. She needed to know if she was really her little sister.

And she needed to know if the evil that Hope hosted was in her too.

But as the little girl pulled away to see who it was that was holding her, their eyes met. No words needed to be spoken. There were no words that Hope knew to describe what was running through her mind. The connection between them was strong. The fear, the curiosity, and the bold questioning that Hope knew her own eyes carried.

But there was no evil inside her. She was just a sweet, little girl with the world before her.

Hope glanced left. Every inch of her wanted to run with the girl. To hide her. To keep her safe.

"You better come out before I find you."

Surely the darkness would hide them. There must be a doorway or something, an alley maybe, where they could hide until the evil mother had passed. She ran, and Polly, her sister, felt the movement and held on tight with both arms around Hope's neck.

But something stopped her.

Where before the darkness inside her had torn open the envelopes in her father's office, where the evil that her mother had passed onto her through birth had embittered her father and all he stood for, a light now shone. It was a light that cast many shadows, tall and long, which seemed to stretch on to all corners of her mind. In the shadows, they could hide. In the shadows, Polly could have a new life free of danger and suffering. In the shadows, they could be sisters.

But Hope knew that it was only in the light that Polly could have a mother. It was only in the light that she could grow free of the questions that Hope herself had come to live with. It was only in the light that she could find her own way in life.

She whispered once more into the girl's ear, taking the time to breathe and inhale the young girl's scent, to savour and remember. She coaxed the girl's face toward her own and found her eyes, bright and red even in the dim street light.

"In years to come, you'll thank me. I hope. I hope you'll understand."

"Polly? Where are you?"

The little girl's head snatched toward the sound of her mother as she stepped into view in the road. She turned back to Hope, eyes wide with fear and panic.

"I'm Hope. Remember my name. Come and find me one day."

The little girl's head shook from side to side as if she was scared to utter a word but knew what was about to happen. And fighting back the urge to join her sister in shared emotion and fear, Hope wiped her eyes and whispered to her sister for the last time.

"I'm so, so sorry."

She stepped out into the light and called to the woman in the road.

Her mother.

"Here."

The joyous moment of relief gave way to anger and wrath on her mother's face as she strode towards Hope, her face a picture of all that is bitter and vile.

But defiant to the woman's rage, Hope stood her ground.

"Here." She held her little sister up for her mother to take and to care for as only a mother can. "I found your little girl."

CHAPTER EIGHTEEN

A summer storm was building in the sky like the ache in Frankie's heart. He stopped the car beside a farmer's gate. Early indications that he'd found the correct spot were good. As he parked, he caught a glimpse of a church spire. He turned the engine off, grabbed the newspaper, and walked back to the gate with his view of Grafton blocked by a tall hedgerow.

The uniform heads of barley swayed in unison as the growing wind licked the tops of the crop. As Frankie reached the gate, he saw the flattened grass where people had stood to gain a better view. Perhaps the photographer who had taken the photo in the newspaper had stood there too.

The church spire, without steeple and belfry, reached high above the trees. The rooftops of Grafton were visible but partially obscured by the mile of landscape. To the right, standing taller than the village, partly due to the low rise it stood on and partly due to its impressive build, was a large house. It was ancient and commanding, affording the owner a view across the village as a king might oversee his reign from a parapet.

The house was out of the shot in the paper. But holding the photo up in front of him, there was no doubt in Frankie's mind that he'd found the right field. On one of the wooden posts were the tattered remains of the red and white tape the police had used to cordon off the area. It was slightly hidden by the reaching limbs of the hedge as if nature had already begun its efforts to conceal the event.

The second photo in the report showed a picture of Greg. It was a police photo of him standing in front of a height guide. His hair had been cropped short but was somehow still unkempt. His gaunt face pulled his skin-tight to reveal sharp cheekbones. But despite being in police custody and despite the image's black and white grain, his pale eyes glistened with life and his mouth seemed to sneer at the camera. A judgmental man would describe the boy as despicable. But a young girl who might be easily led and influenced might find him attractive. There was a charm about his photo.

A square patch of grass, lighter than its surroundings, marked the spot where the tent had been erected, and a dark area identified the place where Greg had fallen. Dried blood, black and unnatural against the green, marred the dying grass like a poison.

The first tiny drop of rain touched Frankie's face. A second and third pattered on his shirt. Then the ground beneath him fell into deep shadow. Above, the grey fingers that had stretched across the sky reached someplace far away and, in their wake, the dark and brooding army of clouds rolled into action.

Frankie crouched. The footsteps of the police and crime scene investigators had destroyed any chance of envisaging the act save for the faintest of trails in the shorter grass that ran alongside the hedge.

His senses pricked. Frankie followed the trail keeping to one side to avoid destroying the path somebody or something had made. At the bottom of the field, where the hedgerow and drainage ditch turned ninety degrees and headed south, the path cut through a patch of mud. It was the run-off from the field.

And there they were.

Two boot prints in a place where the overgrown hedge and wild raspberries would force anybody walking the route to step into the mud. But they were not the boot prints of a young girl. The right-hand print was far deeper than the left. Pools of water began to collect in the prints as the few drops of rain grew heavier and wet the dry areas of Frankie's t-shirt.

Frankie followed the edge of the field to the far corner until he was diagonally opposite the farmer's gate and his car. He found a stile in the fence and crossed over as the heavens opened. The rain in the trees was the only sound he could hear. Taking a quick glance back at the gate in the distance, Frankie stepped down into the mud to observe his new surroundings.

Standing at the edge of a forest, Frankie had a view across open grassland to his left and thick trees to his right. The ground rose before him and at the top of the grassy hill, the gables of the grand house were just visible.

Thick oak trees offered some protection from the rain. Frankie opened the paper and read the report, dismissing fact for fiction and putting to one side the conjecture that reporters use to fill out a story. But one fact stood out amongst the few.

Police are investigating car tyre marks found nearby. They are urging any passers-by to recall if they saw a car parked by the field and to report the colour, make, or model. At this stage, any details would be gratefully received.

The ground where Frankie was standing was boggy. Anybody crossing the stile would have to step into the mud. And besides Frankie's own print, there was only one other. A right boot, its print deep as if the person carried something heavy on their right shoulder.

Frankie felt that he was on the right path. But from that point, the trail ended. It also indicated that the police hadn't looked in the corner of the field, assuming the car tracks to be the killer's means of escape.

The path cut through the forest and at times was lost to the debris that littered the ground, leaves, pine cones, and branches. If he had to describe the walk, Frankie would call it pretty with its meandering paths, wildflowers, and utter silence. Yet he was surprised to find the path untrodden. There were no boot prints and no scattering of leaves or branches with fresh dirt peeking through. It was like nobody had ever walked into the forest, or at least they never took that particular path.

There was a flash of lightning before a strengthening wind began to whip at the trees above. The downpour found weaknesses in the canopy and dripped heavily onto Frankie's shirt. Through a break in the trees, the grim clouds above shone a darkness over Grafton.

There was a crack of a broken branch to his left, deep inside the forest, too far to see.

Frankie stepped off the footpath, ducked beneath the low hanging branches of a tree and entered the forest. His trained eye scanned the trees for movement but found none save for the far-reaching limbs of a thorn bush that blocked Frankie's view of the forest beyond.

There was a peace inside the forest that was otherwise lost to the monotonous hum of cities and towns. Even the village of Grafton, as quiet as it may be, was open to the winds that tore through from the North Sea fifty miles to the east. Frankie walked with care, avoiding dead branches on the forest floor and seeking bare patches of earth. He moved from tree to tree, perpetually alert to any noise or movement. A pair of squirrels chased through the tops of two tall oak trees, emitting chatter-ing-like laughter. Then a wash of rain swept across the forest and the silence was lost to the heavy drops that fell on the scattering of dead leaves.

Frankie peered deeper into the forest be-yond through the thick lines of thorn bushes. A tiny stream trickled across the face of the hill, following the same path it had carved for centuries beforehand. A small pathway had formed from the legs of man and game through the foliage. Frankie eased through the gap and the branches fell into place behind him. He leapt across the stream and scrambled up to the hard mud to take in his first view of this new part of the forest. It felt darker. Maybe because the walls of the forest were thick with undergrowth offering no real escape. Perhaps the canopy was thicker too. But the trees grew sparser with larger gaps between them.

And then he saw the circle of rocks.

At the far end of the forest, encircled by thick oak trees, a series of twelve rocks were set in the ground like teeth in gnarled and rotten gums. Each rock, taller than a man and wider than two, were hewn flat on the side. They were all two arm lengths from the neighbouring rock and standing in the mud to form a perfect circle. The ground between them was flat and debris-free save for a single rock similar to the twelve but laid horizontally in the centre of the ring. Its uppermost surface had been made perfectly flat by the hand of man and smoothed by the hand of nature.

Awestruck by the perfection of the ancient creation, Frankie stepped closer. He ran his hand along the vertical aspects of the closest of the twelve uniform rocks.

No birds sang.

No squirrels chased.

No boughs moved with the wind.

Only the showering rain on the canopy above.

And, behind Frankie, the familiar sound of a shotgun being racked.

CHAPTER NINETEEN

The cool air licked the wounds on Hope's wrists as the chains fell against the wall behind her. To move her arms, to rid her shoulders of the incessant aching, and to scratch the bites of the tiny insects that had plagued her face since she arrived...

It was bliss.

But she said nothing. Instead, she watched as the man lumbered through the darkness, his huge form silhouetted against the bright light from the doorway and his heavy grunts sounding in rhythm with his tired steps. He found Beth in the shadows and she nodded. A sliver of light had found the edge of her profile and she stood, unafraid, as he ducked into the doorway and scraped his way along the tunnel.

Hope exhaled as the door slammed.

"Thank you."

"Don't thank me, Hope. You earned it. Right now, you're a butterfly emerging from a cocoon. You've cracked the shell and you're peering out. It won't be long now."

"And you? If I'm peering out of my cocoon, where are you?"

Beth gave a laugh of triumph, short and proud.

"I've broken free of *my* cocoon, Hope. All that remains now is for me to spread my wings. To show the world my new colours."

"So why don't you? Why don't you go? Why do you stay here?"

"I will. When the time is right, I'll leave."

"But, Beth, you're free. Help me get these chains off my ankles and we can both go. We can escape."

"You should eat."

"I don't want to eat, Beth. I want to know why you don't just leave."

A tin plate dinged in the silence and Beth rummaged in the small bag the man had left.

"Here. Eat this."

The faintest of light reflected off the plate. With one swipe of the back of her hand, Hope lashed out, sending it scattering across the dirt.

"I don't want the food, Beth. I want to get out."

She knew it was wrong the moment her hand connected with the plate.

"I'm sorry."

But Beth said nothing.

"Beth, I'm sorry. It's just my temper and these chains on my feet and..."

A swell of emotion threatened to break behind her eyes.

"It's this place, Beth. I have to get out. I can't stand it." In the few seconds it had taken Hope to spit out the words, her breathing had spiralled. It was as if someone or something was crushing her lungs. She could neither get air in nor out. "I'm sorry." Those were the only words she managed to utter between breaths and she bent double to try and regain some composure.

Until a flash of pale skin in the dark preceded a hard slap against the side of Hope's face, rocking her sideways.

A silence followed. And although she

couldn't see Beth, her eyes burned into Hope's conscience.

"Have you finished?"

With her cheek still ringing from the slap, Hope searched for her and found only a sense of where Beth stood. She was close by, within arm's reach, and waiting for Hope to reply.

"I don't know how you stand it, Beth. That's all. I'm sorry. This isn't easy. I know my father will be worried. And you know what? I want him. For the first time in as long as I can remember, I want to be with him. I want to tell him I'm sorry. I need to make amends."

"And your boyfriend? Greg, wasn't it?" Hearing his name stung Hope's eyes. They burned with a brief desire to fill then cooled. A hand squeezed once at her heart but re-ceded and vanished as if it had merely passed across the organ. "Do you still mourn him? Do you still long to be in his arms? To welcome him into your body?"

She wanted to say yes. She wanted to yearn for him. She wanted to tell Beth how wonderful he made her feel. But where Greg had once ruled Hope's heart with his strong arms, where once there was warmth in his eyes and smile, Hope found only the cold bite of shadow.

"No."

"You don't miss him at all?"

"A part of me wants to. But no. I should be feeling something. I should be grieving him. But..."

"But what, Hope?"

Urged on by Beth's words, Hope sought the grief that she should have felt. It was as if she had plunged her hand into the swirling waters, but before her grasping fingers could grip the words she sought, the cold bite of the water had numbed her grip. She groped but found nothing.

"I'm cold. I want my dad."

"Eat. You need some strength."

A soft hand found Hope's and steered it toward the tin plate Beth offered.

With one hand holding the plate, Hope ran her fingers over the food. It was cold and had the texture of dried flesh.

"What is this?"

"It's meat. It's fresh and it's cooked. Please, Hope, do not waste any more. It's all we have."

Taking one of the lumps of meat between her fingers, Hope raised it to her face. She sniffed and found her mouth moistened. She touched it with her tongue, feeling the grain of the flesh.

And something inside her snatched the morsel from her hands.

She chewed like a wild dog, feeling for the next piece before the first had been fully chewed and swallowed. Some carnivorous sense within her fed on the iron taste that watered her gullet.

"That's it. Eat. You need strength, Hope."

The meat was tough, forcing Hope to hold onto each piece with her grimy hands and tear strips off with her teeth. The effort was demanding. So much so that the only sound she could hear was the grinding of the meat between her back teeth, along with her own hungry breathing struggling to maintain the pace.

It was only when she found no more meat left on the plate that she tried to speak, still chewing the last piece, and sucking the moisture and blood from between her teeth.

"Is there more?"

"No. Not today. Tomorrow maybe. Maybe not. How do you feel?"

Swallowing the last of her meal, Hope

wiped her mouth with the back of her hand. Her breath caught up with her feeding then slowed, and as her tongue ran around her teeth, finding strands of hard flesh in those hard to reach places, she saw Beth in the shadows, equally hard to reach.

She eyed the girl, a patch of black in the surrounding gloom, distinguishable only by the soft movement of her head and two barely visible glints of her eyes.

And just as Hope had seen Beth, Beth saw Hope.

As the feverish effects of the carnivorous feast wore off, and the taste of blood diluted with each empty swallow of Hope's saliva, strength found her. Emboldened by the swelling in her tummy and the sticky remnants of some poor beast on her fingers, she stood tall over Beth.

But Beth was unafraid.

In a single step, she stood before Hope, her breath grazing the skin on Hope's chest. Perversely, Hope enjoyed it. And although the smell of Beth's breath was sour and repugnant and hot like vomit, the joy that came with the close proximity outweighed her disgust.

"You mentioned your father."

Warmth.

"I miss him."

An ache.

"What would you say to him? If you had just one chance. Just one word. What word would you tell him?"

The obvious answer for Hope was to say she was sorry. But he deserved more than a mere apology. A single word could not convey how she wished she could take it all back. The hate, the spite, the videos and photos that had caused him humiliation. The invasion of his privacy when she had torn open his personal effects in selfish greed and misguided entitlement.

"I wouldn't say a thing."

"Not a thing?" Beth's shape twisted in the dark. She cocked her head in surprise and waited for Hope to explain. "You wouldn't ease his mind? Or try to heal the wounds in his heart that you have created?"

"No."

"Then your mother's evil runs through you like poison, Hope. You will never leave this hole. You will never breath-"

"I would say no words to him because

there are no words of such magnitude." Hope waited to make sure Beth had finished her rant then continued. "I would say nothing to him because of the damage my words have already done. Words alone cannot heal the rift between us."

She waited for Beth to question her remark. But no question came. It was a sign she had captivated her, and that the next phase of Hope's transformation would be underway.

"Go on."

"There is nothing that can heal the damage I have caused save for one thing and one thing alone."

"And what is that one thing, Hope?"

"Love." She smiled as she pictured the scene. "I would hold him and hug him like he has been waiting for me to do for eighteen years."

CHAPTER TWENTY

"My name is Frankie Black and I'm looking for my friend."

With his hands behind his head and his back to the gunman, Frankie turned, searching the reaches of his vision for a sign of the man's position and size.

But the steely barrel found Frankie's nape, cold and hard, and he stilled, waiting for the gunman to talk. The man pushed with the length of the gun, forcing Frankie forwards, accompanied by a grunt-like word.

"Walk."

The voice was gruff and deep and came with the sound of saliva. It was a voice, Frankie surmised, that was rarely used and belonged to a man with a barrel-chest and hands like dinner plates, only thicker.

Leaving the stone circle behind and keeping his head hung low, Frankie walked. Through bushes and trees, on paths and through thick brush. Up rises and down hills, Frankie walked, with the weight of the shotgun resting on his neck as a reminder that one false move might be his last.

But the walk was not a submissive notion for the gunman to think he had the upper hand. Nor was it in any shape or form a weakness on Frankie's behalf. The walk was twenty minutes of opportunity for Frankie to learn everything he needed to know.

He stumbled once and learned that the gunman was faster than Frankie had thought. The barrel of the shotgun remained on the back of Frankie's neck the entire time. With his head hung low, Frankie learned that the man wore a size eleven or twelve boot, easily big enough to have been the prints Frankie had seen in the mud earlier.

The small hills gave Frankie a chance to widen his step, and he learned that the man suffered with his breathing but had the stamina of a packhorse. There was no relent in the threat of the shotgun, only an increase in his raspy breaths.

Finally, Frankie learned that the man was no stranger to the woods. The shortcuts they had taken from path to path were the types that only a local or landowner would know. A shortcut to bypass a boggy patch. A shortcut to avoid a fallen tree. A break in the trees to find a small clearing like a crater where the trees would shelter the sound of the gun, where a gap in the trees allowed the rain to collect on the ground, and where the earth was soft enough to bury a man's body.

But where anxiety and trepid anticipation should have gripped Frankie, and fear should have been writhing through his body, he found his thoughts to be only of Jacqui. There would be little pain. Death would come before even the man had released the trigger.

His mourning would be over. Frankie would, once more, be with Jacqui.

And he welcomed the thought.

Although thoughts of his devastated little boy were crushing, they did little to sway Frankie from the path he was about to take. So much so that, as his mind planned escapes to overpower the man, he reasoned that such an action might result in severe injury, paralysis, or prolonged suffering for all. Jake's life would be irreparably altered by tending and nursing his father.

If Frankie were to go then the only course of action was to greet his fate head-on.

And Jacqui looked down at him, a rock among the suits and umbrellas.

But she did not smile.

A rumble of thunder crept across the canopy and seemed to explode above where Frankie was standing.

The rain pattered on the trees and the ground, and it soaked his shirt, sending a shiver through him, wild and electric. Rain dripped from his face and arms. It rolled down his back as a little pressure from the barrel of the gun gestured for him to kneel. Frankie raised his face to the sky above, welcoming death with open arms.

It was time.

Sparing a thought for his boy, Frankie rolled his neck, closed his eyes, and, using every piece of mental strength he could muster, he pictured Jacqui's smiling face. He saw the Grand Mosque in Abu Dhabi and Jacqui in her abaya. Then an image of the market place in Mumbai where Jacqui had haggled over the book. Then where she had sat beneath the glorious sun in the Maldives, her face in the woven shadow of her wide-brimmed hat.

"Do it."

The cold clung to Frankie's skin and his teeth clenched together as he braced for the impact.

Jacqui smiled back at him, a rock in the river of suits, and she waited there, her expression unclear. It was as if she questioned if Frankie was going to follow her or not.

"Come on. Do it. What are you waiting for?"

But despite every muscle in Frankie's body tensing, readying itself for the closure, despite Jacqui urging him to follow her from the black and white confines of another place and time, nothing happened.

Turning slowly, so as not to alarm the gunman, Frankie searched for the tell-tale boot that had betrayed him. But he found nothing.

Gone was the cold gun barrel that had kissed Frankie's nape for what felt like an eternity, numbing it with the cool chill of steel.

He turned further, his arms still raised and his clothes soaked through.

A drop of rain dripped from his eyelid as he searched the trees behind him.

But the gunman was gone.

No matter how hard Frankie tried to recall the scene in his mind of Jacqui coaxing him on, he could not find the memory. She didn't look down at him. There was no rock among the river of suits.

CHAPTER TWENTY-ONE

Walking hand in hand with her father, Hope smiled at his touch, embraced his warmth, and traced the outline of his fingers with her own as the sea breeze found the wetness in her eyes.

But they were not her own fingers. They were grimy and calloused with dirt ingrained into the skin. And where once there had been fingernails, there were deep voids, lined with scar tissue, shiny and grotesque.

They strode as father and daughter might. Buoyed by memories with their bare feet sinking into the cool sand in that place where the creeping tide lures people in with the offer of an endless horizon. Then it takes it away without so much as a blink of the sun, leaving only footsteps in the sand.

There they were. A pile of clothes folded with care and attention to detail.

With love.

Like her father had done. Regardless of the terrible things Hope could say and do, there was always love. There had always been a place for her.

The foot that swung and kicked the pile was grimy and calloused. There was dirt ingrained in the hard skin. And where once there had been toenails, there were deep voids, lined with scar tissue, shiny and grotesque.

A corner. White. Glaring against the yellow and brown sand. Bright against the jeans pocket from which it protruded.

She didn't reach for it. It was just there in her hands.

And there was no beach. Only dirt.

She hadn't unfolded the paper; it was just open, waiting for her to read.

There were no clothes. Only memories and dreams of everything she'd lost.

Torn envelopes.

That hand around her heart.

An open safe.

That hot, acidic saliva.

Her father's face, worried, caring, and disappointed.

But she was bound. Bound to a wall for eternity to suffer his onslaught of kindness, undeserved love, and affection.

"Wake up, Hope."

But she knew if she woke, he would be there. He would punish her with kind words, spoil her with gifts, and she would choke on her own steaming guilt.

"Wake up, Hope. It is time."

Hot breath on her face.

Her father's face soured.

"It's not me, Dad."

"Wake up, Hope."

But it wasn't her dad. It was Greg. And he was mad.

The charismatic eyes that had pulled Hope in were gone. As was the affection and comfort he had once offered. In its place was wrath, silent although he mouthed a scream. Harmless although he lashed out with both fists.

"It wasn't me, Greg. I didn't do it."

"Hope?"

"Greg?"

She stirred, opening her eyes to find a blinding light and the man with his face deep in shadow and the same breathless rasp.

A kiss.

CHAPTER TWENTY-TWO

Scrambling to the top of the low rise in which he'd knelt, Frankie used a tree to support himself in the slippery mud and pulled back a branch to afford himself a view out of the forest. The large house was some way off to his right. The village of Grafton lay sprawling beneath him perhaps a mile away. Between Frankie and the village was a small copse of trees dotted across the landscape, along with three mounds like small hills, too uniform to have been formed by anything other than the hand of man, but too vague in shape or form to serve any purpose.

The gunman was nowhere to be seen.

There were no boot prints in the mud and

no broken branches. Despite his size and apparent ill-health, he'd slipped away under the cover of the rain while Frankie's mind had been occupied with death and Jacqui.

"You're an idiot, Frankie Black."

His muddied boot found the tarmac road. His jeans clung to his legs and his white t-shirt had turned transparent. He ran a hand through his hair, wiped his face with his forearm, and took in his surroundings. With the forest behind him, the opposite side of the road was occupied by a small row of shops. Beyond were the rooftops of houses. Frankie was happily surprised that, despite the larger chain stores putting many local shops out of business, Grafton had retained its independence with a bakers, a butchers, and a grocers. Three independent shops run by three different families.

Above the bakers, written in the type of font that was on the front of Jake's children's books, was the name *Wainwrights*. Below it, in smaller, italic text, was the words *Baker and Cake Maker since 1932.*

The next shop along was a butchers. There was a bike outside. It was an old-style bike that Frankie seldom saw. There was a basket on the front large enough for a few bags of deliveries to local houses. Above the shop, written in large italics, white on black, was the name *Price and Sons Meats*. Swine hung from a hook in the window and joints of fresh meat were on display set on top of a carpet of faux grass. As Frankie walked past on the forest side of the road, he saw the red-tiled floor sprinkled with a dusting of sawdust.

Frankie moved on.

Jones the Grocer, read the next sign. It was dark green with white text but well-worn unlike the previous two shops, which appeared to be have been painted within recent years. Bright fruits of all colours and sizes filled the spaces. Around the edge of the shop, the grocer had pre-packaged baskets for sale in the window, enticing customers to buy more than they needed.

Frankie crossed the street as a small van pulled up outside the butchers. As Frankie ambled along the road, aware that he was soaked to the bone and drawing attention to himself, the butcher emerged and opened the van's rear doors, and called out to the driver.

"What took you so long? Your mother was worried."

Then Frankie reached a small newspaper shop. It wasn't part of the row of amenities but stood detached from any other building. There were notices in the window that Frankie pretended to read while he honed in on the butcher and the driver, who was eying Frankie with a gormless expression. He was a young lad and wore a thick jumper, dark pants, and boots. He was large in stature with a crop of unkempt, dark hair, and he had the demeanour of a teenager who had only just woken up.

The butcher confirmed Frankie's suspicion that the driver was, in fact, his son.

"Grant, don't just stand there. We're late. It's dead. It's not going to walk in here by itself."

Frankie smiled as he read a little notice that had yellowed with the sun and age.

Rooms to let.

Frankie continued on his walk. He hadn't gone far when the lane rounded a small bend, which came to a crossroads. On his right was a small cottage almost perfect in every detail. Ivy masked the yellow Lincolnshire stone and an avenue of rose bushes led the way from the lane to the front door.

It was, in Frankie's mind, an idyllic picture of the great British countryside.

To his left, on the opposite side of the crossroads, was an old pub. Between the ground floor and first-floor windows was a long, black sign that appeared as ancient as the pub itself. On it, in large, white lettering, was the name, The Red Lion. Thick, black beams framed the wattle and daub plasterwork and the entire building leaned to one side as if holding the red-tiled roof up for so many years was finally taking its toll. It looked like the building could fall over at any moment.

But the locals seemed confident that it had a few more years before it crumpled. Through the window, Frankie saw a man standing at the bar. He checked his watch. It was eleven fifteen. So, with the memory of the gunman still heavy on his mind, he decided to join him.

The door opened inwards and easily, and Frankie stepped onto a flagstone floor. Rain dripped from every inch of his clothing and his boots oozed brown water, puddling where he stood framed by the old doorway.

If there had been music on an old record

player, it would have stopped with the needle dragging across the vinyl. But there was no music. There were only the dull, hushed, gravel tones of the men who paused their conversation and eyed Frankie with apparent disdain.

"Are you going to close that or stand there looking like a wet dog?"

It was the barman who had spoken. He had a dishcloth draped over one shoulder and leaned on the bar opposite the punters. The barman wore a knitted tank-top over a check shirt with his sleeves rolled up. He had more facial hair than hair on his head; it was an angry red, thick and covering every part of his face from his neck to his ears.

In the centre of the four men was a man quite different in appearance to the others. Frankie deduced him to be in his late fifties. He sat on a wooden bar stool while the others remained standing. He wore a green barber's jacket, a flat cap, and brown, leather shoes. They were the expensive type that could be worn with almost any attire and still fit well. In his free hand, he cradled a cane. It was the type that elderly people used but of rare and exquisite design. The curved handle had been inlaid with rings of shiny gold and the length of the cane had been carved with care and love by expert hands.

The fingers of his other hand blindly traced the rim of a coffee cup.

His eyes watched Frankie assess him.

"You deaf or just plain stupid?"

It was the barman again.

Frankie smiled.

Another voiced his opinion.

"Oh, you're stupid then, are you? Well, you heard the man. Close the door."

The men watched with unabashed intrigue as Frankie approached the bar. He peered over the counter, aware of the men to his right studying him and waiting for him to say something. Mounted in the corner of the ceiling behind the bar was a small TV. The closing credits of a daytime quiz show were rolling by.

"Can I get you something?" The barman raised an eyebrow as if he expected Frankie to burst into flames or begin a magic trick.

"The coffee smells good."

It was too early for Frankie to drink. Alcohol would bring with it the dreams and the images he'd held at bay.

"The coffee is for guests and friends I'm afraid. We don't sell it. This is a pub."

"What if I rented a room for a few nights? Would I be classed as a guest then?"

"If all you want is coffee, there's a coffee shop in Addleton."

"I saw your ad in the window of the newsagents. I think I'll stay for a few nights."

"You're not from around here, are you?"

"No. No, I'm not." Frankie met his eyes, locked him in, and smiled. "How about that coffee then?"

CHAPTER TWENTY-THREE

"What's happening?"

Hope wiped the tears from her eyes with a grimy arm and pushed herself up off the floor. With her wrists free, Hope had managed to lie down. Sleep had come with ease despite the cold, hard floor and the insects that crawled over her skin.

Confusion followed. Her dream still lingered in the shadows as the bright light from the doorway burned her retinas like a flame seeking fresh air to breathe. She sought darkness to cool her eyes, turning away from the light she had longed for. And, for the first time in her captivity, she saw the room in all its deathly glory.

There was no bed where Hope had envisaged. There was no small desk like the one she had in her own bedroom in her father's house. There were no framed photos of her father or Greg. For the latter, she was indifferent. But a photo of her father might have been all the comfort she would need to see her through.

All the hole had to offer was stone and dirt walls, ancient, broken, and moist from the rain from above that was cleansed by the earth. They were Beth's words. Hope recalled them with a new understanding.

Set into the walls were hollows so deep the light did not dare to reach. Instead, it shone only on the edges. She looked harder, closing one eye to the light, and peered into the hollows. They were two feet deep and as long as a human.

She turned from the light and moved away from the man but watched as he began to trace the chain from her ankles to the wall. The chains were fixed by bolts set into the stone between two more of those strange hollows.

But these hollows were graced by light and located opposite the bright tunnel.

And the horror of the truth stared back at her in the form of the deep, sunken eyes of a human skull.

Hope threw herself away from the pile of bones and groped for stability. Her hand found the man's huge boot and she flinched, seeking refuge but restrained by the length of the chain. Morbid curiosity worked its charm and Hope found herself staring at the bones. She hoped that they were the bones of animals and that her reaction had been exaggerated by fright.

But the more she scanned the remains, the clearer they became.

The skeleton had crumbled, its sinew and tendons long decayed or eaten by scavenging rodents. But the form was still true enough to make out the position in which the body had been laid, curled like a foetus. The dark hollows of empty eyes stared back at her, accusing and unmoving.

"What is this place?"

She sought an answer from the man but received none. It was Beth who spoke. Her voice came like a song, soft and smooth, but monotone like the thoughts of another recited.

Beth stepped out of the shadows to stand

beside the man, whose presence no longer shamed or embarrassed Hope but whose size and silence was sinister enough to invoke fear in her deeper than she had felt before. Beth, a picture of elegance and purity, framed by sunlight, haloed like an angel, was unafraid.

"It's time, Hope."

She held out her arms in offering and, for the first time, Hope witnessed the smooth contours of her skin, pale and tender like that of a child but with the fullness of a woman. Her lank hair had been pulled back and lay across her slender shoulders. The contours of her ribs stood prominently above her starved stomach. But when Hope looked deeper into the picture of innocence and beauty, she found signs of a previous life, tainted and pocked with the scars of needles.

She held a garment up in offering. It was the gown Beth had been wearing.

"This is for you. It is the next part of your transformation."

"For me? But what about you?"

Then it dawned on her and the fear of solitude came with a heavy heart.

"No. Are you leaving? You can't leave me."

"It is my time. You are nearly ready and I am ready to spread my wings."

"You can't leave me here alone. Not with him." Hope pushed herself to her feet and the man stepped forward, giving a little grunt with the effort. But one hand from Beth stayed him.

"It's okay. She won't harm me."

"Beth, you can't go with him. You don't know what he'll do. He hasn't even got the decency to talk. For all you know, he could be some sick pervert. Look around you. Look at the bones."

"The bones, Hope, live here. They are the bones of the worthy and they've been here for centuries."

"I don't understand."

"It's where they buried the worthy. You're transforming, Hope. You're close. You're worthy." Beth offered her the garment once more. "Take this. Remember everything I've told you and soon there will be another."

"Another? Another girl, you mean? Another girl like us?"

"Not like us, Hope. She will be dirty. She will need cleansing. She will need somebody to show her the way. That's you, Hope."

"No. I don't understand. This is all wrong. It's sick."

"Don't you feel the difference, Hope? Don't you feel cleaner and purer? Don't you feel better for sharing those things? Don't you see now the things you have done and the harm you have caused? And doesn't your heart long for your father? To right your wrongs?"

"Yes, of course, but-"

"So show her, Hope. Then you can leave too. This was the last part of my transformation, to show you what you need to do. Show her the way, Hope. Do as I have done. Have patience and guide her. Then you too can spread your wings."

Offering the garment with finality, Beth smiled.

"You can do this, Hope. There's good in you. Let this place consume all that is evil, and leave here as clean and pure as you entered the world."

The fabric was rough, unwashed and stained with Beth's grime and that of her predecessors. Hope dared not to imagine how many there had been. She took the sheet but did not wear it at first. Instead, her hand fell to her side, limp and lifeless as Beth stepped up to her and closed her arms around Hope's shoulder.

Hope was rigid with the fear of the unknown, the turmoil of the emotional roller-coaster that had been her imprisonment, and the shock of the devastating news that Beth would be leaving. She hadn't considered her ever leaving. Although Beth had mentioned it once. She hadn't considered being alone and how that might feel. But, most of all, her fear lay with the silent and brooding eyes that filled the voids within the walls. She knew that once the door was closed, she would not see them, but they would still be watching her.

The girls lingered for a moment until the selfish fear that ruled Hope's mind gave in and joy for Beth replaced it. Her muscles relaxed and Beth squeezed harder. She found her own arms reaching out and Beth buried her head in Hope's shoulder. She found a warmth like she could not remember in Beth's arms. And Hope released the barrier.

Tears followed. More tears than Hope could ever remember crying. Her last friend in the world was leaving, escaping, and Hope was proud of her.

"What will you do?" Hope breathed the words into Beth's neck, unwilling to let go.

Not yet.

But it was Beth who pulled away and the immediate wash of cold found Hope's naked skin. She covered herself with the sheet, which she considered more of a rag than a garment. But, as rough as it was, it still held the warmth of Beth and all the girls before.

"I have to save somebody. A girl. A girl like us as we are now. I have to save her."

"Save her from what? Won't you find your friends?"

A forlorn smile shone through Beth's saddened eyes and she shook her head. Just once.

"That life is over for me now. Just as the life you once led is over, Hope."

"I don't understand. You won't see your friends? I won't see my father again?"

"No. But, Hope, remember this. What I am about to do is the kindest thing a person can do. There is no bigger sacrifice I can make. And for that, a girl will live, and the memories of me will be good and pure."

"Beth, no. What are you saying?"

The man grunted, unsettled by Hope's outburst, but his advance was quelled once more by the raising of Beth's hand. Fighting emotion, Beth held Hope's stare. Her tears rolled free but she did not cry out or wail.

"I have to do this, Hope. Think of a girl. Think of your sister. Somewhere out there, there's a girl just like her. All I have to do, to stop her from leading a life like my own, or like yours, is lay myself down."

"Beth, no."

"It's time, Hope. I must leave."

Reaching for Beth's hand, Hope held it tight.

"Think of Polly, Hope."

Her grip loosened.

"If you could do one thing to make amends for all that you have done, how far would you go?"

Her hand fell to her side.

"It's your time now. It's your time to show the next girl how to cleanse and how to transform."

The man's huge mass filled the small tunnel in the doorway. He crouched as he walked, his movement shading then releasing the bright light, quietening then revealing the incessant sound of the rain.

Beth turned in the doorway with one hand on the door, her face masked in shadow, and a soft glow lit the edges of her skin.

Although Hope could not make out her features, and although the distance between them was too far to see her face, Hope knew. She knew with all her heart that Beth had made peace with the world. The Beth that stood there lingering was a far different Beth to the one who had entered the hole before Hope.

The thought warmed her.

A gentle form stepping out into the world, cleansed, transformed, and smiling.

CHAPTER TWENTY-FOUR

"So are you a friend or a guest?"

Frankie watched for a reaction from the man with the cane who spoke. But he saw none save for a wry smile of confidence and a swirl of his coffee.

"Are you a guest?"

The man laughed and looked at the decor with distaste, and his companions raised wry smiles.

"No, I'd guess, if you had to classify it, Mr-?"

He raised an eyebrow expecting Frankie to fill in the gap. But Frankie had heard enough of the man's voice to form an opinion. Well-spoken, expensive clothes, and the

Bentley in the car park with the driver waiting in the front seat. He was a man of wealth. Aristocracy at its finest. Or worst, depending on which way you looked at it.

"Black. Frankie Black."

"Well, Mr Black, how long will you be staying?" asked the landlord, looking up from the guest book, pen poised and anticipating Frankie's response.

"A few days. Maybe a week."

"I'll need to know." The landlord tapped his book with the end of the pen. "For my records."

"Cash upfront?"

The word cash seemed to appease him a little but still, he loitered, waiting for an answer.

"Put me down for a week."

"And what is your purpose here in Grafton, Mr Black?"

"Do I qualify for that coffee now, Mr-?" It was Frankie's turn to gather some information.

"Armstrong. And I'll do you a coffee when we've completed the paperwork. Formalities. I'm sure a man like you can understand."

"And what do I call you, sir?" Frankie

turned his attention to the man with the cane. "If you aren't a guest then I can only assume you're a friend."

"You have a way about you, Mr Black."

There it was. The game Frankie had been seeking. The turning of tables. The power struggle. He who leads with questions maintains anonymity, at least until enough information had been gathered to tailor their own responses to suit.

"Maybe that's why I'm single." Frankie winked at him, poking at the inbuilt camaraderie that exists between men, friends, and strangers alike and their inability to understand the opposite sex. "You're not the first to say that."

But Frankie's pursuit of male bonding to loosen tongues was well-matched.

"Well, Barry..." The man stood and tapped his cane on the bar twice, a habit Frankie had witnessed once in an officer from his military days. "I must be off. Thank you for the coffee, and please do have a think about I said. It is very important."

Without waiting for a response from the landlord, the man nodded once at Frankie, eyed the weather outside but did not adjust his attire, and then pulled open the old door.

As he did, the butcher and his son walked into the pub. The older man removed his wet coat and seemed to bow to the aristocrat's stern gaze. The butcher's son, however, eyed Frankie with the same thousand-yard stare conveying a severe lack of intelligence.

"Awful sorry, sir. Grant here got stuck in traffic coming back from Lincoln. It's market day, see."

But the explanation did little to appease the well-dressed man who remained clearly unimpressed.

"John and Fred will fill you in with what we discussed. In future, try to be on time."

He turned to offer Frankie a final glance then made to leave.

Frankie called to him, "I didn't get your name, sir."

The man stopped in the doorway. He made a show of raising the collar of his coat to the weather outside and turned to face Frankie. It was a ruse to buy time and recall the most impressive introduction he could make.

"I, Mr Black, am Lord Grafton, and while you are here, you are a guest in my village."

He waited for Frankie to respond. Despite the provocative responses that Frankie could have said in lesser men's presence, he said nothing. He simply replied with a nod of his own and a look of disinterest.

"I'll be seeing you, I'm sure, Mr Black."

Lord Grafton retrieved a hat from one of the hooks beside the door, removed an imaginary speck of fluff, and tipped it once at Frankie before donning the hat and stepping out into the rain.

"I get the impression that I interrupted something, Mr Armstrong," said Frankie.

The remaining men moved closer to the bar and Barry Armstrong leaned on the ale taps.

"It's nothing that can't wait." He placed the coffee on the bar in front of Frankie. "Sugar?"

CHAPTER TWENTY-FIVE

The door slammed.

Beth was gone, taking with her the bright light that had reached into the hole with its timid curiosity, leaving Hope alone in the darkness with dark eyes staring out at her from hidden places within the walls.

Her fingers grazed the coarse fabric of the sheet and she slid down the wall, tucking her knees beneath her chin, and wept. She had cried in front of Beth. She had cried at Beth's story. And she had cried with Beth. But never had the full wrath of her emotions been unleashed.

It came as a sob at first. A single stab of sorrow, nasal and involuntary, but preceded a rush of heat to Hope's face, a run of snot from her nose, and a burst of melancholy desperation that nobody else could hear.

She slid to one side until the tiny, sharp stabs of grit and dirt hurt her cheek, but she didn't move. She couldn't move. Her cries came, and before the echo replied, the next was bursting from her throat. Her stomach pulled up with each wretch and whimper. Her eyes squeezed tight with every release of anxiety and still, the dark eyes looked on from unseen places in the walls, watching her in silent and morbid fascination.

She thought of Beth, remembering the relief when Hope had first heard her voice in the dark. The loneliness had gone in an instant of hope and comfort.

But now unwelcome solitude had returned.

She thought of the words Beth had said. It was as if the horror had been shared. Together they would fight whatever lay in store for them.

But the pain was not to be shared. Recalling the anger she had felt when Beth had spoken more when she had coaxed Hope into revealing more than she had ever revealed to anyone, Hope considered her behaviour with condemnation and regret, loathing her temper and emotions.

And the silence.

The silence Beth had used to torture Hope, which Hope, with her emotional mind, had assumed to be punishment. But now she knew. It hadn't been punishment at all. It had been Beth dealing with the final phase of her own transformation. She had been sitting in silence listening to Hope ramble and rant about how unfair it all was when, all along, Beth had known her fate and was in preparation.

If only she had been kinder. If only she hadn't displayed the cruel and selfish side of herself.

The side of her mother.

The evil side.

The faintest of smiles began to break through the anguish that held her face taut and rigid. She remembered Beth and her patient words. Her ability to bring Hope along, to drag her from the clutches of her mother's ingrained evil and allow the good in her to shine.

And it *had* shone. It had breathed the

stale, ancient air and shown Hope its strength. That there was a chance of her leaving this place cleansed. That's how Beth had put it. Cleansed. Transformed.

She understood.

A younger Beth played in Hope's mind. Her skin was pale and her hair was long and clean, unlike the lank, greasy locks that Hope had seen clinging to her grimy skin.

She was beautiful. In Hope's mind, the young girl had been visually perfect. And the adoring boys followed her wherever she might go, pubescent and willing. In Hope's mind, as she imagined a young Beth and her band of boys, a shadow followed her. The loving but overpowering foster mother's hand tried to steer her, just as Hope's father had also done.

The carnage was defiance. The trouble-some mind was a result of rejection. But the fire in that young girl's eyes as she watched the house burn was as cold as ice.

The silence Beth had utilised was the puckering of that dying flame. It was the evil leaving her and a path of righteousness pre-senting a new way. A way to end the memo-ries and the regret of a young, poisoned mind while at the same time saving the life of one more.

It had been the ultimate sacrifice.

And that same sacrifice awaited Hope. One day she too would be led from the hole, naked and unafraid, ready to offer everything she had for the chance at retribution. She pictured Polly. She would be older now. Old enough to understand perhaps. Old enough for their shared mother's evil to be working its way into her fragile and easily manipulated mind.

Perhaps death would be sweet?

Perhaps death for Hope would end the line of evil her mother had spawned?

Perhaps death for Hope would save a girl like Polly?

The tears were still wet in her eyes but her sobbing had subsided. An image of Polly came to Hope. It was that night. The night she had seen her for the first time, followed them, and held her. It was the night she had discovered that she had a sister.

But would she die for her?

Would she pay the ultimate price for the little girl to live?

If there was a chance of stopping her mother's evil then the answer was yes.

"Yes."

She spoke the word out loud.

To the empty room.

To the dark eyes that stared at her from hidden places in the walls.

To the sister she hadn't known.

"I'll pay the price."

Then she whispered but only to herself.

"I'll do whatever it takes."

Her whisper was answered. Not by the eyes that stared from hidden places within the room. Not by the empty echo of her forgotten chamber.

But by the rattle of heavy chains and a key turning in the padlock.

Heavy metal on wood.

Breathless grunting of an as yet wordless man, threatening in stature alone.

And light so bright it once more found the scars in Hope's eyes and woke the dead from their place in the walls.

But there was no fear left for Hope to reveal. He laid a girl down beside Hope. She was at peace, asleep or drugged. The man stood over Hope saying nothing and she nodded in response to his unspoken question.

"I'm ready."

A grunt and wheeze came in reply and the man lowered himself to one knee. He collected the chains from Hope's ankle and, with the bunch of keys he'd used to open the door, clicked open the padlock.

Freedom.

Cool air once more found Hope's flesh, her old wounds and grazed skin.

Beyond the man there was light. She could see trees for the first time. Perhaps they were the same trees she had heard? There was green grass, and the beginning of a blue sky showed itself through thick trees. She heard the birds sing but it was so far away the song could have been a memory.

She could roll away from him and run. He was large, so large he had to crouch to get down the tunnel.

But Hope could be fast. She could outrun him. She could find someone to help her. To help the girl, whoever she was.

But someone would die. A young girl who had yet to venture along the path of evil.

And the evil that her mother had passed

to her through childbirth would live on inside Hope. And suddenly, the light at the end of that short tunnel seemed so far away.

She flinched as a hand touched the abrasions on her skin. But the man's firm grip held her still and, for the first time, Hope saw his face. He had a beard, long and tangled, and his skin bore the weathered features of age and experience.

But in his eyes, there was something else. Something beyond which Hope had envisaged in the many thoughts of who he might be. He stroked Hope's tender skin as if he cared about her pain and held her gaze as if conveying some unspoken message.

There was a kindness. No, it was more than that. A hint of sadness in his eyes. Like he was sorry.

He wore the same forlorn look when he shackled the new girl's ankle. And when he stood her on her own two feet to bind her wrists with the chains, he lowered her gently until the steel took her weight with the least amount of discomfort. She stirred once and her body contorted against its restraints.

Then, as a final act, he placed a small bag of meat where Hope's friend had once stood.

Beth. It was a cyclical, sickening deed. He meant for Hope to sit where Beth had been.

He grunted once and his huge mass waddled through the small tunnel.

For all the kindness and compassion in his eyes, he did not look back as Beth had done. He did not offer words of hope, opportunity, or retribution.

The door closed with the same muted steel on wood and dulled rattle of rusty chains.

And the light that had illuminated the faces of the dead sank back to go with him to wherever Beth might be.

The silence returned with its internal dialogue but in a new voice. No longer were her thoughts vocalised in her own tongue, in her own accent, bitter and sharp. But Beth's voice spoke to her, conveying her own thoughts and speaking as only silence can speak.

A rattle of chains from Hope's left, somewhere between the places where the dark eyes stared out.

A gasp of fright, of uncertainty, and breathing so heavy surely a terrifying scream would follow.

And it did.

Beth's internal voice quietened as the new girl's terror sang around the walls only to stop as quickly as it had begun.

She offered short, stabby breaths, and Hope could picture her beneath her hood, breathing her own stale air, wondering, trying to recall what had happened, what she had done wrong.

There was a sense of peace. The girl could have been so far away. In another world. She knew so little of what was to come.

For Hope to announce her presence would be the end of the silence.

But Hope was ready for what she had to do. She closed her eyes, accepting her fate, joyous in her own sacrifice yet saddened for her father.

She whispered, "You're not alone."

CHAPTER TWENTY-SIX

The butcher collected his pint from the bar and joined the men who had been standing with Lord Grafton. They had moved to a table, perhaps out of earshot, or perhaps they were just a little more relaxed with Lord Grafton gone.

The boy remained standing and staring at Frankie. His head was cocked to one side like he was searching for something, trying to understand him, giving him the appearance of a dumb brute. Frankie was about to open his mouth to talk to him when his father called him over.

"Leave him be, Grant."

Like a puppy, his head jerked toward the

sound of his father's voice, and he moved over to sit beside him. But still, even from the table, he watched Frankie with caution.

"This is a nice, old pub, Mr Armstrong," said Frankie to the barman. "Have you had it long?"

"It's been in the family for generations. It was my father's and his father's before that. They let it get a bit run down so we don't see much business. But we gave it a lick of paint and put in a pool table."

"And it's picking up now?" Frankie looked around the saloon wondering what parts had been painted.

"Slowly. It takes a while for word to spread. This is a long game, Mr Black. There are no overnight miracles."

"Sunday roasts?"

Armstrong's brow furrowed.

"Sunday roasts, Mr Armstrong," said Frankie. "It's a country pub. People like nothing more than to have a pint with a Sunday roast with their dog by their feet."

"Dogs are welcome. This is farm country. Every man has a dog."

"But no Sunday roasts?"

Barry Armstrong offered an attempt at a

laugh and revealed yellow teeth between his thick beard.

"No. My culinary skills don't stretch that far, I'm afraid."

"So get a cook or a chef. Put some signs up. Five ninety-nine, dinner and a pint. That's what they do, isn't it? The other pubs?"

"So I hear."

"Just a thought. Might be good for business. I don't suppose, now I'm officially a guest, that I could get a towel, please?"

Armstrong reached for a key on the wall below the TV, giving Frankie a chance to lean over the counter and look at the man's feet. He wore black, leather shoes, a size nine at best, which was small for a man of his girth. Frankie assumed the man had once been much smaller and fitter. But easy access to an endless supply of the black stuff had possibly gotten the better of him. The buckle of his belt was hidden beneath the bulge of his belly, which stretched his knitted tank-top so that Frankie could see the weave in the material. There were six wall hooks in total. Once he'd placed Frankie's key on the bar beside his coffee, five keys remained.

"Room two." He flicked his head towards a

small door to the right of the bar. "Up the stairs, first door on the right."

"Slow, is it?" Frankie left the question hanging.

He was close to getting the answers he was looking for. He sipped at his coffee.

The first signs of Armstrong's temper began to show. He exhaled through his nose and pulled his dishcloth from his shoulder, busying his hands with drying glasses from the previous night. He ignored Frankie's question and began his own line of enquiry.

"What do you do then, Mr Black?"

Changing the subject was a clever tactic for avoiding confrontation whilst maintaining politeness. It gave the person the upper hand by not answering a question and placing the onus on the other person to respond. But, in Frankie's mind, unless it was done with tact and skill, it only served to identify a flaw or a weakness. Something to hide. In this case, Frankie deduced, the pub was in financial trouble and Lord Grafton was paying a visit either with a cheque book or the heavy end of a hammer. He'd seemed very proud of his village, and to have the main attraction fall into financial difficulties would unsettle the herd.

"I'm retired."

The response was Frankie's usual one, and more often than not, it invoked one of two possible results. Either the person seemed surprised and questioned further into how a man as young as Frankie could be retired. Or it inspired jealousy and the person doing the questioning hastened to tell them how much they enjoyed their job despite the lack of financial security.

"Good for you."

It wasn't a genuine response. It was flavoured with embitterment. That was normal. Frankie guessed the latter of the two scenarios was about to play out and leaned in with interest at the reasons why Mr Armstrong could be so happy in a place that looked as if might fall down any second. Judging by the lack of funds for a chef and poor attempt at decorating the place, the pub barely made enough money to keep Mr Armstrong in stretchy, woollen tank tops.

"I can't see myself doing that for a while. No. I love this place. Been here all my life and wouldn't know what to do if I walked away."

"You must have seen a few things then?"

"That I have."

"Do you get many people passing through?"

"To where?"

"To wherever. Do many people stop here in Grafton?"

Armstrong seemed shocked at the idea. He leaned on the bar as he had done when he was talking to Lord Grafton.

"There's nowhere to pass through *to*, Mr Black. The people that come to Grafton mean to come to Grafton. There's no through road. We're off the beaten track, as it were. A little pocket of peace and quiet. And that's the way we like it. It's the way Lord Grafton likes it too."

"And what is he? Like a mayor or something?"

"No. No, he's nothing official like that. But he has his ways. He knows people. He knows what's good for Grafton too. Mark my words, he's a good man. Without him, we'd have a bypass road through here quicker than you can imagine. There's always a developer or two sniffing around the top field wanting to build more houses."

"That's got to be good for business, surely?"

"We don't need any more houses here, Mr Black. Thank you. We've got enough. As soon as they come sniffing, Lord Grafton says the right things to the right men and they sniff somewhere else. We owe that man a great deal. I can assure you."

"The top field? You mean the one by the main road?"

"That's it. Always sniffing, they are. It'll happen one day. But not while we've got Lord Grafton on our side and, by God, I hope I'm dead and buried when it does happen."

"That's the field where the boy was killed, isn't it?"

Snap.

Like the flicking of a switch, Armstrong closed off and the hum of men's chatter ceased.

"I'm sure I read about it in the paper."

"I'm sure you read about a lot of things, Mr Black. But around here, we don't talk about it."

"So you saw it then? I wonder what really happened. Do you know?"

"None of our business is what happened. Are you finished with your coffee?"

"Not yet." Frankie made a show of taking

a small sip of his drink. "Such a tragedy to happen in a small village like this."

"Grafton has seen its fair share of tragedies, Mr Black, and it doesn't do anybody any good to gossip. Now, if you'll excuse me, I have work to do."

"Tragedies? Really? In a sleepy, little village like this?"

The agitation was showing on Armstrong's face. He huffed a single blast of air through his broad nostrils and avoided eye contact.

"Mr Black." It was the butcher's voice. He called out from the table and his cronies turned to look at Frankie. "You're here for a week. Can I offer you a little advice?"

Frankie said nothing. He shrugged and finished his coffee, inviting him to continue.

"Don't ask no questions. We enjoy our privacy here. We like to be off the beaten track and we don't appreciate strangers coming and waking up old memories. Not everyone out there is as friendly and patient a man as I am, Mr Black. So listen carefully. Don't you go poking your nose where noses don't belong."

It was a stalemate and Frankie knew it. He'd managed to get the men to reveal far more than Frankie expected. If he pushed harder, they would close off. Maybe for good. It was still early and Armstrong, who had proved to have the loosest of tongues, still had a lot more to say. A few drinks that evening from a paying guest might loosen his tongue further.

"I'll bear that in mind. I was just making conversation."

"That's alright then."

The butcher nodded, seemingly pleased that he had the last word on the matter.

There was a scrape of chairs as the men all stood. The butcher emptied his glass in a single, large mouthful and wiped his mouth with the back of his hand. The two other men pulled on their jackets and brought their glasses to the bar for Armstrong.

The boy continued to watch Frankie with curiosity, his mouth hanging open and his hands resting on his lap. There was a sadness there that Frankie couldn't place.

And, once more, the butcher called out to him, this time from the door.

"Grant, we're leaving."

The boy stood and followed his father through the door, who offered Frankie a cautionary look, supporting his earlier warning, and the other men filed out behind him, not paying Frankie any attention.

The pub fell into silence. Save for a familiar voice.

The sound was low but on the TV screen was the figure that matched the voice. Dressed in a floral dress, which was her style regardless of the weather, Penelope Pike was walking beside the River Witham in Lincoln with her microphone in her hand.

Armstrong reached to turn it off.

"Wait."

Armstrong stopped and turned his head to question Frankie.

"Turn the sound up."

"You don't want to listen to that old rubbish."

"Please. I'd like to hear the report."

With a sigh, Armstrong turned the volume up and Penelope's alluring voice, girlish yet commanding, came through loud and clear. Behind her was the bridge where Frankie had had the interaction with Mona and her two friends, but the report was just finishing and Penelope was beginning her closing statement.

"So, as Lincoln reels from yet another possible abduction, the city's people are asking if it's time for the local police to take action and put a stop-"

Armstrong hit the power button and returned to feigning his work.

"I was watching that."

Armstrong refused to turn and face Frankie. He began shifting papers from one pile to another.

"Mr Armstrong, why did you turn that off?"

"If you'll please, Mr Black." His voice was low and had lost its defensive aggression. "We've had enough of them reporters around here. Bad news is all it is, and we don't have room for any more bad news. Now, if you'll please, I have work to do."

CHAPTER TWENTY-SEVEN

"Who's there? Who was that?"

Her voice was rough. It was hard like the girls Greg had introduced to Hope. Drug users and girls who slept rough.

"Answer me. Who's there?"

She was angry, as Hope had also been. But the darkness would encourage fear to shine through, and Hope would begin the girl's transformation. She thought back to when it had been her standing there, chained, blinded, naked, and afraid.

It wouldn't be long.

"Don't mess me around. What the hell is this?"

Hope waited. She didn't smile. She didn't

bask in her new power. But she also didn't tease the girl with her presence. Doubt would toy with the girl's mind as it had her own. She would question her own sanity and wonder if she really had heard a voice.

"I know you're there. I can smell you. I can hear you breathing. You're as scared as I am. Are you in chains too?"

Hope held her breath and her heartbeat found a new rhythm.

"Just tell me where we are. Do you know? How long have you been here?"

Fear came.

It rose from the bones that were lying in the secret places in the walls. It hung in the cold, stale air. And it seeped from the new girl like a poisonous gas.

But it was Hope that it found. It was Hope that breathed it in.

The reality of where she was, what she had to do, and that she was locked in a hole with a girl who, by her voice alone, was clearly as wild as they come, stirred something inside her. It was as if she had regressed. She hadn't come so far after all. She hadn't transformed in the slightest. She was still just a scared, little girl locked in a hole.

The choice not to speak was no longer controlled by Hope. It was the result of the fear that gripped her and held her fast.

Her feet were stuck as if concrete had set around them.

And her legs, trembling under her own weight, threatened to give in and send her to the ground in a weakened heap.

But she had to be strong.

It was like some inner battle was taking place between her emotions. A part of her wanted to curl into a ball and wait. But she knew that if she did she would never leave the hole. But how nice it would be to close her eyes, sleep, and let the world fade away. If she could never utter another word to the new girl. If it would all be over while she slept.

She thought of the bones and those dark hollows where there were once eyes.

Part of her, the part that was fighting for life, knew she had to find some inner strength. To get out of the hole and her nightmare, she would need to complete her transformation. She would need to stand side by side with the man and present the new girl.

But to do that, she would need to tame her and coax her into confessing her darkest sin.

Hope was sure she would have many.

And the girl would need to confess her greatest moment, a moment of purity and kindness.

Hope doubted she had any at all. But she would have to dig deep and find those memories. Only then would she begin to see the light.

As Hope had done.

And then the man would come to take her away. To where she didn't know. It didn't matter. As long as it would have clean air, light, and warmth, and as long as the end would come swiftly, it was the best Hope could ask for.

"Please."

It had begun.

"Please talk to me. I know you're there. Why don't you just talk to me?"

But what to say?

A sniff, wet and unashamed.

She was scared.

Just as Hope had been.

Hope imagined the tears that would be running beneath the hood.

Her mouth readied to speak to her. But what to say?

She pictured the torturous imaginings the girl's mind would be dreaming up. The not knowing, the silence, and the frustration of doubting her own sanity.

The girl's body finally gave in to the fear and anxiety. A stream of liquid marked her spot on the ground, loud in the dead space. Hope could sense the shame of her dignity being stripped away, leaving her to exist as an animal.

A sob.

It was the first but would not be the last. She had done well. She had lasted longer than Hope. It had taken longer for her to break.

And although Hope had been on the cusp of easing the girl's mind, through her fear, a balance shifted. She felt it. Just as the fear had found her, from the eyes in the walls, from the cold, stale air, and from the girl, it left her like a tangible spirit.

Hope felt strength return to her body, a strength she would need to bring the nightmare to an end.

"What have I done?"

The girl's words were thick with tears and emotion, and Hope felt a warmth.

"Why me? Why am I here?"

Her breathing grew loud. She was hyper-ventilating.

Just as Hope had done.

"Help. Help me. I'm in here."

Her screams sang around the hole, circling like birds of prey only to return bearing no reward.

Just as Hope's screams had circled.

Hope smiled.

Some dark part of her enjoyed the surge of power. The end was near. All Hope had to do was break her, to hear all her sins, and to witness her atrocities.

But climbing from the walls, returning to feed on the cold, stale air, was silence. It spoke between the girl's sobs and above her ragged breathing.

Hope listened as if she now understood why Beth had welcomed it. Because with the silence, her power grew.

It was an ally.

With silence on her side, Hope could break the girl. And to break the girl would mean freedom and an end to the pain.

"Please talk to me. Whoever you are."

Hope smiled while the silence replied.

"Just say something. Anything at all.

Just..." A burst of breath, frustrated and angry yet yearning to be heard. "Just tell me I'm not alone and I didn't imagine your voice."

Biting her bottom lip to refrain from easing the girl's mind and letting the power slip away, Hope searched for the right words to say. Words that would tell the girl she wasn't alone but still maintain the balance.

As Beth had done.

She smiled.

"When the door slams, your world is damned."

CHAPTER TWENTY-EIGHT

The afternoon was darkened by the thunderous clouds that loomed overhead. A blue sky loitered on the horizon like a timid puppy watching the bigger dogs roll and tumble. The pub door closed behind Frankie and the cold air raised pimples on his arms. He braced against the cold and walked back the way he'd come as the patter of rain grew into another deluge.

At the newsagents, he caught the eye of a lady behind the counter. She was tapping her pen as if deep in thought and tracked Frankie as he passed. He nodded once with a silent greeting and continued on his way. Frankie crossed the small alleyway that disappeared behind the row of three shops. He assumed it was private parking for the owners of the shops or the tenants of the upstairs flats, and moved on.

The door to the fruit and veg shop opened to the sound of a little bell and a young mother with a little boy walked out. The boy carried a toy and the woman held a small bag of fruit. Frankie nodded good day to the grocer, recognising him as one of the men who had been with Lord Grafton. He looked up while he was re-arranging the fruit, filling in the new empty spaces. The owner also eyed Frankie, tracking him as he walked past.

The butcher shop van had been moved and the door had a small sign in the little window to tell customers the shop was closed. It was the type of sign that had the opposite message on the reverse side which the owner would display on his return. It was midday, according to Frankie's watch, and as he peered in through the window, the misty, light rain became heavy drops. The sound on the tarmac lane grew louder. There was a glass counter to display the packaged meats with a selection of knives, presumably for the butcher's convenience.

But there was no sign of either the butcher or his son.

Frankie set off, faster than his previous amble, and wrapped his arms around himself to retain warmth. He passed the bakers, which was open, but the baker himself, the second man who had been with Lord Grafton, was too preoccupied to look up.

On the far side of the road, Frankie passed the set of wrought iron gates that led up to the manor house. They were closed but not locked and on each of the supporting pillars was a security camera, presumably so that Lord Grafton could identify guests before they entered the grounds. The grounds were bordered with thick hedges laced with ripening berries too thick to see through. The only gap in the obstruction was the small public footpath that led to the grounds of the manor house and no further.

With the heavy rain, Frankie was now once more soaked to the skin. His clothes were clinging to his body and his heavy boots had allowed some damp to moisten the toes of his socks. There was a side street leading away from the main road and manor house. It was lined with ordinary houses built from

Lincolnshire stone and with red roof tiles. Each property appeared to be uniquely designed but was still a far cry from the little cottage Frankie had seen on the corner opposite the pub.

The final, and perhaps the most important part of the village, was waiting for him at the north end. The church was medieval with a spire and no belfry. It sat in the glorious silence and peace that old churches command. A dry-stone wall bordered the sacred grounds and, as Frankie passed, he searched for the older of the headstones that were visible from the road. There was a broad oak tree at the edge of the graveyard. Its thick boughs and heavy canopy offered Frankie a place to wait out the worst of the rain. There was still at least a mile to the main road where his car was parked so he entered the gate and perused the graves as he made his way to the tree.

Armstrongs and Wainwrights dated back to the early eighteen-hundreds, along with Davidsons and Tylers who were buried before them in the late seventeen hundreds. But set beneath the cover of the tree, the gravestones were so old Frankie could barely make out the dates and the names. He rubbed at one with his thumb to clear the moss that had settled in the groove of the carved epitaph.

A pang of guilt gave a gentle stab but curiosity teased him on.

He cleared some more, bending on one knee, and under the protection of the tree, he worked the moss and dirt from the date. The year of the death read, *1631*.

Glancing around him to make sure nobody was looking who might object, Frankie continued to work the gravestone.

The next line read, *Born 1582.*

"Forty-nine years old."

Curiosity winked at him from the faint lettering at the top of the stone.

Starting on the left, he scraped the letters clear.

He knew it would be a Grafton. Something inside told him so.

Perhaps it was the grandeur of the headstone or the secluded and privileged spot in the graveyard.

Lord Montgomery Grafton. Below the name, *Our Saviour, Who Now Sleeps With The Angels.*

The surrounding graves all belonged to the Grafton family. There were mothers, brothers, and descendants spanning the centuries and, to one side, were three identical headstones of equal size, shape, and deterioration. They belonged to three girls, who had, by Frankie's calculations, been aged nine, ten, and twelve, and had died the same year. According to the dates, they could easily have been Lord Montgomery Grafton's daughters. But it was his grave that held the most prominent position.

It was impossible not to imagine the village four hundred years earlier. The church would have been the same only newer, but still ancient in historical terms. The graveyard may have been less populated and the road might have been just a simple dirt lane. And in the centre of it all, as Frankie imagined it, Lord Montgomery Grafton would have been held in the same high regard as his descendant. Frankie wondered if the pub was the original and if, back then, it had stood tall and upright as opposed to the dilapidated ruin it had become. He wondered if the original Lord Grafton was as sly and despicable.

A few of the cottages surrounding the village green may still have had features dating back to the sixteenth century but Frankie surmised that the village's residential area had evolved over the years. The colours of the roof tiles were often signs of evolution. Bright red tiles marked the newer houses while faded, dull roof tiles and thatched roofs indicated the older buildings.

A flash of colour caught his eye and he stepped back with instinct and that pang of guilt.

He felt an overwhelming feeling of intrusion, although he had done nothing wrong. To be among a family graveyard in a small village such as Grafton, he couldn't help but feel like an outsider.

He peered around the tree as the gate closed with a gentle squeak. A man entered the graveyard. His face was hidden by tree boughs and his jacket collar. In his hands, clutched to his chest, was a small bouquet of flowers.

Watching the man's shoulders hang as he walked between the rows of headstones, Frankie's stomach rolled and hung like he was on a rollercoaster, teetering on the edge of a drop that would never come.

And Jacqui stared up at him, a rock in the river.

The ancient graves mattered no more. All who had loved the persons buried there had long since passed. But for the man and Frankie loss was new, painful, and un-welcome.

Frankie waited, keeping to the shadow of the great oak while the man said all he had to say and laid down the flowers with care. He watched as the man walked between the rows of modern headstones where moss had yet to fill the carved letters and their names were still prominent against marble and stone.

But recognition roused Frankie from the dreams of Jacqui and her photo on the wall as the man turned to leave. It was the butcher. He walked away with his hands stuffed into his pockets and his eyes red with the un-abashed tears of loss.

Frankie watched him. He felt him and shared in his mourning.

It was only when he was closing the gate behind him that Frankie felt the gaze of another.

Standing on the corner, waiting obedi-ently like a puppy, was Grant Price. He was staring at Frankie as he had in the pub. Frankie wondered how long he had been watching him, as he had been watching the boy's father.

And that pang of guilt returned.

Expecting the boy to report to his father, Frankie slipped out of view and made to leave. But when the older man reached the boy, nothing was said. The boy turned and followed his father until they had rounded the bend in the road and had disappeared from view.

Frankie went to the grave where the fresh flowers had been arranged with care and love. Green grass grew where once there had been fresh earth, and Frankie stood, with the rain coming down in sheets, to read the epitaph.

Stephanie Marie Price. Below the name were the words, *Our daughter and angel who was taken too early*.

The girl had been just fourteen years old. Despite the man's words and despite his son's almost childlike obedience and backward appearance, Frankie felt a connection to them. He understood the loss that had been etched in the boy's expression. The girl had been his sister. But why the boy hadn't joined his father at the grave, Frankie couldn't fathom.

Frankie left the graveyard, looked back

once at the girl's grave, and was about to take the long road out of the village when a car pulled up beside him. It was a Volvo that looked as if it had once been a deep green but had faded with age.

He stopped and watched the window wind down with laborious effort to reveal a fresh face with cheeks reddened against the cold.

"You look like you could do with a ride somewhere."

CHAPTER TWENTY-NINE

"Who are you?"

"My name is Hope."

A gasp of air. It was a relief. Or the subsidence of fear.

"Oh, thank God. I thought I was going crazy. Where are we?"

Silence replied. Hope listened as it pulled the girl along on its leash.

"Are you like me? Can you see? I can't."

"I was once like you are now."

"But can you see? My hands are chained and my ankles too. Who's doing this? Do you know? Did you see him?"

The peace that filled the spaces was

bright with new energy. The more the silence spoke, the greater the fear became.

Where once it had been Hope who sought the answers, she was now fascinated by the power. She could picture Beth watching her, standing in the very same spot with Hope chained to the wall at the very beginning of her transformation.

"Are you there? Please talk to me. You said you were once like me? What does that mean? Are you free to move? Can you help me? I need to get out. I need to breathe. Please, Hope. Are you scared?"

"When the door slams, your world is damned."

A tease to feed the fear and frustration.

"What does that even mean? Are we going to die here? Is *that* it? What is this place?"

The hem of the sheet stroked at Hope's leg as she stepped forward, feeling for the rough ground with her bare feet until, step by step, blind in the familiar darkness, she inched closer and stood in front of the girl.

"I can feel you. You're beside me, aren't you?"

The chains rattled and snatched as the

girl reached for her. Hope winced, remembering the bite of the steel on her own flesh.

"I can feel your breath."

As Hope had felt Beth's.

Hope smiled.

"Is it you? Is it you who will kill me?"

"No."

A gasp. That sweet relief conveyed in a single stab of breath.

"Then who are you?"

"I am Hope."

"That doesn't help me. Why are you talking in riddles? Oh, God. I just need to sit. Can you help me?"

"I can help you."

"You can remove the chains? Could you? Would you? My wrists are hurting and my ankles, I think they're bleeding. Help me. Do you have the key?"

"Tell me your name and I'll help you transform."

"Help me what?"

"Transform."

"Into what?"

"Into something beautiful. Into a being as pure as the day you were born. It's the only way you'll ever leave this place."

"Who are you? I don't understand."

"It will all become clear. I was once like you."

"But now?"

"Now I'm transforming. I'm close. Tell me your name and I can help you too."

"You can help me transform? What do I have to do? I'll do anything to get out of here."

"It won't be easy."

"I can do it. Whatever it is, I can do it."

"You're going to have to close your eyes and reach into your soul. You're going to cry. You're going to hate. You're going to remember the things you shut away, and then relive every last moment."

"I don't understand. This is all so scary."

"Start by telling me who you are."

There was a pause, a sniff, and she cleared her throat, readying herself to learn more.

"My name is Mona."

CHAPTER THIRTY

"Do you always pick up strange men?"

"Not always, but-"

"But? I could be anyone."

"It's raining. Would you prefer to walk? Would that ease your conscience?"

She smiled and eased back into the road, straining to see through the fogged windows. She rubbed her hand across the inside of the windscreen, veering to one side as she did.

"It takes a little while to heat up," she said. "We'll be able to see where we're going in a mile or two. How far are you going?"

"The top of the road will be just fine, thanks."

"Ah, come on. It's not that bad. There's

life in the old girl yet." She tapped her hand on the dashboard as if it was a faithful pet.

"I'm serious. My car's at the top of the road."

"You left your car there and didn't take a jacket?" She looked across at Frankie's shirt, which was transparent and clung to his chest.

"I didn't expect to walk so far, and I certainly didn't expect it to rain so hard."

"I hear you. Summer is well and truly over." The car lurched to the left as the front left wheel caught on the grass verge. So the woman snatched the wheel to the right and continued in a series of corrections until they were heading straight. "So where did you walk to? It's quite a way to the main road."

"Ah, you know, just around to get some fresh air."

At the top of the road, she pulled to one side and slowed to a stop, peering through her open window to make sure she was close to the verge but not in the hedge itself.

"That's your car? Wow. You must think I'm a heathen."

"It's my Dad's. *Was* my Dad's. I don't use it often. But if I know it's going to be a nice day and I'll be in the countryside then I'll stretch its legs."

"Wait. You parked there and went for a walk?"

"Yeah."

"You went to see the murder spot, didn't you? Did you know him? I'm sorry. I saw your face. That's partly why I stopped. You looked like you were going to break down at any moment."

"Am I that transparent?"

"No. But, you know, I've seen that face before. A thousand times." The depth of the conversation reached a new low and she smiled as if to hint that she recognised the lull. "In the mirror."

"You saw *my* face in the mirror? That's a rough morning."

"No, I mean, I've been there. I lost someone too. Don't ever hide that face."

The door opened with a loud creak. Frankie offered a smile and nodded once.

"Thanks for the ride."

"Don't listen to what the papers have to say about your friend." Her face dropped when she realised she may have indirectly of-fended Frankie. "I mean, they said he was wanted and, well, all kinds of things. But if you knew him and missed him then that's the memory you want to keep."

Struggling to maintain his smile, Frankie eased himself out of the car into the rain. He went to close the door but stopped, thought for a moment, then leaned in.

"He wasn't my friend. Just so you know. I didn't know him."

The woman's face flushed with embarrassment.

"That's none of my business. I'm sorry if I said too much. You just looked sad. I just put two and two together and came up with seven. I'm sorry. I don't do this much."

"Pick up strange men? That's a good thing. It doesn't need an apology."

She stared ahead through the fogged and rain-beaten windscreen. The window wipers did little to carve a view, but she looked as if she was focused on something far away, waiting for Frankie to close the door.

"For what it's worth, I'm looking for a friend. A girl."

"Oh. Well, then I really am sorry. I said far too much and-"

"No. No, she's a friend's daughter. She's

missing. I..." He was close to telling her what his job was but caught himself mid-sentence. "I said I'd help find her. I thought the two might be linked."

"You thought your friend's daughter might be linked to the criminal that was killed here?"

"I'm just clutching at straws really. He's pretty desperate to find her."

It was only when Frankie was leaning in and the conversation had moved on that the rollercoaster that held his stomach upside down relinquished control, and Frankie was able to see the world clearer. The woman appeared to be in her early forties. She was young enough that, if Frankie was asked to guess, he would suggest mid-thirties to be polite. She wore jeans and a waterproof jacket with a thick, white, roll-neck jumper showing from beneath. Her hair was either brown or dark blonde and just wet. It was hard to tell.

"But you're right," said Frankie. "You should know that you're right. You should trust your judgment."

"I am?"

"I lost my wife. I was passing the cemetery and..." Frankie took a breath to finish the sentence and choose his words with care. "I was reminded. That's all."

"How long has it been?"

"Too long. I was passing and curious. I'm not entirely sure why, but I find old graves fascinating."

"Me too. Do you think it's because deep down we know that one day, two hundred years in the future, there might be some guy standing in the rain looking at our graves?"

Frankie gave a laugh and she seemed to ease, her embarrassment abated.

"It's possible. I've never really thought about it."

"But you are now?"

"How can I not?"

"Let's hope he's wearing a jacket. If they still wear them in two hundred years."

"I was just looking around and somebody came along to visit a grave. Do you ever get the feeling that you're intruding when you're in a graveyard? As if the people that are there are there to mourn and you're just a sick spectator?"

It was her turn to laugh, and a smile followed, broad and honest, unlike her previous shy smirks. Her teeth were bright white, immaculate, and her eyes sparkled a little with memories.

"No. It's usually me who's there to do the mourning, wondering why people are hanging around in graveyards, and why they can't leave me alone to cry."

Not wanting to push the line of conversation into personal realms, Frankie continued with his story.

"It was the butcher from the village. I felt terrible for him. I thought about all the pain I've been through and, well, I figured he must be going through the same. No-one likes to see that."

"That's Jim."

"Jim?"

"Jim Price. His family have been here for generations. Grafton is a bit weird like that. I've lived here for eight years and I still feel like an outsider. The baker is the same, and Lord Grafton, of course. They've all been here for generations."

"It was Jim Price's daughter. Sorry. I looked at the grave."

"Morbid curiosity?"

Frankie shook his head. "At first. But no. It was more than that. Shared grief, I think. It was either that or some selfish means to put a stop to my own mourning."

"The human brain is a wonderful thing."

"It is."

"Stephanie Price. That was her name." The woman looked through her fogged windshield again, staring at something far away and long ago. But she roused herself and cleared her throat. "Do you have a name? Or do I just call you *wet man?*"

Pleased to have the conversation steered away from death, Frankie grinned. He held out his hand after wiping it on his wet pants.

"Frankie. Frankie Black."

"Nice to meet you, Frankie." She let go of his hand and dried it on her denims then blushed as she realised that Frankie was wet through and a wet hand was the least of his worries. "I guess you better..."

"Yes, of course." Frankie smiled, not wanting the conversation to end for two reasons. She had been so easy to talk to and was fun, so he'd smiled for the first time in too long. And secondly, she was a friendly distraction from the torment. "Thanks again."

He smiled one last time and turned to

walk back to his car, fishing the keys from his pocket.

"Hey, Frankie Black."

He'd hoped it would come. A huge part of him hoped he would see her again, but the guilt that ruled his heart voiced its disapproval with a dull stab to his chest.

He turned, rain falling from his top lip and the cold wind seeking new places on his skin to shiver.

"I can tell you a lot about this place. If you're interested, of course?"

"Now?" He gave her a crazed expression and looked up at the rain.

"Later. Five o'clock. There's a pub not far from here in Addleton. The Red Robin. You can buy me dinner in return. I wouldn't want to offend your sense of male pride."

"Buy you dinner?"

"Yes. If you want. And I'll tell you all about this place and its dirty, little secrets."

"At the Red Robin, you say?"

"In Addleton." She had to raise her voice to be heard above the rain on the metal panels of her old car.

"That could be a problem." Offering her his best, dejected face, Frankie slid the tips of his fingers into his pants, both for something to do and to find some kind of warmth somewhere without showing how cold he was.

To his surprise, her dejected face was nearly as good as his own.

"Okay. I thought I'd ask. You can't blame a girl for trying. Good luck finding your friend."

Embarrassed, she fumbled with the gear stick to find first gear and the car lurched forward from the side of the road.

"Wait."

Frankie waved his arms to stop her and moved closer to be heard above the engine. He banged on the back of the car with the flat of his hand and the brake lights flicked on, bright red and arrogant in the dark afternoon. He moved to the passenger side once more and leaned on the car.

She was ready with a flurry of excuses why she had to go and that it was all okay.

"Stop."

She stopped, her eyes wide, almost fearful yet curious.

"You said you can't go to dinner," she said. "I'm sorry. I shouldn't have asked."

"Stop." He spoke louder than before, smiling to reassure her he wasn't being aggressive. "The problem is, I can't take a lady to dinner..."

She opened her mouth to speak but Frankie raised his hands to silence her. He smiled and waited for the shy smile to show, although it came buried in a flush of cheeks.

"I can't take a lady to dinner without first knowing her name. It's my male pride, you see."

CHAPTER THIRTY-ONE

"Tell me, Mona. What's the worst thing you ever did?"

"The what?"

Once more, the silence replied but with spite in its tone and a bite in Mona's wrists as she fought against her restraints.

"What do you mean?"

Her skin was cool beneath Hope's fingers. Her stomach was cold and taut, her ribs prominent and proud, but her breath was as foul as decaying flesh.

Hope placed her hand on Mona's chest and, despite the flinching and writhing, she felt a racing heart thundering like a train.

And she thought of Beth and the greatest thing she had ever done.

"What are you doing?"

"Feeling."

"Feeling what? Get off me. Don't touch me."

"I'm feeling for a heart. You *do* have a heart, don't you?"

"You're insane."

"I want you to think hard, Mona. Think of all the things you ever did that kept you awake at night. Those guilt-ridden, shameful things that you'll carry to your grave."

"You want to hear a story? Is that it? I've lived on the streets for five years. I can tell you things that'll make your blood run cold."

"Yes. Those. Keep them in your mind's eye. I want you to release them. One by one. I want you to be rid of the terrible things you did. It's the first phase."

"The first phase? The first phase of what?"

"Your transformation. Let them go. Let this place cleanse you and you can be free. I didn't believe it myself until I saw it. It's our only chance, Mona."

"So if I tell you, you'll let me go?"

"No. If you tell me, I'll remove your hood. Think of those dirty, little secrets. But it has to be the worst. The darkest thing. I know there's one in there."

Hope thought of the swirling waters and how one memory had shone above the rest. She thought about how it felt to rid herself of the memory and the peace that followed.

"You can see it, can't you? I know you can. Reach in and grab it. Don't let it go. No matter how hard it tries to be forgotten, grab it and hold on."

"I can't."

"You can see it, can't you?"

"There's so many. How do I know which one?"

"Because it's the one you're ashamed of the most. It's the memory you wished you never had."

It was Mona's turn for silence. Hope found her shoulder in the darkness and rested her hand upon it. This had been the hardest part for Hope, and she helped Mona through it as if guiding her through a fog. She spoke softly, not wanting Mona to lose her grip on the past.

"Do you have it?"

"Yes."

The rough tones of the hardened girl had vanished. They were replaced by a gentle whisper. Somewhere inside, there was innocence. Somewhere inside Mona, there was hope.

But the evil inside Hope wanted to hear it. Selfish and repugnant, it needed her to confess. It needed her to begin her transformation.

She waited for the tale to start, basking in the girl's anxiety.

As Beth had done.

"Where does your story begin, Mona? How did you end up on the streets?"

An exhale.

Hope pictured her finding the right place to start. Mona searched for the right words to use to set the tone, just as Hope had. She bit her lip with anticipation.

"I haven't always been bad. I *was* a good girl. I could have done well at school. I could have been somebody."

"You still can."

"No. Not now. I used to live with my

mum. My dad died when I was a baby. Mum worked hard. She did well. She raised us, my brother and me. We didn't have much but we never went without. She was a good woman, hard as nails, but she was good."

"Do you think you have the same good inside you? Do you think your mum passed that kindness onto you?"

"Maybe one day, a long time ago, I might have thought that. But not now."

Her voice trailed off like she was remembering the good Mona that once was. But there was doubt. The memory was too foggy.

"Mum's boyfriend came to live with us at our house. I didn't mind. But my brother didn't like him. He was older than me and I think he resented him. Maybe he was just more attuned. I don't know. As far as I was concerned, things were good. The best they had ever been. Pete, my mum's boyfriend, had a decent job, which meant that Mum had a bit more money. We started to have nicer dinners, weekends away, you know? It was like a breath of fresh air and my mum was a different woman. She'd laugh and smile, and we'd have Sunday dinners together. She still had to work. Mum always worked. Even though Pete said she didn't have to, she wanted her independence, I think. And as I got older, she could afford to give me money to go to the cinema with my friends and get me all the things a teenage girl needs. You know?"

The story elicited a pang of jealousy within Hope. Money had never been an issue for her father, but talk of a mother and growing up with somebody who knew what it was like to be a girl, who understood the changes that were happening to her, must have been wonderful.

"You were lucky."

"In some ways." Mona's voice darkened. "But it was the beginning of the end for us. I heard my brother arguing with my mum once, but when I walked in, they stopped and wouldn't tell me what it was about. The arguments became frequent until, one day, I came home from school and my brother was gone. He'd just packed his things and left. My mum worked nights at one of the factories so I told Pete that he'd gone. Then Pete hugged me and he told me that when people grow up, they leave home. It's natural and I shouldn't be worried. But something wasn't right."

"Did you ever see him again?"

"No. In my dreams I did. Sometimes I thought I'd see him through the bus window as Mum and I went shopping. But it was a fleeting glance. Never a positive sighting. Mum was sad but she put on a brave face for me. She used to tell me that he'd been around to our house in the following weeks, but that I'd just missed him, and maybe next time I would catch him. I missed my brother. Then Pete started coming to my room while Mum was at work. He'd never done it before, but he'd just hang around as if we were best friends. He told me he enjoyed my company. I used to do my homework and he'd lay on my bed and read the paper. Then he'd tell me to get my pyjamas on while he cooked dinner and he'd put me to bed."

As the story unfolded, Hope pictured the scene. She knew the type of man Pete was, and she'd heard or read about hundreds of similar stories. But instead of easing Mona of the burden, she let her tell her tale, knowing that the darkest secrets would follow.

"As time went by, we grew closer, Pete

and I. He'd make me whatever I wanted for dinner and he'd sit and make sure I did my homework while Mum was at work. I never really thought anything of it. Until he started watching me. He'd watch me get changed into my pyjamas, which was nothing at the time. I thought nothing of it. But then more time passed and that became the norm. He became more touchy at bedtime, stroking my hair, you know?"

"No. But I can imagine."

"Then he began to lay with me until I went to sleep. I would pretend to sleep just so he'd stop. Just so he would leave me alone."

Hope had heard enough. Nobody needed to relay the kind of story she thought was coming, regardless of the promise of freedom.

"It's okay. I get it. He began to touch you and told you not to tell your mum-"

"No. Never. He was far more cunning than that. He would get showered with the door open. Or walk through the house with nothing on, pretending to cover himself if I saw. I think he enjoyed it, being seen, you know?"

Hope thought of Greg and how he'd co-erced her into a wild afternoon in the field with the risk of getting caught. How he'd told her that it made him feel alive. The irony.

"He caught me looking at him, at his thing, you know? I was just a kid. I didn't know any better. I mean, my friends and I used to talk about boys. But it was all innocent. I'd never actually seen one before."

It was the silence's turn to speak as Hope's imagination ran wild with disgust and Mona's memory lingered on the sordid details.

"Tell me something else, Mona. You don't have to finish the story. We both know where it ends."

"Do you? Do you really think you *know* me? You think that maybe my curiosity got the better of me and I touched him. Or maybe I let him-"

"No. Sorry. I just didn't want to put you through the memory."

"Well, you have. You asked for the deepest, darkest thing I ever did. And yes, what he did to me was deep and dark and I hope that he's out there somewhere suffering for what he did, but what he really did was create a monster. Yes, it went further. And yes, my curiosity grew until I had trodden a path from which I'd never return. He gave me money to keep our secret quiet."

"Mona, stop."

"No. I have to tell it. I have to say it out loud. That's the rules, right? So the hole can cleanse me?"

"Yes, but-"

"I ran away. First chance I got, I was out. My mum wouldn't believe me when I told her and Pete slapped me when I tried. So I ran away. I didn't look back. But I got hungry. And I got scared. So I did those things again. Everything Pete told me to do. I did it out of spite and for money. I did well at first. I was new to it all. Come wintertime, I'd work for a bottle of something to keep me warm. I wasn't even sixteen and I was drinking a bottle of whatever I could get every day. But after a year of sleeping rough, there are not many men who would come near me. And I don't blame them, to be honest. I had nothing. I was dirty, riddled with God knows what, and I couldn't get through the day without a bottle. It's not a good place to be."

"I met people like you. It's a hard life. Couldn't you go home?"

"Home to what? To the lies and the arguments? No. No, I fell into a dark place. On a freezing cold November night when you can't find anywhere to get your head down, it's enough to drive a person insane. Your whole body shivers. Violent shaking. But, one night, I saw a new girl. I hadn't seen her before and she was in my spot. She was younger than me and clean. That's how you can tell, see. Clean skin. Clean hair. No dirt under their nails."

Hope imagined Mona's top lip curling with distaste beneath the hood. She could taste the stale air and feel the claustrophobia pressing in like an unseen weight.

"Green as grass, that one. She wouldn't have lasted. No. I probably helped her. Did her a favour. It's no life for a young girl."

"What did you do?"

"So now you want to hear my story?"

"I *have* to hear it, Mona."

"I robbed her. While she was sleeping. I took everything she had. She was everything I used to be and I took it all. Don't judge me. I was hungry and, in the cold, I wasn't myself."

"I'm hardly a judge, Mona. Why do you think I'm here?"

"I took all her money, what little there was, and I took her sleeping bag. Brand new, it was, and thick as any duvet I've ever slept under."

"So what happened?"

"That night? I slept like a baby."

"And the girl?"

"They found her the next morning, stiff and blue. She froze to death."

CHAPTER THIRTY-TWO

The Red Robin pub was buried deep among Addleton's country cottages with pride of place on the village green beside a lawn bowls club. A small river ran behind it and as the evening sun tried to make amends for its performance during the day, the fields beyond were cast with hues of orange, yellow, and red. Pollen hung in the air above the crops and flying insects danced, fed, and bred before the setting sun closed the curtains on their one-night show.

Dressed in a clean t-shirt and clean pants, Frankie put his foot on the wheel of his Aston Martin, spat on a tissue, and cleaned his boots as best he could. A few people sat in the beer garden wearing sweaters and enjoying the evening sun on their faces.

Beside the door was an A-board. On it, in bright, coloured chalk, someone had taken the time to design a sign advertising a Sunday roast and a pint of beer for only six pounds ninety-nine.

The door was already open, inviting Frankie into an old hallway that was lined with beams, thick, dark, and ancient, but well-maintained. It had somehow retained a bright, welcoming feel. When Frankie stepped into the saloon, he imagined no scratching of needles across records. Nobody turned to see who he was as they had in the Red Lion, and the thrum of discussions never ceased. It was as if he wasn't there at all.

He ordered water from the bar, took two menus, and found a window seat with a table. From there, he could see across the car park and the pub, and be ready for Jane.

A sense of betrayal hung in his mood, internalised yet brooding like the dark clouds that had filled the sky earlier that day. The voice in his head repeated the same thing over and over.

It's not betrayal. Nobody could ever re-place Jacqui.

Which then turned to justification.

Jane knows the village. She can help me.

"I see you haven't cheered up yet."

And there she was standing opposite him.

"Jane, I..." But the words failed him.

"I think you'll find the words you're looking for begin with 'take a seat' and end in 'I'll get you a drink.'"

That smile, minus the glittering eyes.

"What do you want?"

He seethed at himself for his choice of words.

"Shall we start again?" said Jane.

Dressed in clean jeans, brown, leather boots, and a small, black, leather jacket, she looked fantastic. Her hair, which Frankie could now see was actually a light brown, had been pulled to one side to rest on one of her tiny shoulders.

And that unrelenting smile.

"Hello, Jane."

"Hello, Frankie."

"Please take a seat. I'll get you a drink. What would you like?" He found a formal, polite and well-spoken tone for his second attempt at the greeting, and it elicited the required response.

That smile.

"I'll have a gin and tonic please."

Leaving her at the table, Frankie went to the bar and ordered two gin and tonics.

It's purely business.

He fought the urge to turn around and look at her, choosing instead to study the other people in the room. Two men enjoying a post-work drink to wash the dust from their throats; Frankie placed the van in the car park as theirs. Three teenagers, one of whom looked old enough to drink, but the others were questionable, theirs was the small hatch-back parked away from the other cars, Frankie guessed, perhaps due to a lack of experienced parking skills. A man and a woman had taken another window seat. The woman fingered the rim of her glass, disinterested, while the man gesticulated an anecdote. A shiny BMW had been reverse parked close to the doors of the pub, which Frankie deduced to be his, cleaned to impress the woman and parked close enough for her to be able to see it from the seat he had chosen.

And then Frankie looked over at Jane.

He expected to find her staring back at him doe-eyed. But she wasn't. She was staring out of the window wearing the look of someone who never walked alone. Someone whose conscience teased them at every opportunity with memories, sharp and bitter.

"Is it my turn to cheer you up?"

Frankie set the drinks down and took his seat with no effort to pursue his comment or see if she was alright. If she was wasn't okay, the chances of her telling him were slim anyway.

"This is a nice place," Frankie continued. "Mr Armstrong could do with taking a few lessons from these owners."

"Barry, you mean?"

"Yes. Barry Armstrong."

"I haven't heard anybody call him Mr Armstrong before. It makes him sound official."

"Instead of?"

"The lazy git he really is."

There it was. Returning with warmth, her smile seemed to wake the happiness across her entire face.

"Thanks for meeting me," she said.

"No. Thank you for the ride. Did you reach wherever you were going safely?"

"School? Yeah. And if you're referring to my window wipers, I know. I have to get them fixed."

"Are you studying?"

"I teach history."

"History? You don't look like a historian."

"And what do historians look like?"

"Oh, I don't know. Glasses and a tank top. Maybe a bow tie."

"You should rework that stereotype, Frankie. Or stop believing everything the movies tell you."

"My son would love you." He heard it as the words came out and saw the look on Jane's face. But he had to go on. He couldn't drop the sentence half-way through. "He loves history."

"Right."

"No, seriously. Anything ancient and secretive. He's always playing some video game or watching a movie where ancient skeletons are exhumed and the main guy is searching for treasure."

"I've studied history for a long while now

and, I hate to say it, but I'm yet to find any treasure."

"Don't tell him that." Frankie closed his eyes. He'd done it again, insinuating that she might one day meet Jake. "It would shatter his dreams."

"Maybe he'll move onto war games or zombies?"

"I think I prefer the historical ones. Much less gunfire and explosions."

"The treasure may be hard to come by but there *are* secrets. You should tell him that British history is steeped in darkness. It's fascinating. Three thousand years ago, Britain was a wild place." She leaned in and lowered her voice. There was a passion in her tone so Frankie too leaned in, keen to humour her. "Men would hunt deer and boar, wolves would stalk the men, and they worshipped the sun and their environment. They had to become at one with nature. They had to understand it. They took everything they needed from the wild, and as the seasons rolled past and the herds migrated, they would follow, nomadic and ever-moving."

"Hunter-gatherers?"

"Yes. Mostly. I find them fascinating.

They had a link to nature that is long forgotten now. And they knew that to keep on taking, they would have to keep on giving back somehow. They worshipped the sun because the sun was life. They wore the skins of their kills and ate the marrow from the bones because they knew that to waste life would anger nature. And they sacrificed so the cycle may continue."

"Sacrificed? Pigs?"

"Mostly. Or deer." Jane leaned in, conspiratorial and hushed. "Sometimes humans."

"Why would they do that?"

"Nobody knows exactly how a person would be chosen, whether they were willing or if it was by force. Can you imagine that?"

"It's crazy. I'm not sure I need Jake to know about all that just yet."

She laughed.

"Is it as crazy as our religions?" Jane continued. "We have God, a separate entity that we worship. Some believe in him more than others. Some rely on him for comfort and guidance. Some just need to know that he's there. But early man didn't have anything like that. They had the moon, a strange, bright circle in the sky. And the stars, a hundred million eyes blinking in the night. And they had the sun, a fierce and burning thing that grew hotter in the summer and barely warmed their faces in the winter. Can you imagine how they felt when the land was cold and the animals were sparse? Can you imagine them questioning if they had angered nature somehow? And in the summer, when the sun shines so bright and water runs dry, what would you have done?"

"Do you really think that's what they did it? Sacrifice people? And animals?"

"There are many reasons. There's a legend in these parts that they would sacrifice people from elsewhere to protect their own or to keep their villages safe."

"I might buy Jake a war game. I don't need him getting ideas about sacrifices."

She smiled. It was a courteous smile that encouraged Frankie to move on. They hadn't met to talk about his son.

"Do you teach in Grafton?"

"No, in Branston."

"I know Branston. That's not far from here. I passed there earlier on."

"So you're not from around here?" she asked.

"What makes you say that? Am I missing something that only Lincolnshire people have?" He felt his chin and his nose as if one of them might have fallen off, and she laughed louder this time. It was still a soft laugh but it was genuine.

"The opposite. There's something extra about you. I can't put my finger on it."

"If there was anything extra, I can assure you it was washed away earlier."

"So where are you staying? If you're not from around here, are you staying with your friend? The one with the girl?"

"No. I couldn't. I'm at the Red Lion." He had a feeling she would remark on his choice of hotel so he continued before she could voice her opinion. "I was wondering if you could tell me a little more about Jim Price and..."

"What he's been through?"

"Is that being nosy? I don't mean to pry. It's just I thought it might help. You know? Paint a picture of Grafton."

"It's not a secret. But there's not a lot to tell. I used to teach his son, Grant."

"The dopey kid?"

"He's not dopey and he's hardly a kid anymore. But I used to teach him. He even used to come to our house after school for extra tuition. He had learning problems. He'd spend a few evenings at our house and the other nights at Lord Grafton's manor."

"Why there? Is Lord Grafton a scholar? He doesn't look like the teacher type."

"No, but he had an affection for the boy and didn't have children of his own. I imagine he spent the evenings boring the boy with tales of Grafton and his ancestors."

"And Jim Price? Did he ever see the boy? Seems odd to me."

"You have to understand, Frankie. They've been through a lot. I shouldn't tell you this, but Jim Price was in prison for a while and I think that's what triggered, or stunted, something inside Grant. As much as Lord Grafton is devious and has all manner of officials in his pocket, he does try to help the villagers. That much I'll vouch for."

"What did Jim Price do? Why was he put away?"

"Personally I don't believe he did anything, but he was found guilty of assault. Some woman at the market said something and pressed charges. He was away for a long time."

The news was of no surprise to Frankie and supported the hardened appearance of the man.

"And his daughter?"

Jane sighed and inhaled.

"It was last year in the summer. Nearly a year ago to the day. I was working in the primary school in Grafton, taking a break from the older kids, you know? Reigniting my sense of empathy and compassion with younger children. Teenagers can be hard, Frankie, especially when they're not your own."

Those types of comments always reminded Frankie of Jake and made him question what Jake was like at school. Would he be one of those difficult kids? Maybe. If Frankie let him slip.

"The first girl went at the beginning of summer. It was tragic. The whole village was rocked. We all searched the fields around Grafton and the police ran enquiries. But the fact is that one day she was there and the next she wasn't."

"What do you mean? Went?"

"Disappeared. Abducted. Ran away. No-one knows but-"

"You assume abduction because she was just the first?"

She nodded.

"They took her from her home?"

Jane sipped at her drink, making a poor attempt to hide her shaking hands.

"Jim's girl was next. The village was on lockdown. Parents wouldn't let their children out of their sights. But still, somehow, whoever it was who took her managed to slip through the nets. It was awful. I can remember, Frankie. I can remember that selfish, thankful feeling. I told myself it was okay. It wasn't *my* baby. I slept with her at night to make sure she was safe and she came to school with me. But still..."

"If it's too hard-"

"No. No, I have to. It was an ordinary day. We had friends over, my husband's colleagues. We had a summer garden party." She averted her eyes when she mentioned her husband then brought them back to meet Frankie's like they were equal somehow. Him with his son and her with her husband. "Nobody saw it happen. One minute, she was playing with the dogs. The next minute, she was gone. That's how quick it was."

"I'm so sorry, Jane."

"Don't be. The entire village was in uproar. We cornered Lord Grafton. After all, he's always roaming about telling everyone how Grafton is his village and boasting about how he does this and that for us, stopping housing developments and such. So we told him. Get the problem sorted out. We thought back then that whoever was doing it was one of the locals. It had to be. Nobody comes here, Frankie. They have no reason to."

"And did he do anything?"

She stared at him. There was no smile. Just a bitter expression.

"It stopped."

"The abductions?"

She winced as he said it. Something about that word stabbed at her. But she nodded.

"And that was that. Of course, Lord Grafton added the success to his list of what we should be grateful to him for and nobody knows what it was he actually did. But it stopped."

"Just like that?"

"I miss her."

Three words. The same three words that haunted Frankie day and night.

Something inside Frankie told him he should say something. He should comfort her. But before he could even think of the right words to say, a tear had formed in her eye. Jane dabbed at it with her finger but the effort wasn't enough. By the time she had found a tissue in her bag, the single tear had become many. Embarrassed at showing her emotions in public, she turned away, and the lump in Frankie's throat began to swell like an angry, infected bite.

"I'm sorry." Recovering from her little show of emotion, Jane cleared her throat. She'd somehow managed to avoid smudging her make-up. Her red eyes were the only sign she'd been crying. "I don't even know you. You must think I'm crazy. I should go."

"No." He stopped himself mid-sentence. He'd sounded too eager, too keen for her to stay. "I understand what you're going through. You've heard that a thousand times, I'm sure, and so have I. But really, I do."

"It's been a whole year since she died. I should be able to handle it by now."

"No, you shouldn't. There are no rules. I

thought I was all cried out. I thought that after the funeral and after I'd shut myself away for a week that I was done. I was over it. I felt sad when I saw her photos, I heard her voice in my head, and I think I always will. But it wasn't until recently that it hit me. I don't think I mourned at the time. And now it's hit me like a train. Sudden, you know?"

"You've been holding it all back for all this time. That's such a man thing to do."

"I had no choice. I have a son. He needed me. I couldn't just fob him off onto his grandparents when they had just lost their daughter. So, I had to be strong. For him."

She nodded. But nobody really understood. Not anybody that Frankie had met anyway.

"So, I cried with him. I took him out of school, and we looked at photos of her. I think it helped. We met the loss head-on, and I think he's stronger for it. One day he'll thank me for that. But for that whole week when I cried, I don't think I cried for me. I cried for him. And, after that, I just had to be strong. I had to get him through it."

"Is he okay now?"

"He is."

"What's his name?"

Frankie felt his own smile, but it stirred a flavour of guilt. Jake was alive and her daughter wasn't.

"Jake."

"That's a nice name."

"My wife was Jacqui. We named him after her. What was your daughter's name?"

She too smiled, no doubt remembering her face just as Frankie had pictured Jake's.

"Polly."

CHAPTER THIRTY-THREE

"How did it make you feel?"

Hope allowed the girl some time for clarity to seep into the memory as it had done when Beth had asked the questions and Hope had been chained, hooded, and frightened. The essence of the memories could be told to provide an outline, but it was only when the silence ensued that the memories truly came alive. The details needed to form and it was the details that invoked the most regret.

But Mona needed little time. Perhaps the details had already formed. After all, Mona's victim had not been a despicable, thieving junkie like Hope's. Nor had she been a cruel and imposing foster parent that had cast her out into the cold night like Beth's. She had been just a young girl, innocent and afraid.

"Sick."

Mona spat the word with utter distaste.

"Sick to my stomach. So sick I didn't sleep for days. So sick that I considered finding her family and confessing. But what could I do? By that stage, I was just an alcoholic living on the streets and offering five minutes with any reprobate who was desperate enough to part with a few pounds for my cold and calloused hands. It was the lowest I'd ever been. What was I going to say even if I could find them?"

"I can't imagine."

"So I had to live with it. I had to carry on, knowing I took everything from that poor girl and that she might have lived if I hadn't been so selfish. If I hadn't been a drunk with no scruples. I wondered what might have happened if, instead of robbing her, I had helped her. We might have been friends. Who knows? She was this pure thing. So much better than me. It was me who should have died. Not her. Can you imagine the horror of freezing to death? Alone and afraid, shaking with fear and the cold as, one by one, your organs shut down until all that's left is the smallest of heartbeats. And then nothing."

"No. I can't imagine."

"I do. I do nearly every night. You asked me what the worst thing I ever did was. You told me that I had to find the one that stood out among the rest. But, for me, there was only one memory. Only one regret. And the memory is perpetual. Anything else I did was just a mistake. I can see her blood thickening when I close my eyes at night. I can see ice crystals forming in her veins as the blood slows to a trickle. I can see the shallow rise and fall of her lungs as the ice reaches over them, suffocating her. I can see the colour of her kidneys fade to blue then harden as the cold claims her body."

She stopped and the image she conveyed was clear in Hope's mind. A frozen girl curled into a ball as the cold sucked the last remaining breath from her body.

"But, most of all, I see her face. Her lips are blue. Her skin is white. Her eyes are wide with pain. The only sign of life is the glistening of her final frozen tears."

"You're hard on yourself. You didn't mean to-"

"I killed that girl."

"Life killed that girl. You survived. You can still make amends."

"And how do you suggest I do that? I'm haunted by her. Ever since that night, I've tried to do good. I've tried to be a better person. When I find new people on the streets, I help them. I show them the bakers that give out food at the end of each day. I show them the café that will give you a coffee if you knock on the back door and ask nicely. I help them get clothes. I show them where they can sell things they find and the best places to sleep. I'm a good person inside. I just did a terrible, terrible thing. I was bitter. I was full of hate. But I see it now. I don't need a stupid hole in the ground to cleanse me. I'm already cleansed."

"But you can still do more. You can still make a difference."

"How? What can I possibly do?"

Her words trailed off as the tears came and her throat thickened with remorse.

In contrast to the image of the frozen girl, Mona's heart was racing. Hope lay her hand flat on her chest then squeezed her shoulder. Her touch seemed to rouse Mona. She flinched at first then relaxed when Hope squeezed once more.

"When you leave this place, you can do so much more. We're here for a reason. We're here because of the things we have done. But we've been given a chance, Mona. You have to believe me. I've seen it. I've seen a girl as guilty as you and I. She left here with her head held high. She walked out of that door proud of what she'd become."

"Become?"

"She'd transformed."

Mona's exhale needed no explanation. It spoke a thousand words, all of which were of despair and disbelief.

"She came in here like you and me, heavy with guilt. But she left here as pure as that poor, sweet child who froze to death."

"There was another girl? Before me and you? And how many before that?"

"I don't know," said Hope. "But she showed me the way, Mona. She showed me how we can right our wrongs. How we get out."

"What do we have to do?"

Finding the hessian sack in the dark, Hope groped for the corners so she wouldn't pull Mona's hair. Then she tugged it free and remembered the sensation she had felt when Beth had done the same.

"Thank you."

She was enjoying the touch of the cool air on her face, savouring the moment.

Just as Hope had done.

"What do we need to do? I need to sit down but these chains are hurting."

Hope's fingertips grazed Mona's cheeks, pushing a thick curl of hair from her face and tucking it behind her ear. She moved in closer, allowing the fabric of her gown to press onto Mona's naked skin, offering a little warmth and comfort before she delivered the next requirement.

"Tell me the best thing you ever did."

CHAPTER THIRTY-FOUR

The summer sun lit the far reaches of the western sky and, overhead, darkness was closing in. The first stars shone against deep blue hues and barely a breath of wind rustled the treetops.

Frankie stopped the car in the car park of the Red Lion and watched as Jane's Volvo, which had followed him from Addleton, lumbered into the parking space on the far side of the road outside the cottage that Frankie had thought was pretty.

He switched off his lights, marvelling at life's little intertwines.

A part of him hoped she would look his

way. A larger part of him hoped she would offer him a coffee in her shy manner. But the voice, Jacqui's voice, hoped the night would end there.

Would she look up? Would she glance across at him?

She locked her car and made her way through the little path that was lined with rose bushes then opened her front door.

"She didn't look."

He spoke out loud to himself, almost in surprise. But a slice of what he said was directed at Jacqui as if proving that the meeting had been nothing more than two people sharing their losses and tales of grief with the hope no-one else would have to suffer as they had.

The lights flicked on in the cottage, offering Frankie a glimpse of the inside. There were pictures on the wall and a frilly lampshade.

And then she looked.

He was positive she had looked, just as she had closed the door.

Then she was gone.

But the night was far from over.

There was nothing to be guilty about. He'd done nothing wrong. Those two thoughts and all the other mental justifications a man tells himself, and the voice, weaved through his mind, rolling, spinning, and returning with less ambition. With each second, the excuses weakened or diluted with doubt.

Then the upstairs light came on.

There was a chance of one more glimpse of her before she closed the curtains. But he shouldn't. He knew he shouldn't look. She'd spent the first half of the evening telling him about the daughter she had lost, and he'd reciprocated with stories of Jacqui and Jake. To sit outside her house in the dark was inappropriate, however plausible his reasons.

A distraction came in the form of Jake. Frankie had realised mid-thought that he should call Tom to make sure they were all okay. He checked his watch. Ten o'clock wasn't too late. Jake would be in bed but Tom would be enjoying the evening with a nightcap.

The phone call was answered on the second ring, which meant that Tom was in his armchair beside the phone and hadn't had to rush across the room to pick it up before it woke Mary or Jake.

"Hello?"

"Tom, it's me."

"Frankie, son, is everything okay?"

Kindness was always hard to swallow in moments of self-pity.

Frankie cleared his throat and found the facade he wore with his father-in-law. It wasn't an inaccurate image of himself or a deception. But it was the image of the old Frankie, the strong Frankie that they had trusted with their daughter's life.

"I'm okay, thanks, Tom. I'm sorry to call so late. I hope I'm not disturbing you."

"Not at all. I'm just enjoying a little sip of whiskey before I go up. It helps me sleep. How's Lincoln?"

Jane's shape moved past the window, unhurried and delightful.

"Frankie?"

"Sorry, Tom. Yes. It's nice."

"Wild countryside. I was up there a few years back. Beautiful landscapes, as I remember."

"The views are..." Realising the inappropriate insinuations considering who he was talking to, Frankie sought to move on but kept an eye on the figure in the window. "The views are a welcome distraction, Tom. That's for sure."

She disappeared from sight.

"I was just calling to make sure Jake was okay. I should have called but something came up. Is he okay? He's not causing you any problems, is he?"

She returned, edging around what Frankie imagined was a bed that filled most of the small bedroom. She bent and a tall lamp flicked on. Then she reached and switched the main light off.

"No problem at all. He's a pleasure, Frankie. How's the case going?"

The subtle question had a hidden meaning that Frankie understood only too well. Tom was far too tactful to ask Frankie how he was coping directly.

"I'm getting through it, Tom. I spoke to someone today. Shared my feelings. I think it helped."

"That's good. It takes time. Now, listen, don't you worry about Jake at all. He's doing okay. If only we can drag him away from those damn historical adventure games."

The dim light of the lamp revealed less of the room than the main light. But to its detriment, it focused the attention on Jane. She pulled off her t-shirt, folded it, and laid it down somewhere, perhaps on a chair. Then she unbuttoned her jeans.

Frankie looked away.

"It could be worse, Tom. It could be war games with explosions and gunfire."

She had to be teasing him.

As if with the utmost deliberation, Jane slid from her jeans, her hands grazing her slender thighs as she stepped out of each leg.

Again, Frankie turned away.

"Yes. I guess you're right. If we need anything from you, we'll call. But otherwise, just get yourself back in the game, Frankie. I'm glad you took the job, son."

He hadn't meant to but his deprived and lonely subconscious looked at the window.

She was standing in her underwear folding her jeans, taking her time as if to show Frankie what he might have if he wanted it. Maybe? Or maybe she was just folding her clothes with no purposeful teasing.

"Thanks, Tom. Thanks for being there. I really appreciate it."

Jane reached behind to unfasten her bra.

Frankie closed his eyes as Jacqui's voice returned to him, tempting him to move on with his life.

He opened them again to find the view gone. The curtains had been pulled and the light from the corner of the window blinked off as he imagined her settling into bed and switching off her lamp.

"Goodnight, Frankie. You know where we are if you need us."

Frankie inhaled, long and deep.

"Thanks, Tom."

He hit the button to disconnect the call and took one final glance up at the window. He thought he saw a flicker of the curtain.

Does she want me to go?

The choice between a boring room alone or a nightcap with Jane was an easy one to make. It was a gamble but the signs were all there. A loud laugh came from the pub and, peering in through the window, Frankie saw the bar full of men. If he were to have a beer, there would be no chance of finding a seat and capturing Barry Armstrong for long enough to glean any information anyway.

A little, wrought iron gate sat beneath a

rose arbour at the edge of the little cottage property. It clinked, loud and metallic in the quiet when he opened the latch and the gate squeaked when he pushed it open.

He wondered if Jane had heard.

He looked up. No lights had come on. Perhaps she was waiting there for him to knock.

The front door was green. Even in the dim light, Frankie could make out the colour. There was no knocker or bell. He considered a rap on the letterbox but instead thought a friendly knock would be best.

Two knocks? Short and sweet?

Or maybe something chirpy like a rat-a-tat-tat?

"Get it together, Frankie."

He raised his hand, his eyes still watching for the movement of a curtain or a light to come on, and he went to knock.

But he stopped.

He cocked his head listening to the silent night. There was a noise in the trees behind the cottage. Somewhere far away.

But then nothing.

It could have been a bird. An owl or a small animal.

Knock-knock it is. Straight talking. No nonsense.

He raised his hand.

And there it was.

A scream so shrill and blood-curdling, it rose the hairs on Frankie's arm.

CHAPTER THIRTY-FIVE

"I got myself a job. It was a new start for me. A guy I knew from the streets had managed to turn his life around and build a business buying and selling second-hand furniture. He was a real inspiration to me. Apparently, he was homeless and used to sell anything he could carry in his cart. Then, as people began to trust him, a guy used to let him store things in his garage. Soon enough, he got himself a van, then two vans and a warehouse of his own. A real success story. Do you know what I mean?"

"I think I do, yes." Remembering the story Beth had told, Hope listened with interest. "And this man gave you a job?"

"Yes. He gave many of us a job. Anyone keen to make a change in their lives anyway. He had a saying. *You make your own luck in life.* It stuck with me. I used to help with the admin side of things. He had to train me but he was a patient man. It was wonderful. Every one of us came from the streets. So we all had this kind of affinity with him and each other. Like a community. We worked late if we had to and nobody complained. It was the first job I'd ever had and the best job I could ever dream of. I'll never forget that man."

"He's still alive?"

"Yes. Yes, he's alive. But, as with anything, as fast as he'd turned his life around and the lives of others, it all came crashing down. All the hard work he'd put in to build that business came to nothing in the end."

Remembering Beth's story, Hope clung to every word Mona spoke. The story of the man who made his fortune selling other people's unwanted things and how, for a short time at least, he'd transformed the lives of those around him.

And how it had all come crashing down.

"He had a wife. She was a good woman at heart. But as with the rest of us, she had a story. And just like the rest of us, he brought her up from the gutter and gave her a life beyond anything she could have imagined."

"Lucky woman."

"Yes. Yes, she was. I spoke to her once at their house. She was humble and generous. So very generous. She told me about her past life and how she'd ended up on the street. She was like me. She came from a broken home. In her teens, she was wild, uncontrollable, and unruly. She wasn't proud of what she had done. But in our company, she could tell us anything and nobody would judge. We all could. That was a huge part of our community. We'd all done bad things, things we weren't proud of, but none of it mattered. They were past lives. We'd moved on. All thanks to her husband."

"Did you feel lighter somehow? By telling your stories, did you feel better?"

"Yes. Yes, I did. It was a relief. I guess it was something like a confession in church. Not that I ever went to church. But I *have* seen movies."

"What was it that happened that caused it all to come crashing down? It must have been bad."

Mona sighed. She took a deep breath and Hope could picture her in the darkness, her face recalling the events that had destroyed the lives of so many hard-working people and sent them crawling back to the gutter.

"They had a daughter. She was a pretty, little thing. So peaceful and polite. Somehow, from these two people that had led lives beyond the imaginations of many, suffered hardship and cruelty, and somehow managed to build a business that supported everyone and turned a healthy profit, this child was created. She was a picture of perfection. The apple of her parents' eyes. There was nothing they wouldn't do for her. She was loved by all of us, as if, somehow, each of us had a responsibility to care for her. I had arranged a dinner for them at their home. It was in a little village outside the city and I wanted to say thanks for everything they had done for us. There must have been thirty or forty of us there and we cooked everything ourselves."

"For thirty people?"

"They could probably have afforded to have caterers come and take care of it all. But you have to remember that we all came from nothing. Money was never squandered. It was cherished. Although they were wealthy, they had a healthy respect for those of us who weren't. And besides, it felt good to do something for them. It was my idea. I arranged it all. I arranged the food and cooking and entertainment. It was a good day. To start with anyway. It was summertime. Drinks flowed and we chatted. Each of us told anecdotes of our previous lives, which raised smiles, caused blushes, and sent eyes rolling. We ate in the garden and played with their daughter. We basked in the glorious sunshine, each of us grateful for what we had and remembering where we had come from."

She quietened. Hope felt the story turn with a strengthening cold breeze.

"But then it all went wrong."

"How so?"

"The dogs were barking but nobody paid them any attention. They were always barking. But this time, they didn't let up. I remember I was laying on the grass with some others, making shapes from the clouds. And you know how suddenly a noise registers? Something you had heard but hadn't paid any attention to? Then the noise stopped. His wife came outside with a tray of canapes and asked if we'd seen their little girl. We told her we hadn't, not for a while anyway. I told her she was playing with the dogs. That was when the dogs' silence registered. I'll never forget the look on her face. She dropped the tray of food and rushed around the house. I looked at my friend and we barely had time to exchange worried glances when we heard her scream."

"What happened?"

"She was gone."

"Who? The girl?"

"Taken from under our noses. We tried to think about how long the dogs had been quiet for, but nobody could remember. We tried to help. We searched the village. We searched the woods. We checked every street and knocked on doors. But no-one had seen a thing. One minute she was there. The next she was gone."

"Oh my God. That's terrible. Did they ever find her?"

"No. It was the beginning of the end. That afternoon had been my one way of saying thank you to the man who had touched all our hearts, and it had wrecked everything."

"It wasn't your fault. You were just doing a

nice thing. How could you know what was going to happen?"

"Because things always happen to me. I really did try to be a better person and he helped me. But maybe I just wasn't meant to be a good person. Maybe I was destined to be bad."

"No. Don't say that. Don't think like that."

"What am I supposed to think? It was the kindest thing I'd ever done for anyone. It was supposed to be my proudest moment. And all that happened was that a family was torn apart and all of our lives were ruined. Jacob sunk into a hole. Nobody could reach him. Not even his wife. The business began to fail. In a matter of weeks, some of us were laid off. Then their house was lost. And, if that wasn't bad enough, he pushed his wife away. He told her he couldn't stand to look at her anymore. Every time he did, all he saw was his daughter's face."

"What happened to him?"

Hope knew the answer but wanted to hear it from Mona's lips. It was like closure of a kind, wrapping a story up.

"He tried to kill himself. Tried to throw himself off a bridge in front of a train."

"But he changed his mind?"

"A friend of mine stopped him. A good friend. I didn't know her at the time, but we became friends over the past year."

Hope wanted to say Beth's name. She wanted to tell her she had known her and that her friend had shown her the way too. She wanted to complete the story. But with so much tragedy in the tale, to add the loss of her friend might be too much. If Mona withdrew into herself, she would never transform, and if she didn't transform, then Hope would be stuck in the hole with her forever. Her chance to repent and to give something good back to the world would be lost.

"And the wife?" It was all Hope could think to say to tear her mind away from the tragedy and loss. Although, in her mind, Beth's memory lived on.

"I don't know. She had been studying when things had been good. She had a career of her own so she wouldn't be reliant on Jacob all the time. It was the only way she could help others and give something back. I don't know what happened to her. I just hope that somewhere out there, she's happy. She was a good woman, and if ever there was somebody made for such a perfect soul like Jacob, it was her. I think of her sometimes. But when I do, she's always alone. She lives a simple life. I see her walking through the woods picking wild-flowers, from which she creates a posy. She uses her hairband to bind them together. Then she lays them on her daughter's empty grave."

The thought brought a lump to Hope's throat. The memories of Beth. The tale of the little girl. And the lost woman who had crawled to lofty heights and found refuge in the lowest of places.

"What was her name?"

In the darkness, Hope heard Mona smile. Two glints of light, tiny in the surrounding gloom, marked her moist eyes.

"Her name was Jane."

CHAPTER THIRTY-SIX

The first time could have been a joke, a prank, or kids messing around in the forest on Lord Grafton's land.

But the second scream came as shrill as the first but was cut short. Then there was silence.

Frankie searched for lights, a sign that he wasn't the only one who had heard it.

But there were no lights, save for the pub with its hushed thrum of merriment inside. He was alone. Even Jane's window remained dark, and there was no flicking of the curtains.

The decision to run took a second or less, and with the area from which the scream had come pinpointed in his mind, Frankie leapt out of Jane's front garden and tore into the woods. Blinded by the dark and with the thin, wispy, low-hanging branches of trees whipping at his face, he forced himself through brush and thorns, discerning a vague path in the dense, achromatic forest. He ran uphill using the areas of dark grey to guide himself between the blackness of the trees. Then Frankie stopped near to where he deemed to be the source of the screams.

He controlled his breathing and searched the bleak shadows around him for movement. The scurry of a rodent through the debris on the ground and the hooting of an owl broke the silence. But the snapping of a branch somewhere behind Frankie gave him focus. He tuned into the area and, as quiet as could be, he closed in. Rolling his feet from his heels along the sides of his boots and then to his toes, he walked with slow and precise movements, like a predator searching the night for nearby prey. His eyes flicked between areas of light grey, searching for the faintest of movements.

Somewhere in the canopy, a bird was startled. The sound of its flapping wings was loud in the quiet night. The fracas woke others who in turn scurried from their roosts creating a moment of chaos that multiplied. Soon the canopy above was alive with spooked birds, cries of alarm, and beating wings.

But the din was brief. The silence resumed as the last of the birds fluttered into its new resting place.

Somewhere in the space before Frankie, something moved. Black on grey. For a fraction of a second, from one black tree to another, it passed.

Frankie moved forward.

His heart thumped a familiar beat as the adrenaline seeped into his bloodstream and he found the rhythm of his breathing, controlled and deep.

He'd entered the forest from east to west, uphill away from the Red Lion, and was now moving north to south, hunting with his senses keen.

The shape that had crossed from one tree to another had gone. Doubt came as he questioned if he'd actually seen it or if it had been a trick of the mind as his eyes sought focus in the gloom.

How long he stood waiting to see it again, he didn't know.

But it was only when he decided to move forward that something caught his eye. In the darkness thirty yards ahead of him, something shined, alien to the environment yet as dark as dark can be.

Nothing else mattered. There was nothing else. The world around him was a blank and blurred wall as he closed in without caution for sound. The closer he got to the shining object, the faster he moved.

Then he ran.

Beneath a clearing in the canopy as a window to the heavens above was a shape, familiar but sickening.

A girl.

She was laid on a flat stone, waist-high, naked, and still. Her pale skin glowed in the dim moonlight but her neck was black like the shadows in the trees. Inky blood pooled where she lay.

There was a pulse, faint but it was there.

Her eyes moved once and stared, moist and lost.

But it wasn't Hope.

It was then that Frankie realised where he was standing.

Surrounding the flat stone, standing tall as

if they were soldiers guarding the dying girl, were twelve stones. They were placed a few metres apart and standing ten-feet high, as thick as the oaks that concealed them in the forest.

He found his phone and dialled the emergency services with one hand and held his other to the wound on the girl's neck, maintaining pressure and preventing the loss of any more blood.

The call was answered with the professional haste he'd expected and he spoke five words. It was all the information they would need.

"Ambulance.   Grafton.   Red   Lion. Murder."

He pocketed his phone, assessed the girl's state, and made the decision to get her to the road. She might bleed out on the way. But by the time the emergency crew found him in the woods, she would definitely be gone.

Hoisting her into his arms, Frankie ran downhill, the only way he knew to get out.

"Stay with me. Don't die."

But the only replies the girl could utter were gargled as blood bubbled from the slice in her throat.

He stumbled on roots and fell to his backside, holding the girl off the ground as he stumbled, and he slid a few feet before his boots found traction. She coughed, spraying a mist of blood into his face. But there was light. Two hundred feet away, the lights of the Red Lion shone like a beacon.

In the distance, sirens sang.

He focused on the lights, shouting at the girl to stay alive and calling for help to anyone who could hear him. By the time he emerged onto the road, a couple leaving the bar after a few drinks had heard his shouts and were standing, bemused and concerned, outside the pub. They ran to him as he crossed the road. Together they laid the girl down. Using his jacket to cover the girl's modesty Frankie instructed the woman to keep the pressure on the wound and for the man to fetch towels from Barry Armstrong.

But the girl began to twitch, convulsing as if her body played host to a battle of life and death. Her wide eyes sought air, thick blood ran from her neck, and her hips convulsed as life ebbed away.

Soon the entire pub was standing around them despite Frankie's attempts at keeping them away. Some still held their drinks, shaking their heads at the tragedy. Others just stood and watched, helpless yet curious. Frankie sent two of them running to the church to point the way for the ambulance driver in the hope it would save seconds.

And soon, the ambulance came to a halt beside them, the doors opening even before the vehicle had stopped.

Frankie took control and moved aside for the men to do their work, talking them through the facts and giving them all the information they needed as a police car drew up behind the ambulance.

"Teenage girl with a neck wound. Ten minutes since the incident. She's lost a lot of blood and can't speak. Name unknown. Blood type unknown."

As they lifted the girl onto a stretcher and carried her to the back of the ambulance, Frankie followed.

Then, just as they were lifting her inside, her bloodied hand grabbed Frankie by his shirt.

The men paused, confused.

Her grip was weak but her intentions

strong, and she met Frankie's eyes with her own wide and frightened gaze.

"Sir, we have to-"

"Hold on." He raised his hand. "She's trying to say something."

With wet blood on her fingers, she grabbed Frankie's wrist and he let her turn his hand palm up. Trembling though she was, and with just her own dying blood for ink, she drew on Frankie's hand three circles. Then she closed his fist and the paramedic carried her into the ambulance.

But as they closed the doors, Frankie felt eyes on him.

The ambulance pulled away, turned, and accelerated through the village. All Frankie could think of was the girl, dying alone in the back.

Still, there were eyes on him. As the ambulance disappeared around the corner, he felt them. Penetrating and accusing.

He turned to find the local people huddled together and two policemen standing close by.

"Are you Frankie Black, sir?"

"Yes, I am."

"And you say you found the girl?"

Frankie looked at his blood-stained hands. "Yes. In the forest."

And without warning, the incident turned on its head. He shook his head.

"Wait a minute."

But the locals began to voice their opinions.

"It was him. He doesn't belong here."

"No, it wasn't me. I just found her."

"Do you mind telling us what you were doing in the forest so late, Mr Black?"

"I heard the scream. I ran to help."

Then Jim Price stepped forward, his voice low and guttural with distaste. His obedient son stood beside him.

"We saw him, officer, about fifteen minutes ago. Didn't we, Grant?" He looked at the boy, who had fallen into the lost and sad gaze that seemed to search inside Frankie's very soul. He nodded his confirmation and Jim Price continued. "We saw him sitting in his car in the dark. He was watching a woman getting undressed in that window over there."

CHAPTER THIRTY-SEVEN

"What's wrong? Was it something I said?"

The churning inside Hope's stomach slowed and her mind conjured so many questions.

Mona began to panic at her silence.

"Talk to me. What did I say?"

But even as Hope searched for the words, all manner of possibilities ran through her mind, weaving in and out to the soundtrack of her mother's pitiful cries as she called for her daughter along that dark street so many years before.

"Do you remember where it was?"

"No. Just that it was a little village outside the city."

"And the girl. What was her name?"

"She's dead. What does it matter?"

"Her name. Tell me her name, Mona."

"Polly. Her name was Polly." Her voice softened, shattering the tension. "She was the sweetest little girl you ever saw."

Solidified. There was no longer a slim chance that the characters in her story had only sounded similar. It was real. It was the little girl she had met once. The girl she had held and with whom she had shared the tiniest of moments. A kinship.

"Did you know her?"

Searching only for the sound of her voice in the silence of misery, Mona prompted Hope, trying to pull her back from where she had fallen.

Doubt crept in like a predator. A pack of predators. They emerged from the hidden places in the walls, taking slow, tentative steps, their claws silent on the dirt, but their eyes keen in the darkness. The pack broke apart to encircle her and, in turn, they attacked with the sole purpose of bringing Hope down, to eat away at her desire to do one last good thing, to resurrect her soul and leave this world good and clean.

And she let them feed.

She let them tear away the fear and power of the hole in strips of tainted memories, leaving only Hope, exactly as she had entered the room. Everything Beth had told her had just been words. They meant nothing. The stories Hope had told her and the tales she had dragged from her chasm of spite and hate, to pronounce them and cleanse...

To transform...

It had all been lies.

Not on Beth's part. She could see that. Beth had been brainwashed by the weight of however many tons of soil and rock loomed above her. Her mind had been stained. She'd been convinced that she was evil.

Maybe it was the eyes in the walls that had turned her just as they had been so close to turning Hope.

"No. I do not know her. But one day, maybe, I will."

"Was it something I said? You sound..." Mona stumbled, hesitating while a suitable word presented itself.

"Transformed?"

"Yes. You sound different. Did I do well? Can you remove the chains now? I need to sit down. My legs ache like I've walked a thousand miles yet all I've done is stand here and tell you my story."

Her ebbing doubts, tired and satiated, left Hope with a sense of clarity and purpose like she had never known.

She stepped up to Mona and felt for her hand.

"I see now."

"You do?"

"I see the wrong in all of this. I see that our minds are tricked with the weight of our own guilt. It's funny how fear and uncertainty shroud reality. I feel as though a light has been turned on. Now I understand."

"I don't understand. You're scaring me a little."

"Mona." The smile of Hope's face was its own being. She couldn't control it or stop it from spreading despite the darkness.

It felt so good.

"We have to get out of here."

"Escape? But how. I'm chained and you aren't. Don't leave me here. Please don't leave me here. It's only your voice that helps the time pass. Knowing you are there, even when you don't speak, it helps."

"I won't leave you. I have an idea. It's dangerous but you have to trust me. It's been a full day now. The man will return soon with food. He will be looking to me to see that you are..." She could barely bring herself to say the word and almost laughed at the notion and how foolish she had been. "Transforming."

"And am I? I feel good. Like I said, just telling somebody about what I did makes me feel so much better. It's like a shared secret."

"No, Mona. You aren't transforming. But we must let him believe that you are."

"I'm not? But I did everything you asked."

"No, Mona. There's no such thing. You are who you are, and you've done all those things, terrible or not, honourable or not. You can't change those. All you have is pride and regret, the same as me. I'm proud of the good things I've done but, by God, I regret so much more. It would take a thousand years in this hole to cleanse me, Mona. So no, we are not transformed. All we can do is try, and if we ever get out of here, I'll be the best person I can be."

"Do you really think people can change? I tried. I tried for so long to be a good person. But deep down, it felt as if I was kidding myself. The evil inside me would show its face and undo all my hard work. I think you're right. We are who we are."

"So let's escape. You and I. We can-"

Her idea was halted by the timely rattle of a chain on wood.

"Shhh."

"But how will we...?"

Hope leaned in, glancing back as the rattling stopped, and clutched Mona's hand tight in both of her own.

She whispered in her ear, "Trust me."

The shadows swallowed her and the light from outside spread to its limits as it had done when Beth had shared her prison, tantalising and teasing but held back by the force of the darkness inside.

It was, in Hope's mind, good versus evil illustrated in the dirt.

He grunted.

His waxed jacket scraped against the tunnel and Hope reached inside the recess of the wall, fumbling blindly for a chance.

She found it as the huge man stood tall.

Hope slipped a large femur bone beneath her garment.

He found Mona looking afraid and he

grunted once more. Then he searched for Hope who stepped into the dim reaches of light. She mimicked Beth with her confidence, a loyal servant, transformed and ready to die for the cause. Ready to pay the ultimate price so that another may live.

Nodding in silent response to his unspoken question, Hope confirmed that Mona was transforming. By his side, she felt obedient and, despite his overwhelming mass, she felt the frailty of his trust.

And the evil inside her smiled, feeding on her deception.

He dropped the bag of food to the ground as he had done with Beth. Morsels of tough meat, unsavoury, unrecognisable, and rank.

Then the rattle of his keys triggered the thump in Hope's heart that grew in passion and tempo.

A sliver of light found the outline of Mona's face and body. The slender concave of her shoulder against her jaw. The shallow curve of her childlike breast tipped with the button of pink that was stirred by the cold. The ripple of her ribs as her meagre flesh clung to her frame. And the deep hollow of her starved stomach against the sharp edge of her feminine hips.

Mona gasped in pain as the man found the lock. Then she silenced at his grunts in fear of him changing his mind.

Hope recognised the sound of relief as Mona's wrists were freed. The cold air touching her tender wounds was welcomed with the freedom it accompanied. She touched her own wrists in empathy and shared joy.

The femur slipped from her gown and nestled in Hope's sweaty palm. Her timing would need to be right. There could be no mistake.

It was as he turned away from Mona that he straightened and cast his eyes around the gloom. And it was as he ducked to re-enter the tunnel that Hope swung the heavy end of the femur into his face. It connected with a dull crack, and he hit his head against the roof of the tunnel.

But there was no time to watch.

In the seconds that he sought to recover and decipher his attack, Hope moved in. She had seen Greg fight a dozen times, and she had listened to him tell her to never let up.

So she didn't.

Hope delivered blow after blow, smashing his hands that protected his face.

But it wasn't enough. He stood, crouched in the confines of the tunnel. Then he rushed at her with open arms.

Hope, with both hands on the bone, buried it into his face.

He lay still, a huge mass of muscle half in and half out of the light, straddling the border of good and evil.

She dropped the bone to the ground and found his keys, watching for movement on his face, waiting for his eyes to open.

With trembling hands, Hope searched for the key to free Mona's ankles.

The first didn't fit.

"Hurry."

The second slotted into the lock but wouldn't turn. That left only the third.

She switched the keys and felt the lock give. A sigh of relief followed from both Hope and Mona, who rubbed at her sores.

"Follow me."

The need for speed was quelled by a desire not to stir the man. Hope ducked, raised the hem of her garment, and stepped over him, passing from the darkness into the light. But, unlike the man who would forever be in darkness, the light called to her.

She passed him and turned back to Mona, who stood at the limits of the shadows, covering herself, afraid and uncertain.

"Mona, come on." It was a whisper that Hope barely heard herself.

But Mona was frozen to the spot.

"Mona, let's go. Be quick." It was a hiss now, snake-like and urgent.

The man stirred.

"Now, Mona." It was aggressive, a culmination of all the emotions that had developed over the past days in the confines of the hole. A few feet away, the open sky waited for her. But behind her, the fear that had gripped her earlier now loomed over Mona.

Stooped low, Hope ran back to the door, encouraging Mona with her presence.

It worked.

The girl raised her leg over the man, passing from darkness into light in the wake of Hope.

Hope waved her on, silent now in the most treacherous of moments. She checked outside with the thought that there may be more kidnappers and she would escape into the arms of another.

Outside was night time, bright stars, and life. The treetops danced in the wind, swaying to the rhythm of nature, and nothing else moved.

Her first breath of fresh air tasted good. Inside her, a powerful force hushed the darkness. Somewhere out there was her mother, a good woman by all accounts, transformed of her own accord. And her father who needed no transformation, only the love and loyalty he deserved.

She turned back and Mona was in reach. Hope stretched out her hand. But Mona's feet grazed the man's chest.

She stopped, gripped by fear.

The man's eyes opened.

Hope reached into the tunnel and grabbed her wrist.

The man's strong hand clamped around Mona's ankle.

The tug of war developed into a frantic battle, but despite his position on the ground, his strength far outweighed any power Hope could summon.

"Help me." Mona's voice was shrill.

"Kick him, Mona."

But he had an ankle in each hand and pulled with all his weight, digging his heels into the ground. He gave a sharp tug and Hope fell forward into the hole.

Mona's wrist slipped from her fingers.

There was a moment, as Hope lay face down in the dirt, arms outstretched and hands emptied of the girl she was trying to save, when Mona looked back at her, arms mirroring Hope's and her face a picture of anguish and fear.

A silent scream.

And she was dragged into the darkness.

"Mona," Hope shouted, her fears cast aside and her desperation in its purest form.

But from within the hole, amidst the sound of rattling chains, came the quiet voice of defeat. Sounds of sadness. It was a whisper, not an angered hiss or a shout of desperation.

And Hope heard it. She understood.

"Save yourself."

CHAPTER THIRTY-EIGHT

"So at ten o'clock you parked in the Red Lion car park and made a phone call. Is that right?"

Detective Inspector Thorn made a show of inspecting his notes and waited for Frankie to respond.

"That's what I told you the first time we had this conversation. So yes. It's still correct."

"And then you did what?"

"I finished my phone call with my father-in-law and locked the car. That's when I heard the scream."

"What time would you say that was?"

"Ten minutes past ten."

"And you found the girl at what time?"

"Maybe fifteen or twenty minutes past ten."

"So in five or ten minutes, you managed to find the girl?"

"It was about that amount of time."

"In a forest?"

"Yes."

"In the middle of the night?"

"Yes."

"Did you have a torch?"

"No. Why would I have a torch? I heard a scream and I ran to help. What would you have done?"

"I would have called the police."

"She'd be dead. The only reason she's alive is because of me."

"How many people were there in the pub at the time?" asked Thorn.

"At least six at the bar. Plus whoever was sitting down at tables," said Frankie. "Fifteen maybe?"

"So you had time to count them but not enough time to ask for help or raise the alarm?"

"I didn't think to ask for help."

"You're aware of what happened in Grafton last week?"

"Of course."

"So you ran into a forest, in the dark, with no torch, knowing full well that a killer was on the loose?"

"That's about the size of it."

"You're ex-military, aren't you? I read it on your file."

"I have a file?"

Thorn shrugged. "It's actually an interesting report. You were a marine. Why did you give all that up?"

"Family issues." It was a half-truth. Frankie knew it and the police officer knew it.

"It says you were dishonourably discharged. Is that accurate?"

"Like I said, family issues. Do you have any questions I can answer that will prove my innocence? Or will we spend all night digging up my irrelevant past?"

"Do you have a lawyer?"

"Do I need one?"

"Are you guilty?"

"No."

"Then you need one. Right now, I've got a witness saying he saw you watching a woman get undressed through her bedroom window just fifteen minutes before you say a scream was heard. And I've got you with a dying girl and blood on your hands and nobody to prove you didn't attack her. Lastly, initial reports from the hospital say that her wounds are precise. Whoever did them wasn't a frantic, bloodthirsty murderer. He knew what he was doing. So your military file is quite prominent and your presence is more than just coincidental."

"Jeremy Gilmour." Frankie reached into his pocket and found Jeremy's business card. It was faded and curled from the soaking Frankie had endured, but the writing was still legible. "He's my lawyer."

DI Thorn took the card and passed it to a colleague who eyed Frankie as he stood, embittered that rank had been pulled. But the pulling of rank gave Frankie the opportunity he would need to do his own investigations. DI Thorn checked his watch. It was a Breitling, expensive and very tasteful. As was his suit. Frankie had never been keen on expensive clothes. He preferred function over form but could still appreciate a quality hand-made garment. The lining of the suit jacket was bright and distinct. The lapels rolled gently instead of creasing and the shoulders were clearly made to measure.

Frankie sat back in the plastic chair. He pulled one leg over the other and rested his hands on his lap wondering who had decided the colour of police interview rooms. He wondered if there had been a committee or if research had been carried out to see which colours produced the best results. Then Frankie succumbed to the fact that the decision had likely been swayed by budget and that a light blue would be cheapest.

Thorn watched him with fascination. It was as if the guy had seen too many cop shows and was trying to work out which was the best method to get Frankie to speak.

"Do you know what happens now?"

"What happens now is that we wait for your colleague to return and say nothing until he does. Otherwise, it's your word against mine and anything said during that discussion could go against you in a court of law."

"You know your rights? In my experience, people who know their rights only know them because they need to know them. Innocent people rarely need to know their rights."

"Shall I tell you what I also know?"

The officer seemed to be enjoying the interaction. He leaned forward on the table, prompting Frankie to continue with a flick of his head.

"This is just a stabbing, or an attack, or whatever it was. I don't know how you'd class it because I'm innocent. All I know is that the girl was bleeding from her neck when I found her. But she's alive."

"It's a stabbing."

"Right. And she's alive. If she dies, the case will be escalated. That might open up further investigations. People might wonder why the police aren't doing anything about a murder case. There would be a prosecution and evidence and you'd be back on the streets. If you're lucky."

Thorn said nothing. He watched Frankie with a keen eye and feigned disinterest.

"So enjoy it while you can. Are you aiming to make chief inspector?"

"I like what I do."

"But you don't want to be the monkey for the rest of your life, do you? You want to be the organ grinder. A job more fitting for a man who wears tailor-made suits and expensive watches. I'll let you into a secret, shall I? If you try and pin this on me, there'll be a court case. I'll be found not guilty and your chances of hanging that suit up and getting back into your old uniform increase dramatically."

"What makes you so sure of yourself?"

"Easy. I'm innocent and I have the best lawyer in town. All *you* have is conjecture and Lord Grafton on your side."

"I have a little more than-"

"Let's not get into your payoffs right now. Let's talk about me. Me leaving here, to be more specific. Jim Price said he saw me looking into a window watching a woman get undressed."

"That's right. It's not illegal but it wouldn't buy you many friends on the jury."

"How did he know a woman was getting undressed in there?"

Thorn frowned but said nothing.

"Maybe it was him who was looking. Maybe nobody was looking. Maybe nobody lives there. But you haven't even checked yet, have you?"

The officer's expression stiffened.

"I heard the scream and found the body. Her blood *is* on *my* hands."

Thorn smiled. "Get out of that one."

"Easy. If and when you find a weapon, it won't have my prints on it."

"That's if we find what you did with it."

"I'm guessing you'll also look into my address and try to work out why I'm in Lincolnshire and not at home."

"And why aren't you at home?"

"Let me ask you a question. I'll do a deal with you."

"I don't do deals with criminals."

"How about innocent men?"

He shrugged like he was allowing Frankie a chance to tell him what the deal might involve. He would make a good detective. He was selfish and corruptible.

"I don't expect to walk out of here without proving my innocence. But if I tell you why I'm in Lincoln and my lawyer corroborates it, you let me go."

"That's ridiculous. Your lawyer could be in on it. Why would I do that?"

"Because I'm in Lincoln to *find* a missing girl. Not to murder one."

"What's the connection here?"

"The missing girl I'm looking for was reported missing to the police four days ago, and so far the police haven't lifted a finger to find her."

"I still can't see a connection."

"If you don't let me go, she'll be dead within a week. Then it won't be me who's up in court. It'll be you. For negligence, corruption, and bribery."

CHAPTER THIRTY-NINE

Distance.

She needed distance. A place to hide to wait out the night. Or a road to somewhere far away, where she could call the police.

For Mona.

Around her, tall trees and hedgerows proved too thick for her to penetrate. As bright as the night was, there seemed no path for her to take save for the rise of the fields behind her. Beyond the mound that had been her prison.

And she ran.

Hope pushed to one side her thoughts of Mona and how she had been dragged into the darkness. She restrained the guilt that she felt.

She stopped.

Should she turn back?

She could surprise the man.

But he was already angered. He would be waiting. Perhaps he would be looking for her.

She looked back. It was dark.

Perhaps he was already out? Perhaps he was watching her at that very moment?

She gasped.

And she ran.

Her mind conjured up sounds of his heavy boots, his grunts, and heavy breathing. But when she turned, her bare feet slipping on the grass and mud, there was no-one there.

At the top of the rise, the line of trees grew taller, deeper, and darker. Sanctuary lay within the repulsive darkness from which she had escaped. The darkness that had frightened her, stripped her of her secrets and hidden her.

Once more, she would seek the sanctuary it offered. It was as if the taloned hand of death himself offered guidance. A place to shelter beneath his wing.

Silence fell except for a sparse rustle of leaves in the treetops above and the steady beat of her heart, a pulsing reminder of her life and of what she had to do. Hope stepped forward, finding cool, soft mud beneath her feet, and, as her eyes adjusted to the shadows, a dark trail led away to her left.

The path wove between tall, thin trees and around the trunks of grandfather trees that, had they had eyes, might well have seen girls such as Hope tread the same path before her.

But the shadows that formed from their mass gave comfort.

She climbed a rise and descended, twisting and turning. Hope felt empowered. Like all humanity had been stripped from the earth and only she and the man remained. She was free to walk where she dared. But all paths led to darkness. And from each passing shadow, each black space between the giant trees, he lurked, matching her step for step, waiting for the moment when the weight of the night would crush her.

And he would show himself.

It was his world. The path was his. The trees, the night sky, and all the stars belonged in his domain.

There was no sanctuary.

She was trapped.

But she would try. She had to try.

In her mind, Mona was dragged away once more. The scene repeated itself like a sick movie clip. From light into darkness.

Only Hope could save her.

The weight of his world began to push her down. She felt her knees weaken with every tentative step. She felt his eyes on her though she dared not to stop and search for him.

She walked faster, stumbling on tree roots and grappling with the long branches that reached for her from above, tangling her hair with their bony fingers.

Like the fingers that belonged to those hollow eyes.

But her imagination was playing tricks.

The reality of her world shone through in glimpses like the brief flash of the sun between heavy, passing clouds.

And once more, Mona was dragged from view. From light into darkness.

Hope ran.

Her eyes searched for the path, her feet found patches of solid ground, and the fingers above strived to wrap their bones around her, to hold her prisoner, trapped and ready for the man to finish her.

Then there was light.

She stopped and blinked away the tears, praying that the glimpse had not been the imagery of hope.

It was soft. A glow that lit the underside of the trees. A passage to beyond his evil world.

She ran on, chasing the light as it grew from strength to strength then weaned with every passing step as if teasing her with chance and sanctuary.

But the direction was all she needed. Sanctuary and chance were second to the image of Mona's face as it disappeared into the hole.

Hope was all she needed. For Mona, Hope was all she had.

She ran on further, finding the source of the light as flames. They danced in the dark and the trees danced with them. They were accompanied by the occasional hushed whispers of men's voices.

Breathless and relieved, she tried to call out.

But no sound came.

A line of flaming torches stood below her in a shallow dip. Perhaps they were searching for her. Perhaps they were looking for Mona.

Hope tried to call out once more. But still, her throat refused to issue even the tiniest of sounds save for her hoarse and ragged breath.

Then the line of flames changed. Mesmerised by the sight, Hope watched as, one by one, each of them left their place in the procession and ventured onto their own paths. Shapes of the men flashed in the glow. Some large. Some small. There were five altogether circling the darkness.

They were searching for her.

But almost all her energy was spent. Fatigued by fear and uncertainty, she pushed on, stumbling from tree to tree as each of the lights came closer then ventured onto a new path.

She clung to a tree. Sharp debris stabbed at the soles of her feet and her fingers found the grooves in the tree's hardened bark. She slid down to her knees and, as the passing flame of one of the men came into view, she saw the robed figure beyond it and reached out, fingers splayed for him to see.

But he didn't see her. The thin branches of the bushes sprang back into place and the soft, flickering glow of the flames faded with her remaining hope.

She wept.

Unabashed, lost, and disoriented, the darkness claimed the night once more as the flames brought light to some other place.

But there was a sound.

The crack of a small twig.

She blinked away the tears, as alert as a stiff field mouse in the shadow of a kestrel.

Hope turned. In the surrounding gloom before her was a dense black, darker than the hole. At its core was the glint of two eyes, shining like Mona's.

And she knew.

She didn't try to dodge the blow.

She saw his arm swing, wild, angry, and savage.

But the fight inside her was all gone.

She closed her eyes and let the darkness take her.

CHAPTER FORTY

The sun had already crested the eastern sky when Frankie emerged from the police station. He shook Jeremy's hand.

"Thank you, Jeremy. I don't usually ask my clients to help me out like that. But, well, you're a defence lawyer and-"

"It's okay, Mr Black. How are you getting on? I was hoping you'd call with an update."

"I would have. There *is* news and I'm piecing things together, but I can't say too much right now. What I can say is this. There's something extremely sinister going on, and your daughter is mixed up in it somehow."

"Is she alive, Mr Black?"

He considered wrapping the words up in cotton wool or answering with something that would be non-committal.

"Yes."

Jeremy's face seemed to stretch vertically with both surprise and relief.

"She's alive? You're sure?"

"Almost positive."

"Oh, thank God. How do you know? Can we get her back?"

"She's alive but not for long."

"What? What do you mean?"

"The next time you see me, I'll either have your daughter..."

"Or?"

Frankie looked him in the eye and placed his hand on his shoulder.

"You need to prepare yourself, Jeremy. Just in case. I'll do everything I can but-"

"What? No."

"Jeremy, calm down."

"I'm coming with you. I'll help. We'll both find her."

"It's not an option, Jeremy. If you want my help then you need to leave it to me."

They exchanged a look. Jeremy's was of disappointment, helplessness, and all the fatherly feelings with which Frankie could empathise. Frankie's look invited the man to trust him.

"You're sure you can find her?"

"Right now, I'm your best bet." He flicked his head back, gesturing at the police station behind them. "Those lot in there aren't going to do a great deal. Right now, they're looking for whoever stabbed the other girl for a quick win."

"Surely they're looking for Greg's killer as well. They won't just let that go."

"No, they won't. But they aren't looking too hard. He wasn't a nice man and, in their opinion, Lincoln will be better off without him."

"And what are you going to do?"

"I thought that would be obvious, Jeremy." Frankie offered Jeremy a reassuring stare. A silent promise. "I'm going to do everything I can to get Hope back alive."

The man nodded. He was on the verge of breaking down. Everything he loved was in Frankie's hands.

"I'll be in touch, Jeremy. Stay positive."

Jeremy thrust his hands into the pockets of his jacket. He walked away, looked back once, then turned and left.

Once he was alone, Frankie reached for his phone from his pocket and checked for messages.

There was nothing.

Unsure of what he was expecting to find, Frankie wondered if the news had reached Jane yet. He put his phone away and was about to head to the road when a familiar scent was carried past him on the morning breeze. A voice stopped him in his tracks.

"So she's alive, is she?"

He closed his eyes and smiled.

She took slow steps behind him, her heels matching her calm and composed personality.

"If you're going to creep up on me, Penelope, you really should change your perfume. I recognised that scent ten minutes ago. Did you hear what you wanted to hear?"

"Nobody wants to hear about missing children, Frankie. Even me."

"Not even for a prime spot on the national news?" He turned and found her behind him. She was wearing her famous floral patterned dress and complimenting heels, and her wild, red hair was bursting with life and volume.

"Well, when you put it like that, Frankie."

"If you broadcast this, more girls could die. Is that what you want?"

"Of course not. But I do have deadlines. I do have to give my boss something."

"Is this the point where you give me an ultimatum?" He turned away to conceal the humour on his face and to coax her into following him.

"Not necessarily." He felt her hand trace the outline of his back and her thumbs find the spaces between his vertebrae. "So tense, Frankie. Would you like to get some breakfast and maybe you can tell me all about it?"

"Tell you about what, Penelope? My troubles or your story?"

"Oh, come on. You know I'd never broadcast anything about you. But, I have to admit, even after spending the night in an interview room, you look delicious. Do you have time for coffee?"

"You know I don't."

"Oh, because you need to find Mr Gilmour's daughter, of course. How is she linked to the missing street girls?"

"Did I say she was linked?"

"That's what you told him. And the up-to-no-good kid. Greg, wasn't it? They're all linked and you're onto something."

"Penelope, I can't tell you."

She sighed. "That's a shame. I was hoping to have some kind of clarification. My viewers do enjoy it when I report facts before anybody else. But I guess I'll have to just tell them what I *think* is happening. There's nothing like a bit of conjecture to get the tongues wagging."

"You could just wait. At least until we know what's going on."

"I can see it now. A killer is loose in Lincoln. One girl is missing, another is fighting for her life, and a young man has been found bludgeoned to death. That would be quite the story."

She smiled at her own musing.

"And you'd have a hundred reporters here in a flash," said Frankie. "You could say goodbye to your story."

"Unless the ex-military man who has been contracted to find the missing girl buys me a coffee and feeds me some tit-bits. Or even dinner? A night out with the infamous Frankie Black. It would be just like old times, Frankie. You do remember those times?"

"How can I forget?"

"It might buy me some patience. I'm sure I could report back to the office with something that would keep them happy. There's a little Italian restaurant on the hill near the castle. It's much nicer than a grubby, little village pub. Shall we say seven p.m.?"

Penelope stepped in front of Frankie and leaned into him. Her hand lay flat against his shirt, and her face, tantalising in its proximity, teased him with her smooth skin. In her eyes, she begged for him to question how she knew about the dinner he'd had in the Red Robin.

Frankie found her wrist with his hand and moved it away, pulling it down away from him to stop the enticement and to appease Jacqui's voice in his mind.

But the movement brought their faces closer. Something inside him gave.

"Such strength, Frankie Black."

He nuzzled her neck, waiting for the soft moan of pleasure while he enjoyed the scent of her hair. Always the same scent.

He felt her smile against the side of his face and he allowed a few more lingering moments of victory before he kissed her once on the side of the cheek.

"Here's the deal. You hold off on your report, wait until I've found her, and you get the exclusive story. I'll even give the interview myself."

He knew it was the deal she was waiting for. She couldn't resist an exclusive. Exclusives were what had brought her fame. The legendary Penelope Pike, daring to go further than any other reporter in the name of humanity.

"Deal?"

It was her turn to nuzzle him, and she seemed to enjoy the sensation of her skin against his two days of growth.

"You drive a hard bargain, Frankie Black." She kissed him once in return for his earlier effort and slipped her card into his hand. "You have yourself a deal. Call me when you know more."

CHAPTER FORTY-ONE

The stars above showed themselves in brief flashes in the spaces between the canopy of trees and Hope's consciousness. Awareness rolled in and out like waves on a beach, teasing her with recognising the forest then fading to churning dreams where she was home, safe, and doting on her father.

With each passing dream, the longing was stronger, the details greater, and the feelings truer. But each time they faded to reveal a little more of her reality. Dragged by her feet. The shapes of the trees and bushes looming over her. An audience witnessing her defeat with pleasure.

And then, beneath the unwavering

strength of her assailant, Hope slipped away once more to a place she longed to be and a time she wished she could have again.

The street lights cast circles of orange on the wet ground and the fronts of houses. The spaces between remained grey, sad and yearning for the light of the sun.

A voice carried along the street. But it was different somehow. The tone. It wasn't the harsh, cruel tongue of bitter evil. It was the playful tone of a loving mother.

"You get back here right now, you little monster."

The little girl giggled. She hid between the cars and the mother crept around from the roadside, pretending to stalk and surprise her, and to keep the girl from running into the quiet road.

The loving mother captured the little girl in her arms, swooping in and scooping her up. She set her down and fastened the girl's little coat against the cold then raised her skirt to pull up the little tights she wore to keep her legs warm.

But there was no hard slap.

From a street corner, Hope looked on with adoration. She longed to have been that little girl. She longed to have had a mother who cared for her in such a manner.

Giggling and writhing in her mother's arms, the girl broke free and ran.

Hope's heart skipped a beat.

The mother searched left and right as the girl ran into the shadows.

"Get back here."

Again, the tone was kind. Hope felt a contradiction in emotions as the scene played out and the girl ran towards her, smiling, innocent, and free.

She stopped at the corner where Hope was framed in the shadow of a doorway. It was like the little girl had found her through connection alone.

Hope stepped out to meet her.

There was a cute, devious expression on the girl's face. She might run again, taunting her mother by evading her capture. As if it was a game.

But Hope opened her arms and the girl came to her. She lifted her up and sat her on the crook of her arm as her mother's footsteps echoed along the street, louder and faster.

"Where are you?"

The woman was panicked. The kindness remained but it was fraught with urgency.

Hope looked down at the girl, savouring the moment.

"What's your name, little girl?"

But the girl just giggled. Her face was burning hot from her game and her body trembled in Hope's arms.

Trembled with excitement.

"Polly? Where are you?"

"Polly? Is that your name? It's okay. I'm not going to hurt you." Whispering in the child's ear, Hope tried to hold her away so she could look into her eyes. She needed to know if she was really her little sister.

"You better come out before I find you."

A playful tone as the mother slowed to a walk. Hope imagined her searching between cars and doorways. She imagined it was a game the girl played often.

But inside Hope, evil stirred, raising its head and tasting the air with its feverish tongue.

And she wanted her.

She wanted the girl to herself. The desire to have and to hold her for all time, to have what she should have had, to share with her sibling the things that sisters share.

Hope searched the street behind for an escape.

Surely the darkness would hide them? There must be a doorway or something, an alley maybe, where they could hide until the mother had passed. She made to run and Polly, her sister, felt the movement and held on tight with both arms around Hope's neck.

But something stopped her. Something inside her.

"You better come out before I find you."

The voice was kindness and affection. Hope was stayed.

She whispered in the girl's ear, savouring the scent of innocent childhood, "In years to come, you'll thank me. I hope you'll understand."

"Polly? Where are you?"

The little girl's head snatched towards the sound of her mother as she stepped into view in the road. She turned back to Hope, eyes wide with fear and panic of being caught, and of the game being over. She smiled, pleading with Hope to help her hide, to prolong the game.

But Hope was lost in the moment.

She whispered once more, "I'm Hope. Remember my name. Come and find me one day."

Then she stepped out into the light and called to the woman in the road.

Her mother.

"Here."

The joyous moment of relief gave way to faux anger as her mother strode towards Polly, her face a picture of all that is tender and loving.

"Here." Hope held her little sister up for her mother to take and to care for as only a mother can. "I found your little girl."

"Thank you so much."

The mother took the girl and Hope searched the woman's face for detail. But she found none. She studied her eyes for colour. But the darkness hid them. She studied her skin for a mark. But she found none. She searched for some kind of evil. But she found only love.

But it *was* her.

She was beautiful. Unblemished, pure of heart, and standing right beside Hope. And as she studied her face, the clarity of memory gave way to the fog of desire and a dream took over, guided only by Hope's heart.

She didn't walk away as the memory might have convinced her. She didn't look back to watch her evil mother disappear into the night.

"She's a beautiful girl." It was all Hope could think to say, not wishing the meeting to be over. "You must be very proud."

"Yes, I am. Thank you."

She nuzzled her face into the giggling girl's neck and withdrew, aware that such displays of affection weren't always appropriate in front of strangers. For the first time, the woman seemed to take in Hope's appearance. She looked from her feet to her clothes to her hair and smiled a half-smile like she knew that Hope was lost. She could see it in her face. Like she'd been there herself.

"I am very proud. How can I thank you?"

"It's okay. It was nothing. You don't have to-"

"I'm serious. Let me buy you a coffee or hot chocolate. I'm taking her to see Santa. I think they have a cafe."

A thud to the back of Hope's head dizzied the scene and the stars above no longer showed themselves between the spaces of the trees. The night sky was clear, open and wide, and still, she was dragged by her feet, the skin on her back raw but numbed like her mind.

She thought of fighting, of kicking out. But there was no fight left. She succumbed to the darkness and sought the warmth of the dream, searching the corners of her mind to take her back to the time in the street and the sound of her mother's kind voice as she passed through a doorway, the night sky giving way to a blue haze.

But the dream was lost. It faded to black, sinking to the depths of the ocean, out of Hope's grasp. She reached out for it, fingers clasping at nothing but stale, cold air.

And the dragging stopped.

Her feet fell to the floor and the form of the man, lit with a dull, blue sheen, stepped over her body.

"Who are you?"

Her mouth was dry and her words barely audible.

But he just cocked his head with intrigue.

Then smothered her face with his huge hands.

CHAPTER FORTY-TWO

Blue skies shone in death's wake like the weather had washed the previous night's events away to be forgotten like strangers who left without a trace.

Two ladies were walking past the row of shops when Frankie climbed from the taxi and walked through Grafton. Their heads turned as he passed then reunited in gossip as they continued their journey.

Frankie was thoughtful. The discussion with Jane about the three missing girls, including her own. The girl whose throat had been sliced and the precision of the cut. The lack of a police investigation.

He glanced along the empty street, marvelling at how the village had somehow managed to retain its innocence from modernisation and community yet buried deep inside was something sinister and evil laced with secrets, lies, and deceit.

To his right, the Red Lion was waking. Barry Armstrong pottered behind the bar, looking up on occasion as if he was waiting for Frankie to walk inside. But Frankie was in no mood for small talk and finger-pointing.

He crossed the street and entered the forest on the edge of Lord Grafton's property at the same place he had the previous night. The sunlight found the holes in the canopy and cast beams of light in which pollen, insects, and the morning mist floated, danced, and hung.

But the hideous night had tainted the woods. No birds sang. A deathly silence filled the void, rich and provocative of thoughts and imagination.

The path led him up the hill he'd climbed blindly the previous night and stumbled back down with the dying girl in his arms. He found the patches of mud in which he'd slipped and the roots over which he'd stumbled. Frankie ducked beneath low-hanging branches, any one of which could have been the culprit that had clawed his face.

It was only when he'd been walking for ten minutes or more that he heard a distant rumbling. The further he walked, the louder it grew, but it was always distant. The rumbling became a hum that seemed to pulse. It was coming from an area to his left. He rolled the soles of his boots to avoid breaking twigs and making a sound and slipped into the brush. Thick oaks and tall elms barred his vision. But with each step he took, the hum became clearer.

And then he saw him.

Concealed within the henge and bowing to the central stone stood a man shrouded in a long, white gown, hooded so that only his hands could be seen. They lay flat on the stone with his head hanging low in prayer.

And the hum became a chant. The words flowed like water, spoken with a deep voice, but were soothing like a breath of warm air.

Frankie moved closer, keeping the thick trunks of the trees between him and the robed figure, until, just one hundred feet away, Frankie could hear the spoken words.

But they made no sense. It was another language but an unfamiliar one.

From where Frankie was standing, the flat stone still bore the dark, red blood from the previous night. It had pooled at one end before the hewn rock had absorbed it, and small runs had reached the squared edges to form fingers on the side. A torch of wood and oil burned a low flame to the far side of the man. Its end was speared into the ground to provide light.

Around him, not a creature stirred. The breathless morning stayed the trees and only the sun, high above in the featureless sky, dared to venture into the darkness with tentative fingers.

With the man bent to the stone and robed in loose cloth, it was difficult to gauge his size. Frankie wanted to run at him, to catch him off-guard and tackle him to the ground. But although the man stood at the place where Frankie had found the girl, there was no proof that he was indeed the killer.

The hidden henge had been a shock to Frankie but may have been common knowledge for a local man.

A religious man, maybe.

In the palm of Frankie's hand were the remains of the circles the girl had drawn. It was dried and cracked but still visible if only from memory.

Frankie watched with curiosity as the man reached into his robe. He produced a small vessel that was brown in colour like coffee or the tea jars that Jacqui had bought for their kitchen. Rustic, she had called them.

The man pulled a cork from the bottle. He gathered his robes and smeared the stone in a clear liquid until the vessel was empty and the surface of the rock was shiny like glass in the sunlight.

He rose with the grandeur of ceremony then reached his arms to the sky above, uttering a stream of words. And Frankie heard it. It was repetitive and cyclical. And with each cycle of the chant, the words became commands. Although Frankie could not understand the language, the tone often needed no interpretation.

The man raised the torch to the sky then lowered it to the ground. He held it at arm's length.

It was wrong. Frankie knew it. Whoever the man was, the whole scene was wrong. He moved forward, keeping quiet and hidden, as the man brought the torch to the stone and the oil caught the flame with a hungry whoosh.

Silhouetted by the fire, the man stepped back. He raised his arms and spoke once more to the sky above. It was the same sentence he'd been repeating. Only now it had a sorrowful tone.

It was time.

Stepping between the trees into the clearing, Frankie moved into the open space, using the tall henge stones as his final barrier between him and the man. The heat of the fire warmed his face. He turned with his back to the closest stone and readied himself.

The chanting stopped.

The cool air returned as the oil burned away and the fire, starved of fuel, faded.

Frankie closed his eyes, readying himself for whatever may come.

Then he stepped into view.

But the man was nowhere to be seen.

A soft cloud of smoke hung in the sunlit beams but there was no sign of the robed man.

He circled the henge, peering behind every stone.

But he was alone.

The fire died and it was cool again, like the morning of a hot, summer day. Twelve eerie stones rose from the ground around Frankie shrouded in the thin smoke that no breeze would dare claim.

He searched the trees that surrounded the ancient place.

He found nothing.

He ran to the top of the hill to gain a better vantage point.

But his efforts proved futile.

It was a brave bird whose song first broke the silence. Loud and alone in the surreal forest.

But another joined the first as if in reply. Then others announced their presence until the canopy was alive with unseen voices and the tell-tale smoke had dispersed leaving only the illusion of a dream. But the event had been real enough for Frankie to question his mind.

He'd seen it. He wasn't mad. He hadn't dreamed it.

"It was real," he whispered.

But his voice cracked.

"I saw it. I definitely saw it."

Shrill and loud in the natural world, his phone began to ring. Dream-like memories and wild imagination were removed as he pulled it from his pocket and answered the call.

"Frankie?"

That voice. He checked around him, sure that someone was watching. But he found nobody.

"Frankie, it's Penelope."

"I thought we had a deal. Don't tell me you've changed your mind."

He peered along the path hoping to see the robed figure. But deep down, he knew he wouldn't.

"No. The deal is good. But there's something you need to know."

"Need to know what, Penelope?"

"The girl. Beth."

"From last night?"

"Yes. That was her name."

"*Was* her name?"

"She pulled the plug on her life support machine, Frankie. She's dead."

CHAPTER FORTY-THREE

A blast of cold air roused Hope from some-place far away, a place of warmth, love, smiles, and joy.

And the silence that followed gave comfort in solitude.

She gasped in the air, putrid and stale, and searched the room, tasting his fingers on her lips, sour with sweat.

At first, she doubted her eyes, unfocused and maybe damaged. The seconds passed like minutes, and the minutes passed like hours, and all she could see was a soft, blue hue through a woven mesh.

There was a pain in her wrists. It wasn't sharp like a stab or dull like the blow to her head. It was constant and persistent as if its purpose was to wear her down. It was rope cutting into her wounds, abrasive and unforgiving of her movements, no matter how she tried to re-arrange her weight.

"No. Not again."

Her bare feet touched the cold floor. But only just. By frustration and discomfort alone, she found that by standing on the toes of one foot, she could reach the floor just enough to support most of her weight while the other foot rested on top until the cold surface began to numb her skin and ache her toes. Then she would swap feet.

Hope changed her weight to her right foot and counted, giving herself one minute before the change. She likened the process to the changing of the guard she had seen in London, where soldiers of the Queen's Guard would stand for hours on end, unmoving and resolute in the face of discomfort.

"One, two, three."

She whispered aloud and found detail in the sound.

"Six, seven, eight."

The room was hard, void of soft furnishing.

"Eleven, twelve, thirteen."

It was large, as large as their kitchen perhaps. Her father's kitchen.

"Sixteen, seventeen, eighteen."

The numbness began. The smaller toes suffered first while her large toe held strong. She could make a full minute.

"Twenty-one, twenty-two."

The ache spread to the sole of her foot and she trembled.

"Twenty-four, twenty-five."

The ache grew into a sting as if the array of dull sensations collated into a single point, a shard of cold steel in the ball of her foot.

"Twenty-nine, thirty."

Breathing helped. Long, deep breaths.

"Thirty-four, thirty-five."

She found warmth in her own sour breath but it reminded her of another time.

"Forty, forty-one."

A time when she had been chained to a wall, ankles and wrists held by the sharp and unforgiving teeth of chains.

"Forty-five, forty-six."

And Beth had stood before her.

"Forty-nine, fifty."

Foul as she had smelled, Hope had

wanted her, relishing the security of another. A shared fear.

"Fifty-one, fifty-two."

As Mona had.

"Fifty-four, fifty-five."

And there she was. Hope could see her, alone and afraid, with her hopes and prayers pinned onto one person.

"Fifty-seven, fifty-eight."

Hope returned to a room larger than her father's kitchen, cold and hard.

"Sixty."

The cold bite of the floor sank its teeth into Hope's flesh and she changed feet, savouring the brief relief and relative warmth but wincing at the stab of pain in her wrist.

She exhaled, closing her eyes to focus on the task at hand. Survival.

And she began again.

"One, two..."

CHAPTER FORTY-FOUR

Beneath a thin veil on a gurney, a form teased at Frankie. Mental snapshots of what had been. The curves of Jacqui's body, still and peaceful in death. Memories of her laugh, her soft voice, her smile, betrayed by the cold, pale skin of the arm that peered out from beneath. She was sleeping. A long and deep sleep with secret dreams that she couldn't share. Not even with Frankie.

She would wake soon, Frankie was sure, and the pain would go away.

She would tell him good morning.

And she would laugh at his foolish worry, offering her arms for him to step into, luring him in with those eyes.

The corner of the sheet felt thin beneath his fingers. Thin but heavy. Heavy like she held it down, refusing to meet the morning, even with the smell of the coffee Frankie had made her.

Then she moved.

Her hair was as it had always been. A cushion of wild curls and life that, as Frankie pulled the sheet further away, framed her delicate face.

But it wasn't Jacqui's face.

The skin was pale but not perfect.

There was dirt in place of the mischievous freckles.

And in the place of her full and tantalising lips was a thin, cruel, bitter sneer.

Breathless and fighting a racing heart, Frankie couldn't drop the sheet. He tried to pull it back to cover the girl but the same weight that had resisted the reveal stayed it. The wound in her neck was open and inside was black like she was hollow and void of life.

Then she smiled.

Her lips parted.

And snap.

Her eyes opened, green like the trees with fingers of red, bright against her pale skin.

"Help me, Frankie."

It was a tree that caught his fall and he held it as the forest around him stilled and the wild bird song returned as the daydream faded and he found himself again in the forest.

He thought of the girl in his arms. He'd felt the life in her body. He'd felt her fight and her strength. He had done everything he could.

"Why?"

The birds silenced for the smallest of moments as the word faded into the trees never to return with an answer.

Frankie looked down at the henge of stones and its central plinth. Sunlight streamed through a gap in the canopy and shadows filled the spaces between the trees. It was almost magical. The perfect place for imaginations to run wild.

The perfect place to fulfil a dark desire.

"A ritual?"

He studied every stone from every angle and searched the neighbouring trees but found no hint at who the man might have been or the path that he had taken.

But then a thought struck him. A memory. Something Jane had said about sacrifice. It had been a passing statement, almost ludicrous.

Frankie moved immediately, running up the hill out of the low dip that surrounded the stone circle and finding the path that led into the village. He passed the roots that had tripped him and the mud that had caused him to slip. With each keen step, gravity began to pull him down faster until he was leaning back, his arms working to maintain balance, and he burst through the trees onto the road.

He glanced across at the Red Lion to make sure he hadn't been seen then checked Jane's house. Her old Volvo wasn't there. She would be working.

It was in his mind. Another piece of a jumbled puzzle. It was a large piece, but it made no sense and was cloaked in doubt. A part of him was glad that Jane wasn't home. He pictured himself asking her about sacrifices and stirring up memories of her daughter, offering the possibility that her daughter's death had been ritualistic.

Frankie surmised there would have been two possible outcomes.

She would never talk to him again.

Or she would laugh in his face at the preposterous notion.

He crossed the empty road and pushed open the door to the pub. It was still early but Frankie had yet to find the door locked and Barry Armstrong not behind the bar.

But Barry Armstrong was not behind the bar. He was at the table with the baker, the grocer, and Jim Price. Their conversation came to an abrupt halt and all eyes turned to face Frankie.

Sitting on a barstool, his cane in his hand and his head held high looking down on his flock was Lord Grafton, and standing beside him like an obedient puppy was Grant Price.

"Been for a walk, Mr Black?"

"It's a nice morning."

"It's a nice morning for what?"

The man's eyebrows were raised, teasing Frankie to say something he would regret.

"A walk. I find it clears my head, you know? Gives me a little clarity."

"And what was it that became clearer?"

"That this place isn't what it appears to be."

"And what does it appear to be?"

"A peaceful, little village, quaint and picturesque with a close and loving community. Well-kept gardens and chocolate box cottages." He nodded in the direction of Jane's house then wished he hadn't.

"That's how we like it, Mr Black."

Ignoring the cottage and the previous night's accusations, Lord Grafton pushed himself up from his barstool and sauntered over to the window to stare into the forest.

"That's your land, isn't it?" said Frankie.

"The forest?" Lord Grafton held his hands behind his back, cane in the one and the other balled into a fist. "It's been in my family for generations. I leave it open for the villagers, you know? For them to enjoy. They can walk their dogs or do whatever it is people like to do."

He turned back to face the window, leaving a space for Frankie to pursue his line of questioning as if he was permitting it., It was as if every decision or privilege in the village was his responsibility.

"And what is it they like to do in there?"

"Who knows? I rarely venture in there myself. My groundsman assures me everything is in order."

"Your groundsman?"

"Yes. Jack. He's a man of very few words. But if there's a problem, I'm the first to know."

"Like if someone was to be trespassing on your property, for instance?"

"Sometimes. If he feels the individual should be brought to my attention. But he knows the grounds better than me. I leave the outside to him. It's his *speciality*, shall we say?"

"And that's why you were here the other day," said Frankie. "When I first came to the pub. You knew I'd come here."

"There's nowhere else to go."

"And you wanted to size me up."

"No, Mr Black." He spoke as if he was correcting an ill-educated child with his upper-class diction and air of authority. "I wasn't *sizing you up*. I was protecting my village. As my family have been doing for centuries. We've always taken care of our village and I don't intend on being the man to break the tradition."

"Well, you might want to rethink your methods." Seeing an opening in the man's armour, Frankie leaned against an old, wooden pillar and put his hands in his pockets.

"How dare you? I've been the custodian of Grafton for thirty-three years and never have

I witnessed such insolence. And from a stranger, no less."

Frankie's smile had the desired effect. It reddened the man's face further.

"I was referring to the murder."

"The boy?" He gave Frankie a look of incredulity that he should even mention the incident. "That wasn't even within Grafton boundaries. I can assure you-"

"I meant the murder last night. And the one before that. Plus the three last year. I don't know who it is in the police that you're paying off to keep the name of the village from being tainted, but I have a good idea. You seem to have a problem, and that friend of yours in the police is not going to be able to keep it under wraps for much longer."

"How dare you? Who are you? You're a nobody. For all we know, you really *are* the killer. It was peaceful until you got here."

"We both know that's not the truth, Lord Grafton. You don't believe it was me just as much as I don't believe this place really is a peaceful, quaint, little village with chocolate box cottages and a happy, little community."

A door closed behind Frankie. He turned to find Barry Armstrong standing in the middle of the pub. In his hand was Frankie's bag, which he dropped to the wooden floor with little consideration for its contents.

Each of the men at the table turned their attention back to Frankie who, in turn, faced Lord Grafton who seemed to be studying the brass cap on his cane, wiping marks away with his thumb.

"What's this?" asked Frankie.

It was Lord Grafton's turn to smile. He tore his attention away from his cane and nodded at Barry, who moved over to the exit and held the door open.

"Before you go, Mr Black, there are a few things you should know about Grafton."

"Go on."

"We love our village. We love the peace and the solitude. There's a reason we don't have a supermarket or any chain stores. There's a reason there's no through road. I am that reason, Mr Black. We'll do anything to keep our village quiet and off the map. And if that includes seeing off unwelcome strangers then so be it."

"You want me to leave Grafton?"

"You're not welcome here."

"And if I don't leave?"

"Let's not venture down that route, Mr Black. Quit while you're ahead."

"I'm sure my friends in the news would be happy to hear about this place."

"In which case, I'm sure my friends in the police would be happy to hear about certain items of clothing being found at the scene of last night's crime. Stained with the girl's blood, I might add."

They locked stares until Lord Grafton broke it off. He straightened his jacket, gave his cane a spin in his hand, and tapped the end twice on the floor, the way Frankie had seen an officer do years before in another life.

Barry Armstrong wouldn't meet Frankie's stare as he passed but Lord Grafton called out just as Frankie felt the breath of fresh air on his face.

"Mr Black?"

Frankie turned, bag in hand, but said nothing.

"Don't come back."

CHAPTER FORTY-FIVE

The numbers no longer made sense.

"Seven-t-teen."

The spaces between felt like chasms.

"E-eighteen."

And the cold sting of the hard floor now burned with its icy touch.

"N-n-nine-t-teen."

Her warm, foul breath formed a cloud. Although she could not see it, she could tell by the way the blue around her new hood misted with each exhale.

"T-twen-t-ty."

There was no longer any brief moment of warm joy to savour at the changing of her guard. The cold had spread like ivy, reaching further from her toes and fingertips across her limbs, and eventually hugging her body so that each breath brought with it a pain in her slowly dying organs.

"T-twen-t-ty."

Hope was mumbling, incoherent even to herself. By the time the words had escaped her frozen lips, she had forgotten all she had meant to say. Should she have been accompanied by another, as she had been in the hole, and asked what foot she was standing on, she could not have said. Each of them was numb and held no weight.

But still, the words fell from her delirious lips as treacle might leak from an upturned jar. It was her body's way of surviving, keeping her mind in motion, as if it too might succumb to the cold. Blue and frozen like the world around her.

"Thirt-t-t-ty."

The sequence was no longer relevant. She had changed her feet more times than she had counted to sixty, and the time had passed in fitful bursts of unconsciousness and wakened spasms of fear. Where once she feared a final blow or to be drained of blood with a slice to her neck and watch her life pour from her, red across her frozen skin, now she feared a death far slower. Where once she had waited for the man to return and for death to begin in whichever form he chose, she now felt the process take place without him.

Alone.

So many times, she had released the dull ache of her bladder, relishing the warmth on her legs with disregard to pride. It was a treat that she had saved for herself for the first hour. *Or was it two?* A reward for her efforts.

But the numbers no longer made sense and the reward had run dry.

The bitter and violent shivers of cold were no longer distinguishable from the spams of fear that shook her body. Unrelenting, both sensations grasped her in their bony fingers, shook her, and dug deeper, searching unchartered territories to claim her until her body had been claimed in its entirety. Only the tiniest parts of her remained resolute. Like a lone soldier on a battlefield, her heart was surrounded, defending its space with a bitter fierceness, fuelled only by the instinct of survival.

Where once Hope had found warmth in repositioning her feet, the only warmth she could find now was by lifting her feet at the sacrifice of her wrists. But the pain of abrasion and burning flesh was a welcome distraction.

She hung from her bindings, head downcast, searching for detail in the blue haze. Hope turned with the weave of the rope, her mind occupying itself with the new visual information, as much as the hessian hood would allow.

Beside her, where there should have been blue, there was shadow. Its form was almost human. She startled and her feet found the cold floor. She backed up, her arms stretching beyond the agony of the biting rope on her wounds, seeking distance from the human form and gasping with uncontrollable fear.

And there was a touch.

Behind her.

And she froze.

It was another body, hanging and swaying at her touch, rolling around her as if it hung just as she did.

Hope closed her eyes, unable to shake the image of Beth hanging there, death long since having taken her wonderful heart.

Her breath came like the unfathomable stammers of a nervous child.

She exhaled, long and slow, but her breath no longer warmed her face.

Reaching back with one foot, Hope prayed not to find Beth's foot. She searched the cold floor beneath the form with tentative toes.

But she found only space.

She took a step away to stand between the two forms and raised a leg, toes extended and mouth curling with disgust as she felt for more clues.

And there it was.

The touch.

Naked and cold yet not solid.

Soft.

Like flesh.

CHAPTER FORTY-SIX

The front wheels of Frankie's Aston Martin spun in the loose gravel of the Red Lion car park but gripped hard when they found the tarmac road. The town bakers, butchers, and grocers whizzed past in a blur and, as Frankie rounded the bend by the church, the ancient gravestones of the Grafton family sat and watched in silence.

The main road to Lincoln was free of traffic, and once he'd passed Addleton and Shelton, he focused on the meandering road with Lincoln Cathedral on the distant horizon. A few villages later, he saw the signs he was looking for. Then, two miles from Branston,

Frankie began to doubt what he was doing. At one mile away, he was close to turning around. But the school came up on his right while he deliberated and, before he knew it, he was parking the car.

He strode through the gates towards the reception, feeling very aware that, being a man in a primary school, all eyes and cameras would be on him. In the car park, Jane's decrepit, old Volvo sat beneath a tree, its windscreen scattered with blossom.

Despite his own internal conflict, a warm smile greeted him at reception.

Frankie realised he didn't know Jane's last name.

"I'm looking for Jane. She teaches here."

"Jane Osborne?"

"Yes. That's it."

The girl began to move her mouse around, clicking on an unseen screen hidden from Frankie's view. She picked up her phone and sat poised to dial.

Frankie took in the room. It had been painted in a duck-egg blue to waist level then bright white to the ceiling. Much of the space had been filled by awards designed to impress prospective parents alongside artwork from talented students.

To the right of the reception desk were a pair of doors leading into a hallway. It was only when a lady, who reminded Frankie of Jake's teacher, burst through with her arms full of paperwork and bifocals resting on the tip of her nose that Frankie, through the hallway windows, caught sight of somebody walking through the car park.

She wore a long dress with a knitted cardigan. Her hair had been tied up. She hurried, glancing back over her shoulder.

The receptionist coughed, politely drawing him back to her.

"She doesn't have a class right now. You're lucky. Who should I say is here to see her?"

The receptionist caught Frankie off-guard. He glanced at her once, and by the time he'd looked back, the doors had closed.

"I'm sorry. I think I've made a terrible mistake."

He made to leave but the receptionist, confused, raised her voice and called for him to return. Frankie stepped outside, letting the doors close and the receptionist's voice trail away.

In its place came the distinct sound of a squeaky car door and a twenty-year-old engine firing up.

Frankie ran.

He reached the end of the school building in time for the front of the car to show as Jane rounded the sweeping bend to leave the car park. Sprinting, Frankie cleared a small flower bed just as the Volvo straightened up. She indicated left back towards Grafton. Frankie didn't let up. Thirty yards ahead of him, she stopped to wait for a gap in the traffic. He could see her head flicking from the mirror and back to the road, edging out further and trying to encourage another motorist to let her out.

And they did.

The front of the Volvo lifted up just as Frankie slammed his hands on the bonnet, stopping her. Jane's eyes were wide with panic and the other motorist honked once. Then moved on when Frankie stared at him.

Jane turned to face Frankie, trying to read his thoughts through the filthy windscreen.

"I just want to talk, Jane."

"I have nothing to say to you."

"You had plenty to say last night."

"That was before you sat outside my house like some kind of pervert."

"I was on the phone to my father-in-law. What Jim Price said were lies."

She paused. Then made up her mind.

"It doesn't matter. I still have nothing to say."

"I just want to talk."

"I told you, I have nothing-"

"It's about the missing girls. I need your help."

She sat, aghast, incredulous that he might ask for help after what she had been told.

"Why would I help you?"

"Because you might help more girls. More girls like Polly."

He straightened slowly, letting his fingers slide from the bonnet.

"Can we talk?"

She wound her window down a quarter of a turn.

"I don't see what help I can be."

"I need a history lesson, Jane. I need to know about human sacrifice. I think it involves Polly."

The wait seemed to last forever.

Then, although Frankie couldn't hear her, he could tell by the roll of her eyes that Jane sighed as she reached across and pushed open the passenger door.

The Volvo eased onto the main road toward Grafton, creaking and groaning with every lift and drop of its suspension and squeaking with reluctance at every turn of the steering wheel.

Jane sat uneasily in the driver's seat with her eyes flicking from Frankie to the road and back again, paying more attention to his movements than to the journey ahead.

Frankie watched the road on her behalf, aware of her suspicions.

"I promise I won't hurt you, Jane. There's a camera on the school gates. Somebody saw me get into your car. You're safe. I promise."

"I've only known you five minutes and you've gone from being the perfect guy to a dirty creep who sits outside girls' houses watching them."

"You knew I was there."

"I did not."

"I saw the way you were. The way you

moved. The way you undressed. I'm not a fool, Jane."

"So you do admit to watching me?"

"Seeing you is different from watching you. I was on the phone. You can check it if you like."

The tension was easing. Frankie relaxed, content he was winning back her confidence.

"I don't need to check it."

"But I have to say one more thing, Jane."

"Go on."

"You were wrong about me."

It was enough to raise her eyebrows.

"I was never the perfect guy. I'm damaged goods, I'm afraid. A grieving widower."

He smiled, inciting an eye roll, and the tension eased a fraction more.

"So what was I? A distraction?"

"No. Well, not entirely."

"So you wanted to see if you still had it?"

Frankie let her continue, interested in her appraisal.

"Well, for what it's worth, you do. In fact, if you hadn't acted all creepy, I might have asked you out tonight."

"Is that so? What makes you think I would have said yes?"

"Because of my link to the girl you're looking for. It's okay, Frankie. I can see you're not interested in me. Your eyes might want me but your heart belongs somewhere else. That's fine."

"I wouldn't have said it quite like that."

"I prefer to keep things straight, Frankie. In truth, it might have been me who wondered if *I* still had it. If I was still young enough to pull them in like I used to. Let's keep it professional, shall we? You want me to help you. I may have led you on a little. It's the least I can do."

"So you did know I was watching?"

"Gotcha." Jane smiled.

"You knew that I'd seen you?"

"Shall we move on?"

The church steeple in Addleton rolled past surrounded by tall trees and village rooftops. Frankie watched it pass by, marvelling at the glorious Lincolnshire landscape. He spoke as he caught sight of a kestrel hanging on a breeze using gentle adjustments of its wings to balance and stay up high, its keen eyes tracking tiny movements of mice or voles on the ground below.

"Pull over here."

In his peripheral vision, he saw Jane question him with a look, but the car slowed and she eased the lumbering machine into a small lay-by. All the time, Frankie watched the kestrel easing left and turning into the wind.

The car shuddered to a stop and silence lay a blanket over the previous topic, cementing their relationship in place. It would move no further and, for that, Frankie was pleased.

"Something you said last night about early man and rituals caught my attention."

"What exactly did I say? I know I rambled on about a lot of things, but I don't recall."

"Human sacrifice."

She stopped and took a breath, her unspoken question hanging there for Frankie to snatch at. He tore his gaze from the kestrel and looked into her eyes.

"Three girls disappeared exactly a year ago. One of them was your daughter."

Her lips tightened at the mention of the incident.

"Two girls, maybe more, have disappeared almost exactly a year later."

"So?" She shrugged, not making the connection. "The three girls last year were all from Grafton. They were all younger and taken from their homes. The girls you told me about this year were street girls. Teenagers. I don't see how they are connected."

"That *is* the connection, Jane. I didn't see it until this morning. Do you know about stone circles?"

"Of course. There are hundreds of them."

"One in particular."

"On Grafton's land?" She shook her head as if she was loath to facilitate the impending conversation. "Yes. Everyone knows about it. It's ancient. A relic from the past. Lord Grafton likes to tell people his ancestors used to use it, that they've been here for centuries, but it was there long before the Graftons. It's two and a half thousand years old, from a time when humans used to worship the dead and the sun and offer sacrifice in return for seed, crops, and meat. I don't see where you're going with this."

"Lord Grafton knows people. He has friends in high places. Right?"

"Sure. He always has some kind of gathering up at the manor house. Nice cars, tuxedos. You know the sort. A load of old men talking about the past."

"A load of old men watching each other's backs, you mean?"

"I don't understand."

Frankie straightened and caught the kestrel again. It had moved on the breeze and hovered two hundred metres in the sky above the car.

"When your daughter was killed, and Jim Price's daughter, Lord Grafton made a promise to the villagers that he'd do something about it. Am I right?"

"Yes, and he did."

"It's funny how the police didn't follow up."

"They ran their investigations. But they found nothing."

"Of course. So they just dropped a case of three missing girls?"

"Well? What were they supposed to do?"

Frankie sighed. "A lot more than that. That is if a certain somebody in high places hadn't taken matters into his own hands."

"Lord Grafton?"

"This is going to sound crazy and I can barely believe I'm going to say it, but..." He sucked in a lungful of air and formed the sentence in his head. "I found the girl at the stone circle last night."

"I know."

"And I went back there this morning once I'd convinced the senior police officer that if the case against me were to continue, he might be in more trouble than me."

"Right?"

"I saw a man at the stones."

"So?"

"Wearing a cloak or robes or something."

Jane let out a laugh and Frankie closed his eyes to remain focused on the absurd.

"He was chanting, Jane, or praying or something."

The laugh came for real. A stab of laughter that seemed to have undone all the credibility Frankie had developed in his own beliefs.

"So you think that because someone was chanting at an ancient henge that it must have been a human sacrifice?"

"What if, Jane..." He raised his voice then caught himself and lowered it to a whisper. "What if Lord Grafton and his little circle of villagers are getting girls from the city and sacrificing them?"

"You're insane."

"But what if I'm right?"

"So why would Jim Price be involved? He lost a daughter too."

"I don't know. None of it makes sense."

"And why would Lord Grafton risk everything he has?"

"I don't know. Look, I don't have all the facts. I'm just..." He searched for the word. "Brainstorming. I'm just brainstorming. And you're the only one I know who's sane and pleasant enough to bounce ideas off."

"I suppose I should take that as a compliment?"

"I think that Lord Grafton's position is so sacred to him, he's so set on being the master of the village, that he'd do anything to keep the village his. It's all he has. The estate. The high society dinners. He's an aristocrat. A dying breed. He'd do anything to protect that. Without it, he'd be nothing. He would be the Grafton that brought the little empire crashing down. A failure to all the Graftons before him."

Jane nodded, agreeing with Frankie for the first time.

"I think he's scaring the villagers into believing he's doing good. You said it yourself. The place has a history of children being killed and going missing, and that all started with the old Montgomery Grafton."

"You're talking about the three graves in the graveyard?"

"Three girls, Jane. It's a bit of a coincidence, isn't it?"

"That was centuries ago and they weren't killed. They died of the plague."

"But what if the old Lord Grafton, four centuries ago, lost his daughters and reignited the practice of sacrifice? And what if your Lord Grafton is using that little snippet of history to convince the locals he's doing good?"

"He's not my Lord Grafton."

"You know what I mean. He would only need to convince a few key members of the community and the rest would believe in him as well."

"And you think Jim Price is in on it?"

Frankie nodded. "And the landlord."

"If Jim is in on this then so is John Jones, the grocer."

"And his groundsman."

"Jack? He's a grumpy old so and so. It wouldn't surprise me."

"But, if I'm right and they *are* sacrificing street girls, Lord Grafton has somehow brain-washed them into believing they are doing it to protect the village girls."

"But really it's just Lord Grafton's way of making sure the villagers don't get rid of him? He's making them think they really need him?"

"Without the village, Jane, he's nothing. A nobody."

Frankie could tell by the expression on her face that the new line of thought wasn't adding up.

"Who else have you told about this?" she asked.

"Only one other person. Someone I trust. If anything happens to me, I need to know the story will get out there. I need to know the truth will be revealed."

"It's a crazy idea. I'm not sure who's more insane, Lord Grafton or you."

"If I'm right, Jane, it means two things. Lord Grafton is hiding the missing girls some-where on his property."

Her face turned a shade paler. Her silence prompted Frankie to continue.

"And if the pattern is the same as last year, three girls over three nights..."

She gasped with realisation.

"There'll be another sacrifice tonight."

PART III

CHAPTER FORTY-SEVEN

The cold no longer mattered. Her body was shrouded in its icy tentacles and her heart fought its final stand with shots of adrenaline that coursed through her veins. She swung from side to side, feet slipping on the cold, hard floor, to remove herself from the two forms that hung beside her. With her arms stretched to their limits, there was a brief moment when her frozen hands might slip the noose that bound her wrists.

Hope pulled harder but the numbness disguised her progress. She tugged but her feet slipped, sending her back into the space where she collided with her grotesque neighbours.

She screamed. Though hoarse and dry, her throat offered a shrill sound borne of frustration and desperation.

And when her screams fell in defeat, fading like a dying wind, she cried.

Anguished sobs like never before. Even in the throes of fear and anxiety in the hole, Hope hadn't felt such suffering.

She longed for death. But death felt so far away. Like it was savouring its meal with evil delight. Taking joy from Hope's suffering.

Hope remembered something she had heard once about people with illnesses giving up, unable to cope with the excruciating pain any longer, how the desire to live subsided and death took them.

And so she longed for it. Although she had no memory of religion or faith in God, she prayed for God to take her. Desire alone could not stop her heart as it fought against all odds, but God might hear her pleas. After all, she was now cleansed.

She was transformed.

Maybe this is it?

The hope roused her and her feet stopped the dizzying sway of her body.

Maybe this is what I have to do? The final transformation.

Beside her, Hope searched for some sign that the form was Beth. That she was on the path that Beth had described and that it hadn't all been lies. That Beth hadn't been misguided. That it was all true.

There was comfort in the presence of Beth's body, as there had been in the hole. They were together again. Maybe one day soon, Mona would find them both, and she too would transform.

The desire to live subsided in the wake of death's ever-growing shadow. But with it came regret. Through her own transformation, she'd found love for her father. It was a love that, by rights, she should have conveyed a thousand times over and more. But the evil inside her was of substance and had taken her on a different path. Death was welcome. But she longed for the opportunity to tell her father that he had been wrong. The evil he believed to have come from her mother wasn't true. She was a good woman. Hope had heard the stories that Mona had told. She had seen her own memories in the light of good. How wrong her perception had been.

He needed to know. There was so much he needed to know.

But it was too late.

She would die before the opportunity arose.

She would die with Beth by her side.

If only Mona would live. If only Mona could somehow survive and meet him in life.

It was as the bitter cold closed in on her heart that she was left with a dying pang of regret.

CHAPTER FORTY-EIGHT

As if on cue, the kestrel pushed its wings back, sending the predator into a dive, steered only by tiny adjustments in the bird's balance.

"The barrows."

Jane spoke as if in a trance, recalling something from long ago in the far reaches of her mind.

"The what?" asked Frankie.

"The barrows. Large mounds of earth where ancient man used to bury their dead. There are three on the Grafton estate. It has to be where he's keeping the girls."

"I've seen them. Are they graves?"

Jane slammed the old car into gear, checked her mirror briefly, and, as the kestrel rose from the field, its quarry gripped in steely talons, she stomped on the accelerator.

"Ancient bodies." She spoke as if it was a distraction. Her eyes focused on the road ahead. "Years ago, we lived in roundhouses. Tiny settlements. That's why the henge is there. For the local people to worship and to talk with the dead. The barrows are just stone caves buried in the earth over thousands of years."

"Seems like a massive effort to bury someone."

"They did that so they could revisit them. They didn't revere the dead as we do. They worshipped them. Dying was not as final as it is now. It was just the passing from one world into another and one barrow might house the remains of an entire family."

"How did they get in? I didn't see any doors."

"You walked across the field from the forest?"

"Yeah."

"The entrances all face west to the setting sun. But they aren't doors. Not usually. They are more like tunnels. Even I would have to duck to get inside, and you would have to crouch right down."

She indicated left for Grafton, checked her mirror, and slowed the car.

"No," said Frankie. "Not that way. Park there. Where I parked before."

"But this will be quicker."

"If I know Lord Grafton like I think I do, he'll be expecting me back."

"Why *wouldn't* he be expecting you back?"

"He made it clear I'm not very welcome."

"You're a troublemaker, Frankie Black."

She smiled. But Frankie didn't find the humour. His attention was focused on the stile at the far side of the field as they passed the farmer's gate.

"Not really. He's an intelligent man."

Jane stopped the car in the spot Frankie had first parked his Aston and looked at him, questioning his statement.

"He knows I'm onto him, Jane." He handed her Penelope Pike's card. "If anything happens to me, call this number."

She replied with a grave expression, pocketing the card.

"Let's hope you're also an intelligent man."

Then she pushed open the door and turned back to him. "If you're wrong about all of this, I might also be banished from his kingdom."

Joining her outside, Frankie raised his hands to stop her.

"You're not coming. It could be dangerous."

"Don't give me that masculinity talk again, Frankie. I'm tougher than I look. Besides, if you're right, I want to see the man who took her away from me. I want to look him in the eye."

"You'll never understand it, Jane. You can search his soul all you want and you'll never know why he did it."

Ignoring him, she moved passed Frankie and scaled the gate, dropping to the mud beyond.

"Are you coming or are you just going to stand there?"

They ran the length of the field, past the crime scene where Greg's body had been found and along the back hedge to the stile. Offering to help Jane over, Frankie extended his arm. But she was far more agile than her appearance suggested. With her long dress gathered in one hand, she scaled the wooden crossing and leapt to the far side of the wet mud. Frankie followed, spying the large footprints of the man who had held the gun to his head what seemed like an age ago.

Jane led. They took a similar route, keeping to the edge of the forest and climbing a low rise until, after many twists and turns and Frankie's many thoughts about Jane's fitness, they came across the low dip in the ground where the gunman had left him.

"There."

Staring through the trees into the open field adjacent to the forest, Jane pointed at the three large mounds of grass-covered earth. Each one was fifty feet or more in diameter and the west-side entrances were hidden from view.

"I've heard people talk about them but I've never actually seen them myself," said Jane.

"And you say they are two thousand years old?"

"More. Maybe a lot more. Some date back twelve thousand years. Others are more recent. These are amazing, Frankie."

She was lost in the sight, which, to Frankie, had initially appeared to be three small and irrelevant hills. But now he found it hard to look at them without imagining people thousands of years ago carrying the bodies of their relatives inside. But more than that, Frankie realised, as he and Jane stood looking at them, Hope could be inside.

"What's the plan, Frankie? It'll be getting dark soon."

Jane didn't look at him. Instead, she seemed to marvel at the barrows as if she might be able to see through the layers of earth to the inside.

"We have three options."

"Three?" This time she did turn to face him, her face puzzled. "The police?"

"That's option one. But from what I can tell, the senior police officer is Lord Grafton's friend. I'd prefer to keep them out of it if I can. At least for the time being."

"So you want to just walk in there? Even if you find the girl, Lord Grafton will deny everything. A good lawyer will have the charges dropped, and you can be sure that he has a very good lawyer."

"I thought about that. We need to catch him red-handed."

"You want to catch him in the act of sacrifice?"

Her mouth hung open and her eyebrows raised in disbelief.

Frankie said nothing.

"It'll be our word against his," said Jane.

"Not necessarily."

"So? What *is* option two?"

"We wait until dark. He won't risk being seen by a dog walker or something. That's why the footpath is closed off from the village. My guess is that it used to run right through here but it was too close to the barrows."

"Yeah. He closed it off a few months ago. I heard from one of the villagers who used to walk their dogs up here. Something about protecting the heritage."

"He's protecting something alright."

"What's option three?"

Frankie sucked in a breath, parted the trees, and stepped onto the grass. He stopped and looked back at her, seeing her eyes wide with apprehension.

"I do what I'm being paid to do and to hell with the consequences."

Frankie walked on, hearing her scramble through the trees after him. He ignored her complaints and watched as she tried to keep up with him while searching around them as if she expected them to be jumped at any minute.

The first barrow was smaller than the other two. When Frankie approached what appeared to be an opening, he found a pile of crumbled, grey stone and earth covered in weeds and wild grass.

"This has never been excavated. Look at that grass. It's been there for years."

Jane glanced up again toward the house at the top of the rise then across to the next barrow and up at the darkening sky. Frankie nodded, confirming her unspoken concern that Lord Grafton and his men would come to get the girl at night. Time was of the essence.

They ran and, this time, Jane was the first to arrive. The opening to the barrow had been cleared but inside was dark. Frankie likened the mounds to igloos. Rounded knolls with tunnel-like entrances, low and narrow, but with stone and earth in place of ice and snow.

But before Frankie could take a look inside, Jane had dropped to her knees.

"Jane, no."

But it was too late. The tunnel was too low for Frankie. She dragged herself inside, her delicate shoes disappearing into the gloom. Helpless, Frankie checked the house at the top of the hill. Lights were on, sporadically placed across the west side of the old building. He wondered if he could be seen or if anyone was even looking. Then he lowered to a crouch and called in after Jane.

"Jane?"

She appeared head first from the black and dragged herself to her feet before answering Frankie's questioning face.

"Nothing. Not that I could see anyway. The hole is too small for any man to get through."

Together they looked across to the third barrow sitting, ominous and eerie, in the corner of the field. It stood apart from the others and was slightly larger, taller in height and with more pronounced walls.

"Third time lucky?"

Jane raised an eyebrow at him, questioning his choice of the word *lucky*.

Again, they ran, but it was Frankie who reached there first. The entrance was intact, but instead of a dark and foreboding opening, a door had been fitted into the arched space. It had been locked in place by a thick chain and padlock.

There were no words needed. Not even an exchange of questioning glances. Frankie took a single step back then kicked with all his weight.

The door didn't budge.

The chain rattled loudly against the wooden door.

Jane searched their surroundings, nodding the all-clear.

And Frankie lunged again.

This time, the heel of his foot connected with the door beside the chain, and the wood splintered.

"Hurry, Frankie."

Jane peered over the mound through the long grass and looked back at him. She nodded again.

And he delivered the final kick.

The chains fell against the stone, rattling loudly in the relative quiet. The wood cracked then thumped against the inside of the narrow tunnel.

Frankie, with a final nod from Jane, crouched and entered the barrow.

The air was stale and damp.

The stone tunnel scraped against his

back. Ahead of him a darkness, blacker than he had imagined, loomed.

He stopped halfway along the tunnel. It was too tight to turn around.

"Hope?"

There was no reply.

He moved on, feeling the walls to guide him and ducking his head to avoid the hard stone.

But then the wall ended at a right angle. The broken doorway allowed light through, but the night was falling and the tunnel's length was too long for it to light anything except for the first two feet of earth floor.

"Hope, are you in here?"

There was a shuffle ahead. Movement. His head flicked towards the sound and he moved forward, now able to stand in the room. With his hands before him, acting as both a guard and a means to explore the darkness, he reached out.

His fingertips touched stone walls. Damp ran down in a dribble from above. He moved sideways, feeling his way.

Until his fingers found cold flesh and he pulled back as a gasp hissed in the silence.

"Hope, is that you? I won't hurt you."

Breathing, heavy with fear and trepidation, and a whimper, involuntary but bold.

"Who's there?"

The voice was accented.

"I've come to get you out of here. Is that you, Hope?"

He strained to find her shape in the gloom but found only the glint of moist eyes.

"I'm not Hope."

That voice. It was familiar.

"Are you hurt?"

"No. Just my hands. They're chained to the wall. Please help me."

"Okay. Stay still. I'm going to see if I can release them."

Frankie glanced back through the tunnel but saw only the fading light on the long grass outside. He felt for her arms and found her cold skin then traced them down to where two shackles gripped her wrists.

She flinched at his touch, her wounds tender.

"I'm sorry. I didn't mean to hurt you."

"Can you get them off?"

He pulled at the chains and found them bolted to the wall. He pulled them from every angle he could while his mind searched for the voice. But they refused to budge.

"The chains are bolted to the wall. I'm going to need some help."

"No, don't leave me." Her voice was frantic and harsh then softened. "Please."

There it was.

"Mona?" He felt, rather than saw or heard, her head flick at the mention of her name. "Is that you?"

"You're him, aren't you? The man from the bridge."

But before Frankie could respond, the dim light in the tunnel fell into shadow. He turned in time to see the space filled by the giant frame of a man, hunched and forcing himself through the narrow tunnel.

With a single index finger placed to Mona's lips, Frankie silenced her and stepped back into the gloom away from the entrance. His hands found a hole that was cut away in the wall. It was a space large enough for him to crawl into. As he did, the murky shadow that seemed to roll from side to side as the man lumbered along the tunnel grew ever larger until, as Frankie settled into the small space, no light was left. The man stood up straight.

His breathing was ragged, and although Frankie could not see his face, he sensed him searching the darkness.

Frankie lay motionless. His hands explored the space searching for another exit. But there was none. Only the unmistakable remains of a human being. The long bones of somebody's arms and the curved shards of ribs lay by his side.

And by his head, the smooth and bulbous form of a human skull was unmistakable.

The man grunted, dumb and incapable of speech.

And Mona gave a whimper to accompany the rattle of chains and keys.

With nothing to hand save for the long femur bone of the body with which he shared the space, Frankie waited, poised and ready to step in.

But curiosity was a marvellous thing. The desire to step up behind the man and somehow overpower the behemoth in the dark confines of the tomb was quelled by Frankie's urge to see what he would do next. For all his great size and strength, the man, in shadows alone, displayed no intelligence great enough to carry out the synchronised murders.

Heavy footsteps replaced the jangle of chains and Mona's sobs occupied the audible spaces.

Frankie heard the crunch of dirt beneath sizeable boots. But the sound was off-set. He was stronger on one leg than the other. Although Frankie could not tell which, he remembered the boot prints in the mud and how one was deeper than the other like it had carried a great weight. He knew this was the man who had held a gun to his head.

The man's presence was accompanied by his odour. It was a sweet smell like a combination of masculinity, stale beer, leather, and sweat.

He grunted once more as he stopped beside Frankie's hole.

Frankie gripped the femur. Holding his breath would be a mistake if the man lingered for longer than Frankie could wait. Instead, he silenced his breathing with long but shallow breaths so that all he could hear was his heart thump in his ears.

For all he knew, the man could have been crouched in front of him. He may have somehow been able to see Frankie with eyes accustomed to the darkness.

And all Frankie could do was wait, blind to the world and relying on any other sense that offered some kind of clue.

The man moved on. He seemed to be searching the room, feeling the walls and listening as a predator might tune itself into its environment. Tasting the air. Smelling the fear.

He grunted once more in discontent and moved swiftly, familiar with the darkness and with an ability to navigate the space using memory and familiarity.

Another rattle of chains, more vigorous than before, caused Mona to cry out in pain.

"No. Get off me. You can't do this."

A scream and the dull scrape of flesh being dragged across the earth.

Frankie leaned from his space in the wall in time to see the dim light wash over Mona's face as she searched the darkness for him.

Frankie prayed she would not give him away. He willed her to remain quiet. He would find her. He made a promise to her, silent but heartfelt, as she searched the darkness. Her hand reached out, fingers splayed, begging quietly, pleading with her eyes.

And she was dragged from view.

Exhaling, long and loud, Frankie rolled from the ledge, leaving the ancient remains behind. He considered taking the femur. It would be his only weapon, and against such a sizable man, he would need something.

But the dead should be allowed to rest.

He thought of Jacqui when he laid the bone back down. It was a fleeting memory, stirred by the touch of cold. A sharp stab of mourning. A momentary distraction to which his brain responded with a flash of her face in his mind's eye.

But the shard of loss that pricked his heart was dulled with the memory of her smile, which was then torn from his mind in its entirety by the sound of Mona's anguished scream somewhere in the distance.

He scrambled to his feet and stopped at the entrance, feeling the walls to provide a sense of space and listening for movement outside.

There was none, and he moved on.

The light at the far end of the tunnel was fading as if mimicking Mona's life, and the warm sun had fallen behind the surrounding trees, leaving a cool wash of air in its wake and the threat of a summer mist hanging over the undulating ground.

Frankie peered over the edge of the mound and up towards the house. Lit windows peered back like eyes in the dying day. But far to the right, at the edge of the forest, a procession of torch flames moved in unison. He climbed up the mound seeking a better view, just in time before the first flame disappeared into the forest.

And one by one, as the dark forest swallowed them, they blinked out.

"Jane?" His whisper was loud, more like a hiss. But no response came. "Jane, where are you?"

The occasional flash of orange amongst the distant trees on the far side of Lord Grafton's land teased at his conscience. He knew what he had to do and cursed himself for allowing Mona to be taken.

And with that thought, he ran across the estate with disregard for prying eyes to the mouth of the forest that had swallowed the flames.

He broke through the tree line into silence. Then darkness seemed to rise up from between the trees. The ground beneath him was swallowed and the fall of his boot found nothing but space.

He hit the ground on his front and rolled, tucking his elbows in as sharp debris snapped at his flesh. He rolled once, twice, and, on the third, as his body came to a stop and the rough ground sucked at the momentum of his fall, his skull found the blunt face of a large rock.

The surrounding darkness rose up and engulfed him.

Time and space swirled in a dizzying haze. Up and down. Left and right. All merging in a sickening fog until his fingers gripped the soil and the tufts of wild grass. He spat the earth from his mouth and let a string of acidic mucus fall from his lips as the dark world around him settled once more to reveal the gut-wrenching reality of his failure.

He found himself in a place he had been before. Memories stirred inside him, rousing the emotions that he'd tried so hard to quieten. Frankie pulled himself to his knees as the images of Jacqui found prominence in his thoughts.

The market place where she had bartered for a book.

Her smile.

The Grand Mosque in Abu Dhabi where she had marvelled at the intricate design.

Her eyes.

The Maldivian island where she had basked in the sun and relished the wonders of nature beneath the shade of her favourite woven hat.

Her beauty.

Once more, he settled on his haunches and raised his hands as a child might reach out to be lifted for comfort and warmth. The tears in his eyes formed a billion stars. But no hands reached for him and the heavy hand of defeat forced him back to the ground.

He'd failed.

His hands gripped the earth.

Mona was dragged from view, over and over, her feet whisked into the tunnel.

And he'd just laid there watching, too absorbed in his own mourning to save her.

His arms began to shake.

The skull beneath his hand grew warm.

The femur he clutched moved. There was flesh.

Beyond his tiny space, the man grunted.

Mona disappeared from view once more.

But in the darkness, the shiny glints of eyes found him. Beneath his hand was Jacqui's smiling face nested in her wild hair.

And he was with her, in the tomb they would share for all of time, never again to be apart, their bones to become one, indistinguishable as nature sought to bury their remains with earth and time.

"I want to be with you."

"No, Frankie."

Her voice.

Nestled in the crook of his arm, she shook her head. She placed a slender hand against his heart, and her soft, pale flesh began to crack.

"No. Don't go."

Her smile faded.

"Jacqui, no."

Her warm limbs cooled to become lifeless bones that fell to rest on the ground beneath him.

A finger grazed his lips, hushing him as she slipped from his grip.

And she was no more.

She lay in the still calm of her grave, her

perfect beauty etched into the grain of her casket for all time.

And Frankie knelt in a low shallow in a forest with only memories to cling to. But they *were* memories. He had them. Nobody could take them. And, for that, he was grateful. It was as if a fog had cleared. The darkness still encircled him, weaving between the trees above like a phantom.

But Frankie was not alone.

No longer would he walk the earth searching for a soul that once was. No longer would he pine to share one last moment.

He would cling to the memories he had. Some people had yet to find such moments. People like Mona and Hope who had yet to live life.

And as the thought of the two girls pronounced the failure that clouded his mind, confirmation came in the form of a piercing scream that froze the darkness around him.

CHAPTER FORTY-NINE

The light changed around her.

From somewhere above, a white hue shone through the blue, bright as if heaven had opened and her prayers had been answered. The light was blinding to her eyes. But still, her curiosity for death searched for something. A hand or a voice. Something to guide her.

A shadow as something passed from the light.

It was time.

She was close. She could feel it in her dying body.

A touch, soft at first, inquisitive, gentle, and innocent as a hand rested on her head.

She allowed it.

She welcomed it.

With the tender care of a child, the hand pulled at her hood, its coarse fabric grazing her flesh until it had passed. The cool air touched her face and Hope closed her eyes to the new brightness.

A finger felt her cheeks. A thumb wiped away the frozen tears. And a hand raised her chin.

A voice, soft and childlike, sang to her through the haze of death.

"Open your eyes, child."

"You?"

"Easy now."

Hues of blue and the light of heaven dizzied and combined to produce an ethereal world.

"It's time to go, child."

Of all the angels that Hope could have dreamed of, there was only one that she would have chosen to guide her. And she was standing before her now. Lit with the light of good. Braving the darkness to take Hope into the next world.

"I'm ready." The face before her was one of perfection, pale and smooth with the caring eyes of tenderness, and memories of love and loss. "I always knew."

"Hush now. We must leave."

Her fingers were warm against Hope's skin as she sought to untie the knot that held her captive and had tightened beneath her weight, just as death's grip had staked its claim on her heart and life had begun to fade like a dying sun.

She heard the sound of cold steel and the angel returned with a blade.

Hope gasped in fright, but as soon as her mind had conjured images of impending pain, the angel had slashed the ropes that bound her.

She crumpled to the floor. Her hands remained bound but she was free from her incarceration.

The angel stood over Hope, tall, perfect, and bathed in blue light. As Hope reached out her hands for the knot to be cut, she held them in her own. She was warm and took them, nursing each of her fingers until death's grip waned and life flowed once more.

"Stay with me."

Even her whisper was musical to Hope's ears. She clung to the words, hoping for more.

The cool blade found the space between Hope's wrists and she winced. The angel was angered but then sorry.

"I didn't mean to hurt you. Let me see."

The angel dropped the knife to the floor and crouched beside Hope, inspecting the wounds beneath the rope. Then she shook her head.

"We must go now. Can you stand?"

But, try as she might, Hope couldn't even summon the strength to reply. She lay back and felt the bite of the cold through the thin fabric of her garment.

"No. Don't lay down. You have to stand. I'll help you. Come on."

The angel pulled Hope's bound hands over her head. She braced her legs, straddling Hope, and held her beneath her arms.

"Help me, child."

And she pulled.

In her mind, Hope directed every ounce of strength she had to the effort. But she felt no movement. The angel tried once more, pulling Hope across the floor to straighten her legs. But still, Hope's limbs would not do as she asked.

She stared up, beyond the angel, at the

two forms that she had hung beside. She had hoped to see Beth in all her deathly glory, transformed and the saviour of one pure child.

But, instead, she found only the grim carcasses of two hogs hanging there, their legs bound by the same rope that had bound Hope's wrists.

"Beth?"

The angel stopped. She peered into Hope's eyes then followed her gaze.

"They're just hogs. Help me, child. Stand."

But it was all wrong.

"Where's Beth?"

Still, the angel fought to raise Hope as death pinned her down.

It was as if Hope's spirit was separate from her body. Her soul was free to roam and follow the angel. But she couldn't move.

The hogs swayed, their momentum was entrancing.

The angel's face, desperate to move Hope's mortal body, began to cry in desperation.

And Hope looked on, helpless and numb to the world.

But by the will of grace and of lost love, a single word came to Hope, and she repeated it with a soft finality.

"Mother."

And it was as that single word formed on her lips, and the angel's eyes searched Hope's, that death appeared in the bright light behind her, tall, angry, and ready to fight for his quarry.

CHAPTER FIFTY

The meandering trail bent as a slow-moving river meets the wide expanse of the ocean. Long, wispy branches tore at Frankie's face, but he ran on regardless, leaning into the bends and seeking solid earth to place each pounding step.

Twice he stopped to gain a sense of distance and direction, guided only by the low hum of men's voices. The third time he stopped, his beating heart joined in the thrum, and the men's voices, harmonious in a chorus, steered him towards a soft, orange glow over the next small rise.

But once he was there, the soft glow became a sight he would remember for the rest of his days.

Four men stood in front of the twelve large stones clad in robes with hoods shading their downcast faces. In each of their left hands was a flaming torch that created a circle of fire, fierce and bright in the growing dark. It lit the underside of the canopy of trees, turning the scene ethereal.

But laying on the central stone, bound, naked, and afraid, Mona struggled for freedom.

On seeing her, Frankie moved forward, cautious with every step he took, fearful that if his presence was known, the slaughter would begin and he would be too far away to intervene.

From tree to tree, he moved like the dancing shadows that played across Mona's skin and flickered in the forest.

And the chanting began to grow in intensity.

The cloaked figure standing before the stone at Mona's head stepped forward and held his torch high. The remaining three followed suit, blocking Frankie's view.

He moved closer. The silhouetted trees before him stood like a gathered crowd.

And the chanting stopped.

Only Lord Grafton's baritone voice remained. He raised his head and called out to the sky.

And the three men replied in unison and harmony.

Lord Grafton repeated the phrase and lowered the torch to light Mona's body and she writhed as the heat drew close.

Once again, the three men mimicked his movement, replying to his chant in chorus.

From beneath his robes, Lord Grafton produced something. But Frankie's view was blocked.

Crouching, he ran to the next tree in time to see a flash of light reflect from a steel blade.

The chanting, unified now, grew to a crescendo. Each of the flames was held over Mona's body as she writhed on the stone plinth, eyes wide with fear and gasping for the courage to scream.

Grafton lowered the blade as the three raised their torches high in the air.

And the chanting ceased.

Only Lord Grafton remained as the three stepped back to their respective stones.

And the tip of the blade found Mona's skin.

It was enough for Frankie. He stepped from the trees into the clearing. But no man turned to him. No heads raised. No confrontation was offered.

"Stop right there, Grafton."

From beneath the shadow of his hood, the outline of Lord Grafton's face was lit by his flickering flame.

"Mr Black, how did I know I hadn't seen the last of you?"

"Put the knife down. It's over."

"On the contrary, it has only just begun."

He lay the flat of his hand on Mona's forehead, caressing her as if she was the most sacred thing he had ever seen.

"She's done nothing wrong. Let her go. This stops now."

"No. She has done everything right. She is paying the ultimate price for her sins and she will leave this world for the next as pure as the day she was born."

"She has no sins. None that concern you anyway. Leave her be."

Readying himself for the three men to rush at him, Frankie eased himself into a position to reach Grafton should he plunge the knife into Mona's body.

"I've taken all her sins, Frankie. She is transformed. She came to us tainted, a stain on humanity, but now..." He looked up and, for the first time, Frankie found his cold eyes beneath the hood. "Look at her. Her purity will keep the village alive."

"You're insane. She's a human being. Let her go."

"Mr Black, you know nothing of our affairs. But, I'm afraid, this time, your meddling has gone too far."

"I know enough. You think that, by some madness, killing her will save the village from a myth."

"Not a myth, Mr Black. A legend. A legend so great that the modern world cannot possibly comprehend it. Only the chosen few, those of us who have lived to witness the carnage, can understand. We play our part and we live in peace, Mr Black, as we have done for years."

"You're out of your mind, Grafton. It's a

myth. Your ancestors believed it and now you're doing the same."

"You know nothing of my ancestors."

He spat the words with visible distaste. But Frankie continued.

"I know enough that Montgomery Grafton, your forbearer, suffered from the same delusions and he was killed for it. He lost three daughters, didn't he? He lost three daughters and reignited the rituals. I'm right, aren't I? The only difference between you and your deranged ancestor is that at least he knew what it was that killed his daughters. You haven't got a clue, have you? You know there's a killer and you're capitalising on it. Tell me I'm wrong, Grafton."

Frankie stepped forward expecting a response from the three men.

But nobody moved. They held their torches high and cast their faces down, allowing Frankie to stand at Mona's feet. She looked up at him, pleading with her eyes to help, to do something.

But he was outnumbered and the risk was too great with the blade in Grafton's hand.

"Whether you are right or wrong, Mr Black, it doesn't matter anymore. Our village has been plagued with death since the Graftons first came here. Our offerings keep us safe. The lives of a few young girls to protect an entire village. The chance for them to transform themselves, to repent, and to leave this world in a state of purity is more than a life on the streets could ever offer."

"You killed girls and convinced these men you're doing a good thing. Don't give me that rubbish about cleansing. That's what you tell the girls to brainwash them, isn't it? Answer me, Grafton."

"We are not barbarians, Mr Black. The village has been spared for many years. Until now."

"You re-ignited the practice of human sacrifice to save your flock? Do you know how that sounds? Do you honestly believe that what you're doing is right?"

"Right or wrong doesn't come into it. There's nothing I wouldn't do for my people. I am a Grafton, after all."

Frankie looked around at the other three who stood unwavering and downcast.

"And these men? Let me guess. Wainwright, Jones the grocer, and Barry Armstrong. Where's the other one? Where's Jim Price?"

Nobody moved, but from the builds of the men, Frankie could name each of them.

"You'll all spend the rest of your lives in prison. Who will protect the village then?"

"I doubt that, Mr Black. You might say what happens in Grafton stays in Grafton." The landowner smiled and the whites of his teeth showed in the dark confines of his hood.

"You're wrong. I've already put the word out. It's over, Grafton. If anything happens to me, this will be on every news channel in the country. Put the knife down and step away from Mona."

"That's *Lord* Grafton, if you please, Mr Black. And I think your assessment is somewhat premature."

But Frankie had heard enough. He moved behind the two men to his right, circling the henge. Each time he appeared from between the stones, Lord Grafton's sneer followed him.

"You're making a big mistake, Mr Black."

Just five feet from Lord Grafton, Frankie stopped.

"Last chance, Grafton. Let her go."

But Lord Grafton gripped the knife and,

with his eyes held firmly on Frankie's, he let the tip of the blade produce blood from Mona's body.

Frankie jumped at him.

But his advance was halted by the deafening blast of a shotgun being fired and a flash of light, bright against the forest.

Lord Grafton, unfazed by the sound, smiled at Frankie. From the shadows of the trees, a large man stepped into view. The thorny branches of the tangled undergrowth brushed off his long, waxed, moleskin jacket, and his heavy boots seemed to remain free of the flickering light. In his right hand, his shotgun was breeched and pointing into the air. In his left hand was the tail end of a length of rope that disappeared into the darkness.

"You're acquainted with my groundsman, I believe?"

"We've met." Frankie nodded, still admiring the sheer size of the giant man who stood as tall as the henge stones and nearly as broad.

"Don't be rude, Jack. Say hello to our new friend."

The groundsman grunted, turning his

broad head to study Frankie with relatively small and lazy eyes as if Frankie's presence was of no significance to him.

"I believe you were telling me about the word being out, Mr Black?" Lord Grafton nodded once more at Jack, who gave a hard tug on the rope. From the shadows of the forest, her hands bound, a woman stumbled into the clearing and fell to her knees.

The recognition was instant. The hair, the dress, and the brazen manner in which she carried herself, even in captivity.

Penelope Pike looked up at him but failed to hold his stare.

"So what now? You kill all three of us?"

Frankie began to distance himself but Lord Grafton raised the blade from Mona's chest and wetted the tip of his finger with her blood.

"Oh no, Mr Black. That's not how the legend goes. Don't you know? He prefers them alive."

CHAPTER FIFTY-ONE

Recognition formed in the angel's eyes.

It was not the recognition of a mother seeing her daughter. It was the recognition of fear that was etched into Hope's face. Death delivered his blow and cast the woman aside like a paper bag. She slammed into the wall.

Then he stood over Hope, angered and ghastly in the blue light.

He reached down, gripping Hope's throat with one hand, and leaned in until his breath warmed her face. But there was no malice in his eyes. Only the intrigue and morbid curiosity of a child as he might pull the wings off an insect and admire its suffering.

But for Hope, her journey had already

begun. A warmth had found the very tips of her toes and was growing inside her. There was no fight in her heart, no desire to survive, only a yearning to follow the angel.

She lay limply and let her head hang over her back, held up only by the strength of death's grip. The world was upside down, blue and disorienting. Two hogs stood on their heads, upright and alert, watching her pass from one world to the next.

The angel rose to all fours, clinging to the ceiling, her face twisted with malice and hate.

Drunk with fading life, Hope watched as the angel stalked death walking on all fours, dragging herself across the ceiling like a predator with her teeth bared and her lips in an unearthly shape of ferociousness as she pounced.

Air found Hope's lungs, cold and sharp, as the angel collided with death and together they rolled to the floor.

Hope rolled too. Away from the clatter and bursts of blurred arms and limbs. Guttural screams and wild, angered roars filled the space and Hope climbed to her knees, questioning her sanity and her own mortality.

Good and evil fought before her. The desperate scratches and kicks that good delivered were no match for the evil man. He pushed through the angel's vicious attacks, pinning her to the wall, and then slammed her head back with a sickening thud.

And the angel was no longer an immortal hand to guide Hope to someplace else. She was a woman fighting for something far stronger. It was her mother. And death was just a man, large and dumb in his features but strong enough to throw her mother around like a rag doll.

The light at the far end of the room was not heaven. It was a stairway. It was life.

Hope dragged herself to her feet, holding onto the hogs for balance. She swayed as they swayed and they held her until her mind had settled. She watched, helpless to move for fear of falling to the floor, as her mother crawled towards the stairwell. Inside, Hope prayed for help, but she knew that none would come.

The man reached for her mother's ankle as she gripped the stairs. But she turned, slashing at him with the blade and finding flesh with a final wild stab.

The man groaned and stumbled, clutching his arm. His blood was ink in the ultra-violet light and it seeped over his hands like molasses.

"Run, child."

She was beckoning her from the staircase, pleading with Hope to join her.

And so she tried. But the new desire for life was betrayed by her body. Unbalanced and weakened by her ordeal, Hope hugged the wall, her hands guiding every step until she was just an arm's length from her mother, who reached out to help.

Then the man struck again. With the fury and wrath of a raging bull, he barged through the hanging carcasses and groped for Hope's neck with fat fingers and ungodly strength.

His efforts were rewarded with a slash of her mother's blade. It rushed past Hope's face, severing fingers and sending him backwards with an agonised wail. Dark ink spattered over Hope's face and hands and she stared at them in disbelief, finding her garment, glowing white in the unnatural light, adorned with patches of dark, blue blood.

A hand caught her wrists. She winced but it held true. Her mother pulled her to the stairwell and helped her climb each step one at a time. With every step, warmth came, and bright lights guided them.

"Keep going. Don't look back."

Hope climbed the stairs as a child might, on her hands and knees, frail but keen.

"That's it. You're doing great."

But it was as they reached the top step that she heard the riled cry from deep within the man's stomach.

Hope turned.

As if death himself stood on the border of good and evil bathed in blue light, the man clambered after them.

"Faster."

She felt her mother tugging on her arms but Hope was stricken with fear and exhaustion. She couldn't move. Her mother wrapped her arms around her to take her weight. The urgency in her voice grew.

"Move, child. We have to move."

And then, as Hope expected to be pulled back down to the depths of the basement, it was her mother who fell. Hope caught her wrist as she passed. Just as Hope had grappled with Mona in the hole, there was no way she was letting go of her mother now.

The man was one-handed but angry and

wild. At the thought of losing her mother, her angel, Hope's fury lashed out at him with the full force of her weight. She plunged her foot into his face.

The first kick stunned him.

The second enraged him. But together with her mother, they both kicked. And the third tore his hand free and sent him to the basement below bouncing off the hard, concrete stairs.

They fell back onto the step together. Her mother's hand groped for hers and they shared a moment as the fear dispersed and their breath was recovered. Below them, the shape of the man lay sprawled on the floor.

Her mother helped Hope to stand and pulled her arm across her shoulders to support her. She found herself in the backroom of a butcher's shop. Stainless steel surfaces shone in the bright light and the red, tiled floor was dull but clean.

Together they made their way through a door into the front of the shop. The lights were off but the bright light from the back room guided them to the door. On one side, Hope leaned on her mother, and on the other, she slid her hips along the glass counter for support.

"Stay here."

Her mother squeezed her hand. The sensation was wonderful. She moved across the room, injured and dazed, and worked the door lock, rattling the wood in the frame and seeking an escape.

Entranced in delight at the connection and the thought that her mother was alive and not the evil person her father had led her to believe, Hope watched with admiration.

But the good fortune was short-lived.

The room fell dark and an uneasy feeling gripped Hope's stomach. She turned to find the man standing in the doorway, silhouetted against the light, emerging into the darkness, embittered and cursing with the foulness of hell.

"Mum."

Her mother turned at the door, but it was too late. The man was upon her before she could react. He dragged her away and forced her head into the glass counter. Hope lunged. But with an easy back swipe of his hand, the man sent her to the floor.

She turned in time to see him rip her

mother from among the broken glass and run with her, forcing her head down until he crashed it through the shop window.

Glass shattered above his enraged screams.

And Hope pounced again. She reached into the broken glass counter for a cleaver. Then, as the man reached for her mother once more, Hope swiped at his back.

He straightened as his skin sliced open and dropped her mother into the pile of broken glass.

Now Hope was alone with him.

And she was as furious as he was. If ever there was a time to call upon the evil inside her, it was then.

She stepped towards the back room, searching for an escape. But there was no time. He rushed at her with open arms. He blocked her wild swing with his damaged hand and grabbed her throat with the other.

With incredible strength, he dragged her into the wall, pinning her and crushing her airways.

She spat, cursed, and scratched until he forced the blade from her hand.

He pulled back his arm to force her skull

into the wall and from nowhere a heavy pan smashed into his head with the sound of a gong.

His grip released.

But his face remained bitter.

He turned. Before her mother could run, he caught her, turned her, and threw her. Her broken body slid through the broken glass and she lay unmoving.

With only seconds to act, Hope pounced for the last time. She held onto his back and reached around his head, feeling for his eyes. He roared. She clung to his wild thrashes with everything she had as he slammed her from wall to wall trying to shake her off.

But she dug deep, searching for something inside his skull. A weakness.

And there it was.

A tendon or a nerve. Something frail and taut like sinew.

He dropped to his knees as she pulled it, screaming like a child, and she felt his body spasm as she withdrew.

His one good hand covered his face as Hope pounded on the back of his head.

But his tenacity was unmatched. He rolled so that Hope straddled him, and blood pooled in his eyes. Like a dying beast, he whimpered, his cries almost childlike and innocent.

On the floor beside him sat the cleaver, bright against the blood-red tiles.

The handle slipped in Hope's hand and was tacky. He searched blindly for her with his damaged arm. His fingers were missing and his stump of a hand had been hewn in two.

Hope glanced behind her and found her mother lying still in a pool of blood.

And with the memories of Beth, Mona, and the suffering they had endured, she raised the cleaver and prepared to deliver the vengeance that was erupting inside her.

CHAPTER FIFTY-TWO

Convinced by the twin barrels of the shotgun to kneel beside Penelope at the edge of the clearing, Frankie let his hands be pulled behind his back and bound with the other end of the rope that tied him to his old friend.

The ritual began over. This time with a fifth member of the party. Jack the groundsman took his place at the stone before Mona's feet. Both Frankie and Penelope looked on, incredulous and alarmed, as Lord Grafton led the chanting.

"I should have known something like this would happen with you involved, Frankie Black," Penelope whispered, keeping her mouth still to avoid being silenced by the groundsman.

"How did you know where to find me?"

"Your latest girlfriend called me. What were you hoping I would do? Save you?"

Shaking his head in regret, Frankie tore his eyes from the circle of stones and men to the anguished looks of help from Mona in the flickering light. He could only return the look with failure and sorrow as he struggled against the rope.

"She said you had worked it out. She told me the story was mine for the taking. I didn't think I'd be *part* of the story."

The chanting began again. Lord Grafton led as before and the four men around him replied in unison.

Blindly, Frankie found the loose end of the rope with his fingers and closed his eyes as he felt the knot, tracing the path of the rope. But it was a good knot, firm and unmoving.

The torches lowered to light Mona's body. From where Frankie knelt, the circle of blood on her chest glistened, bright and clear in the glow of the flames.

"Tell me you have a plan, Frankie. What is it?"

He stopped struggling and closed his eyes to think above the mayhem.

The usual calm composure and almost seductive tone that Frankie knew her for was gone. In its place, fear had her gripped. It was etched in her voice, her pale skin, and wide eyes.

"So we die here, Frankie? Is that it? Aren't you even going to try and save that poor girl?"

He knew she was trying to agitate him, trying to wake the emotion inside him so he'd fight harder.

"The legend has it that the sacrificed disappear never to be seen again," said Frankie.

The chanting stopped.

"No bodies?"

"Nothing."

"Are you telling me there's someone out there watching? Waiting for them to disappear so he can take us away? Who is it, Frankie? You're not telling me everything."

"I've got my suspicions."

"Do you think it's one of them?" She gestured with her head and flicked her eyes at the five men.

But Frankie neither confirmed nor denied her question. The mystery was still unravelling in his mind and he needed to voice his thoughts as they came.

"Someone who knows loss."

Frankie watched as the first of the flames disappeared into the forest.

"But where is he?"

"Where would you go to get rid of a body?"

"I'm not following."

"Somewhere you could chop a body up into small parts without having to be questioned about the blood?"

Then the procession of flames cut through the forest. The last man to leave was Lord Grafton. He gave Frankie a winning look as he ran his hand across Mona's body and she writhed against his touch, her voice too hoarse to scream.

"We thank you for your sacrifice, Mr Black. Grafton will be safe for a while with such a pure and honest spirit such as yours to offer. Of that, I'm quite sure."

He disappeared through the stones before Frankie could reply, his flaming torch leaving a fading light in his wake.

"Now what? Where's your girlfriend? Can't she help?"

Penelope hissed more than spoke as if she blamed him for her position and expected Frankie to come up with a solution.

"That's what I'm worried about, Penelope."

"This is no time for ambiguity, Frankie."

"Let's just say, whoever the killer is, we'll find out soon enough."

"Not if I can help it."

She watched the final torch disappear into the forest. Then, grimacing with pain, her body tightened. She squeezed her eyes closed with concentration then eased her hand from the loop of rope around her wrists and flexed her fingers in front of her. She rubbed her tiny wrist as she looked across at Frankie with a broad and guilty grin.

Frankie felt his jaw slacken in surprise at her tenacity.

"Escape and evasion, Frankie. You taught me that yourself."

In a flash, she released her left hand and untied the rope around her ankles. Then she set to work on Frankie's bindings.

"It's a shame. On any other occasion, having the mighty Frankie Black trussed and helpless would be the topic of any girl's dream."

"Just get me out of this, Penelope."

He felt the knot give and the bindings on his wrist release, and he exhaled long and deep as he brought his arms to his front and nursed the abrasions. He checked around them, listening for movement, then instructed Penelope to untie Mona. He tossed her his jacket to cover the girl's modesty.

Penelope caught the jacket but stood still.

"Where are you going?"

She looked scared, the triumph of her rescue already over. The shift of power had returned to Frankie, who searched the surrounding darkness, considering his options.

"I'm going to find Hope. Get Mona to the main road and call the police."

Without waiting for a response, he ran into the trees, running up the gentle climb to the path he had used when he had carried a dying Beth in his arms. He burst onto the road opposite the Red Lion and found only silence and calm. The village was ignorant of the sickening events that had just taken place in the woods.

A window shattered far off to his left and

broke the silence. Leaving Penelope to tend to Mona, Frankie ran towards the sound.

He reached the butchers in time to hear the sound of destruction from inside. Frankie slammed the heel of his boot into the door. He stumbled into the shop and fell to the hard floor. Searching for what had tripped him, in the half-light, he saw a body.

Long hair and soft skin. A small frame.

He raised the woman's head to see her in the moonlight. For the tiniest of moments, his heart stopped as the light found the outline of Jane's perfect face.

Her eyes opened, revealing two black holes, dilated and vacant.

"Jane, it's me." Frankie pulled the hair from her face, smoothing it behind her ear.

She whispered, summoning all the energy she could, "I failed, Frankie. I tried to be good. I tried to save her."

"You did fine, Jane. Stay with me. Keep talking."

"I couldn't stop him. I wasn't strong enough."

"You did fine. Don't say that. You worked it out before I did. Where is he?"

Before she could answer, and as her eyes

closed, exhausted from the effort, there was a crash of pans and broken glass from the back room.

He lowered Jane's head to the floor and kissed her forehead, and then burst through the rear door in time to catch the wrist of a bloodied hand held high and gripping a cleaver with all its might.

Hope Gilmour peered up at him, panting, wild and ferocious in fear. Her face was red with blood spatter and a fresh wound across her forehead ran into her eye.

Frankie squeezed his hand on her arm and she looked at him, pleading for him to let her finish it. She tensed, but he held her. She fought, but Frankie held fast.

And as her muscles relaxed, she slumped and her head hung forward with fatigue and trauma. Her grip loosened and the cleaver fell to the floor with a harmless clatter of steel.

But beyond her tangled mass of hair was not the man Frankie expected to find. The conversations with Lord Grafton and Jane all came flooding back in lightning flashes of memories.

Beneath her, dazed, blinded with blood,

and condemned, was the broken body of
Grant Price.

CHAPTER FIFTY-THREE

The paramedic finished applying a bandage to Hope's head and nodded at her warmly. He checked her eyes once more with a small torch, pulling her head from side to side to check for concussion.

"Are you okay to walk?"

She looked away from him and through to the men in front of the butchers tending to somebody with far worse injuries than herself.

"I'll be fine. You should see to her."

Her ordeal had climaxed, leaving her weak and unstable on her feet, but she stood with the man's help and followed him out to the roadside, where the scene before her struck with the power of a cannonball.

She doubled, clutching her stomach, but it wasn't a physical pain that she felt. It was the heartfelt stares of the people who had gathered and were still gathering, to watch as word of the incident spread.

She thought of the hole, the darkness, and the hollow. The dark eyes that stared up at her from the walls.

She thought of Beth, her scream, and the time they had shared.

How her death had been for nothing. Her story of how she had saved the man from suicide. How entwined that man had been with Hope's own life.

And she thought of Mona.

She called to the paramedic, tugging on his coveralls as he opened the rear doors of an ambulance for her.

"There's another girl. In a hole somewhere. She'll be scared. We must find her."

She stared across at the woods, dark and foreboding, but the events had blurred any sense of direction.

"She's in there somewhere. We have to find her."

The paramedic studied her face. He pulled open the door, peeked inside, and then returned to her, opening the space up for her to see.

"Would the girl in question be called Mona by any chance?"

Hope felt relief wash through her. She felt the panic in her face drop.

"Yes."

He gave a quick look around for his colleagues.

"I shouldn't do this but..."

He pulled open the rear doors, and there, wrapped in a red blanket and wearing a pair of green paramedic coveralls, was Mona. She was sitting on the edge of a gurney looking lost and forlorn, her face stained with tears and sadness.

"Mona?"

There was no recognition in her eyes. Only a hope that the voice she had heard belonged to the girl.

"Is that you?" she breathed.

Nodding, Hope leapt up the steps and flung her arms around the girl, feeling her grin spread from ear to ear like the blossoming of a flower. She felt the warmth of Mona's tear on her cheek and she pulled away to look at her.

"Are you hurt?"

Unable to talk, her throat clogged with emotion, Mona shook her head. She coughed then smiled, which bloomed into a laugh of joy and revealed her chest. A single plaster had been fixed to her skin.

"A small cut. Plus these." She showed the sores on her wrists and ankles that mirrored Hope's own injuries. "I never thought I'd see you again."

"I'm so sorry I left. I had to. It was our only chance."

"It's okay. It's fine. We made it. I knew you would."

"Oh, Mona. There's so much I have to tell you."

"It's time to go, girls." The ambulance driver was beaming. He held the door open for Hope to climb down, perhaps sensing that their chat would be a long one. "You can catch her at the hospital."

"Wait," said Mona.

Hope turned at the step, glad for the opportunity to talk to someone who understood what they had been through.

"You never told me your name."

In a fraction of a second, Hope ran

through the conversations from the hole. It was true.

"My name is Hope." It was all she could say without spilling out all she had to say. But Mona held her for one last moment.

"Hope?"

"Yes? What is it?" She hung on Mona's every word.

"The girl before you. The girl who showed you the way."

It was a conversation that Hope had wanted to keep until the end, when they had shared the happiness and joy of survival, and she had shared how Mona's story had changed her life.

"I'm sorry, Mona."

"It was her, wasn't it? I could feel it in your expression somehow. I don't know how. But when I spoke of her, when I told you my friend had saved Jacob's life, I felt you change. I'm right, aren't I? God, I wish I was wrong. But I know I'm right. It was her scream we heard that night."

"I'm sorry, Mona." They exchanged pitiful glances but Hope couldn't meet her stare for long. "It was Beth."

She squeezed Mona's foot and, with the

help of the paramedic, dropped down to the ground.

"I'll see you at the hospital. I'll come and find you. I promise."

Mona nodded. Her smile was a facade of bravery set on a wall of emotion that could crumble at any moment.

And the paramedic closed the door.

Hope watched as the ambulance pulled away and the uniformed police removed the barrier to allow the vehicle through. There was a struggle taking place at the boundary. Two officers were helping someone through the crowd. They lifted the tape for him and the man ducked under, searching the scene, frantic in his movements.

It was as if time stood still for that moment only.

The commotion around them blurred.

The noise fell to a dreamlike hum.

And then he saw her.

She had never felt so lost and alone. So sorrowful. So guilty. But, at the same time, so very pleased to see him.

Her father ran to her and she smiled. But the smile broke down her barrier and tears began to well up in her eyes once more. Her legs began to shake with violence, and just as he reached her and wrapped his arms around her, they gave.

Her father took the full weight of Hope's body, and she made no effort to stand, happy to feel him against her, happy to be wanted by him, undeserved as the love might be. All her effort went into the strongest hug she could summon.

"Are you okay? Are you hurt?"

She couldn't reply. Her throat tightened and all she could do was squeeze.

"I missed you, sweetheart. I'm sorry for everything. I should have been there. I should have done more."

"No."

Her tone was aggressive. She heard it. She felt the strength in his arms loosen their grip in disappointment.

"No, Dad. I'm so sorry. I've been terrible. You did everything you ever could have done and more. It's me who should be sorry."

Her words seemed to appease him. He hushed her and ran his hand through her hair, kissing her cheek and holding her close.

"It's over now. You're safe."

But there was a clatter of metal from inside the shop. Two ambulance men appeared pushing a gurney through the gap. To Hope's relief, the patient's eyes were wide open, taking in the scene.

"Dad?"

His head was buried in her shoulder, hiding his own tears and emotion as he often did.

"Yes, sweetheart. What is it?"

"There's someone I want you to meet."

She had been covered with a sheet, save for her face, but her eyes were open and her head bandaged in a similar fashion to Hope's.

Finding strength in the sight, Hope ran from her father's embrace to the woman's side. She walked with her as the paramedics pushed the gurney across the road.

The crowd around them fell silent and cameras flashed at the first sight of the final victim.

Her father came to stand by her side. Hope turned to find her father lost in a memory, a horrified expression on his face.

"Dad?"

But he was dumbstruck, searching for something, a clue or recognition.

And then it happened.

It was as if a light had been flicked on in her father's mind. Hope knew that a memory they would never ever tell her was being shared by them in silence. In her father's mind, Hope imagined a fight of good and evil, imagining how someone as pretty, angelic, and helpless as her could have been labelled evil. He would be questioning his own mind, doubting the reasoning behind every thought he'd had since the night they'd shared so long ago.

"Get away from her."

"No, Dad wait-"

"She's evil. Get her away."

Hope glanced at her mother in time to catch the expression of understanding on her face, as if she deserved her father's reaction.

"Dad?"

He stopped, unwilling to let her hand go, and Hope moved closer to her mother.

"Dad, you're wrong."

"You don't know her."

"And neither do you, Dad. She's not evil. And nor am I. You don't know what I've been through, and I don't even know if I can ever tell you."

She paused, fighting the urge to cry again,

trying to be strong, trying not to let her father see her crack. But the harder she fought it, the hotter her eyes burned. The further away she pushed them, the clearer the memories became. The swirling pool of her darkest moments dizzied her until her father reached out and touched her arm.

Hope pulled away then stopped. She was alone again. Only two steps from her father and her mother, she could have been a hundred miles from them. She was alone. The swelling in her throat could restrain it no more.

She reached out to her father, searching for him through the layer of tears across her eyes, and his hand came to her, solid and strong as if she was being pulled along a river, and he was the bough that reached from the bank.

And she caught him. That touch. That fatherly tenderness that she'd so often taken for granted. And the warmth that she'd so often ridiculed.

She broke. Hot tears of sorrow, guilt, and regret warmed her face.

And he pulled her in.

"It's okay, Hope. It's okay."

He held her. She'd never felt his strength before and she wanted more. She needed more. Her face buried into his jacket and his kiss found the crown of her head, soft and warmed by his breath.

She spoke through her tears, incoherent even to herself.

"I'm sorry, Dad."

"Shhh. You don't need to say-"

"Yes, I do." She pulled her head away to feel the cool air on her face but clung to him. She looked between them, her mother and her father, and there was hope. "I do need to. There's so much I need to say. But in time."

"You've been through a lot."

"But I promise you this, Dad. Whatever you thought I was, however bad I might have been, it's all in the past. The fact that I'm standing here right now is because of her, my mother. People change, Dad."

She smiled between her parents and laughed, although she was unsure why. Taking both their hands in her own, her tears were borne of something new, something unashamed and proud.

"Please, Dad. Give her a chance. Give us both a chance."

It was the expression in his face that said everything that needed to be said. There was relief that his daughter was safely by his side, and that, for the first time, he could see the love in her eyes.

"Dad?"

Hope stared at him, waiting for his response. For a moment, she doubted the look in his eyes and the decision he was about to make, and those few seconds hung from her heart like a lead weight.

Her father said nothing. He searched her mother's eyes for some sign that what Hope had said was real.

And then he stopped searching.

Hope startled when he let go of her hand, fearing he would leave, but he remained and the seconds ticked by like hours once again.

But he smiled, turning to each of them once with clarity in his eyes. Then he nodded, and together, for the first time in all of Hope's life, her father, her mother, and their daughter embraced.

CHAPTER FIFTY-FOUR

The scene was tender.

Stronger than anything Frankie could articulate but as soft and gentle as only true love can be. It warmed Frankie to think of Jake and the times they had shared with his mum.

From above the shoulders of his daughter and her mother, Jeremy Gilmour blinked away the tears and found Frankie. He held him there, fixed in a stare of gratitude, then softened and absorbed his family in an embrace.

Frankie glanced up at the stars and thought of Jacqui. A part of him hoped she would be looking down on him, proud that he had brought a family together in the wake of his own desperate loss.

But if she wasn't, well, that would be okay too. She would be there when his time came.

The peace and calm of the ancient village had gone. The road through Grafton had been blocked at both ends by police cars. Blue lights danced across the woods that framed the village, joining those from the ambulances that were parked outside Price's Butchers. The blue lights shone through the broken window.

Grant Price was held between two uniformed policemen. Paramedics had bandaged his arm and folded it into a sling and there was blood smeared across his face from the wounds that Hope had inflicted, reminding Frankie of photos he'd seen of soldiers who had been blinded by mustard gas. He was cuffed and Officer Thorn was calling for a secure unit, announcing to the operator that there were five suspects to bring in, all highly dangerous. The boy appeared remorseless, unaware of his actions and how they had altered the lives of so many, but he met Frankie's stare with a lapse in his facade. He stared at Frankie, cold and hard, with bitterness in his eyes.

At the ambulance in front of him, Jane was being loaded in and, despite her father's objections, Hope followed. To his surprise, she pulled Jeremy in behind her.

A family, estranged and each with their own journeys behind and ahead of them.

Frankie wished them well. He wished that one good thing would come of the tragedy and that Hope and her family might find some connection during their healing.

Then another sensation. He smelled her scent before he saw her or heard her heels as she stepped up behind him. He felt her stand next to him and, though he didn't turn to see her, he knew she would be smiling.

"That was touching."

Frankie ignored the sentiment. He knew that beneath the perfectly formed face and wild hair, there was a force much stronger than love within Penelope Pike. The story was always held higher than compassion or sentiment.

"I promised you the exclusive." In his peripheral, Frankie saw her eyes widen in horror at his statement. "It doesn't get much more exclusive than this. I thought you'd be conducting interviews by now."

"I could have been killed, Frankie. I don't think that's any call for celebration. Besides I'm waiting for my crew. They're on their way."

"Well, when they get here, you could do better than to interview that guy." He nodded at Detective Inspector Thorn.

"He's the one that arrested you, isn't he? I saw him at the police station. What's he done?"

"I don't know. But he's corrupt. I'll leave you to find out the details."

"A corrupt policeman? That's not much compensation for nearly being killed, Frankie."

"You were never really in any danger, Penelope. The whole thing is a myth."

They both stared at the boy.

"Why did he do it? He killed his own sister?"

"He was brainwashed from childhood. He grew up listening to tales and legends from Lord Grafton. That's enough to warp the mind of any kid. He'll spend the rest of his life in a secure unit for the mentally ill. He'll probably be on the same wing as Lord Grafton. They're both as insane as each other."

"How did you know it was him?"

"The truth?" Frankie wanted to lie. He wanted to tell her he'd suspected the boy all along. But the fact was that Grant Price had remained so far from Frankie's radar and Lord Grafton had been such a key player in his investigation that he hadn't even given the boy a second thought. He'd been so preoccupied with his own state of mental health that he'd failed to look further than the easiest solution, the boy's father. "I didn't."

"Why do you think he did it? Surely not just derangement?"

"No. His sister was his first. I think he developed a taste for death. A curiosity." Frankie stared at the boy, who had returned to his expression of an innocent and ignorant child. "I think that somewhere inside that cold shell, he believes the legend to be true. He's smarter than he gives off. Grafton and his men kept feeding girls to the legend and Grant would have heard their plans. He would have been the only one outside of their little circle that knew about it. I think Lord Grafton is the deranged one. He was so lost in the fear that he would lose his status, he couldn't see the killer right beneath his nose."

Between the ambulances, police cars had formed a protective circle. Neighbouring villagers had gathered and were held back by uniformed police, one of whom was pulling the police tape to mark the boundary of the crime scene. Cameras flashed and people shouted abuse at Lord Grafton who, in the wake of his undoing, had been handcuffed and led through the village from the manor house to the scene outside the butchers. He held his head high and resolute, and found Frankie's stare, returning it with his own cold and bitter sneer in contrast to the glory smile he had offered Frankie when he had left him to die.

Behind him, his counterparts followed, equally handcuffed and guarded by a handful of armed police.

Jack the groundsman was second in the line with his eyes cast to the ground, trailing after Lord Grafton's feet, following his master's path for perhaps the last time. His huge shoulders were slumped but his face remained void of any emotion.

Barry Armstrong followed with his head hung low, and then Wainwright the baker, who tried to turn as he walked, offering consolation to John Jones, the grocer, who was openly crying in remorse and calling out his defence.

"We didn't mean any harm. We were doing a good thing. Isn't that right?"

His cries went unanswered by the policemen, who each glared at them with distaste and astonishment. One of them shoved Wainwright to straighten up and to stop him from turning around. The public spat and verbalised their disgust. Many of them were either holding babies or the hands of small children of their own.

The men halted beside a police car, adjacent to Grant Price who watched with curiosity at the fall of the greatest power he had ever known. But instead of remorse showing itself on the killer's face, he displayed the gormless expression of a young man devoid of compassion or understanding. It was as if he was studying the faces of the men who had, through ill-guided miscomprehension, been feeding his sick habit. He was quizzical.

His head was cocked to one side.

Frankie followed his gaze as, one by one, the prisoners lined up and cast their own savage looks his way.

"Something's wrong."

Penelope, who had been watching the Gilmour family being loaded into the ambulance and biting her lower lip, looked up at him.

"What is it?"

"A man is missing."

Penelope looked at the men but Frankie didn't need her confirmation. He glanced left along the street towards the pub, peering over the heads of the masses that had come to see the spectacle, and then right towards the church and the manor house.

But the answer he was looking for came from behind.

A heavy boot pounded through the butcher's shop door.

The policemen startled and turned to see the commotion as Frankie pulled Penelope to one side, covering her head with his hand.

The armed police that were guarding the prisoners turned and raised their weapons, and Thorn bellowed his command.

"Put the weapon down."

"Why did you do it?"

The question was angry and aimed at Grant Price, who showed fear for the first time. The officers either side of him held him tight and Thorn issued more commands.

"Put the weapon down, sir. I won't tell you again."

The shotgun that was nestled into the man's shoulder dropped and he held it loose, his finger still poised over the trigger and his shoulders slumped in defeat. Then his voice broke.

"Why? Why did you have to kill her?"

His voice whined, his throat was thick with emotion, and his eyes burned a fiery red. It was the same fiery red that Frankie had seen in the graveyard.

It was the first time Frankie had heard the boy talk. His voice, as Frankie's suspicions alluded, was intelligent and articulate, and his eyes were cold and proud. He turned once to Lord Grafton, who looked on with horror but, after a pause, nodded once in response, as if permitting the boy to speak.

The crowd was silent and tense.

The boy turned, letting his hollow stare wash across all who looked on until he found the face of his father, who pleaded with his son with streaming eyes.

"Why, Son? Why?"

The proud smile that spread over Grant Price's face washed away the gormless expression.

"Simple. I wanted to be a legend."

It was as Officer Thorn issued his third and final warning that three things happened.

Jim Price fired both barrels of his shotgun.

The armed police opened fire, each of them firing three rounds into Jim's body.

And, at the hand of his own broken father, Grant Price's chest exploded.

Both father and son were dead before their bodies hit the ground.

CHAPTER FIFTY-FIVE

A pale, blue sky hung behind soft, gentle, white clouds. Oaks, elms, and sycamores, thick with summer and green with life, framed a mysterious collection of large stones. The space between each stone, which were taller and broader than most men, had been filled by much smaller and flatter rocks to form low dry-stone walls.

In the centre of the circle was a mound of earth, which was covered in well-maintained grass, tended to by local authorities and heritage groups. But the focus of every visitor to the Addleton long barrow that day, and most days, was the dark hollow formed by stones that disappeared into the centre of the mound.

"It's so dark inside."

Jake stood, entranced and searching the dark hole for some kind of detail or clue as to what lay inside.

"What's in there?"

"It's a resting place, Jake."

Tom, always fast with his mind, was the first to think of a suitable response to give a young boy.

"Like a bed, you mean? It doesn't look very nice. It's dark inside."

"Similar to a bed," said Tom. "It's a place where people can come and remember others. Like the pyramids in your video game."

"Remember who? Dead people?"

Tom and Frankie shared a surprised look and Frankie nodded, confirming that his father-in-law should continue. The boy was old enough to know a little more detail.

"That's right. It's where people can enjoy some peace and remember all the good times they had. Death doesn't have to be sad."

Sensing that the last comment was aimed at Frankie as well as his son, Frankie interjected.

"A long time ago, Jake, when somebody died, they were still part of people's lives. They still talked to them every day and they went to see them. They believed that when somebody died in this world, their lives began in another. So having somewhere to go and talk to them was like a connection between the two worlds."

The boy examined the tall stones at the perimeter of the barrow and ran his hand along the rock, feeling the edge that somebody, three thousand years before, had shaped with primitive tools.

"Is Mummy in a new world then?"

He spoke without looking at either of them, fascinated by the structure, and although Frankie knew the conversation would lead to Jacqui, there was no way he could have been ready for it.

"Yes. Yes, she is."

"And is she happy there?"

It was an easy question to answer. Frankie stepped forward and crouched beside his son. The palm of his hand was flat against the stone as if he too was searching for a connection or trying to feel the other world.

"Did you ever see your mum angry or sad?"

Jake shook his head.

"I like to think that Mummy will be happy whichever world she's in," said Frankie. "Don't you?"

Jake nodded.

"And I like to think that wherever Mummy is, she's making somebody smile. Do you remember how she could always make you smile?"

Again, the boy nodded.

"Even when I hurt my knee."

Jake touched his leg as if remembering the incident and, for the first time, he looked up at Frankie.

"So can we talk to her?"

As if sensing Frankie's unease, Tom stepped forward. He hung back but his presence made it easier for Frankie.

"Of course we can. But you have to remember, this place was built a long time ago."

"How long?"

"Three thousand years ago."

"Isn't that before Jesus was born?"

"Yes. A long time before Jesus. But they

believed different things then. They didn't know what we know now."

"Like what?"

He knew what he wanted to say, but phrasing the words with enough detail for Jake to understand and limiting his sentence to avoid upsetting the boy was hard.

Tom nodded.

"Well, ancient man used to come to places like this to talk to their relatives. We would come to a place like this to talk to Mummy if we lived three thousand years ago too."

"I don't like it. It's too dark."

"Exactly. But we don't live three thousand years ago. We live now. And we know that we don't need to be in a place like this to talk to Mummy. We can talk to her anywhere and she will hear us."

"Anywhere?"

"Of course. Everywhere you go, your mummy is watching over you. Everything you do, your mummy sees."

"And I can talk to her?"

"Yes." Frankie laughed for the first time in too long. "She won't always reply but she'll hear you. We might not be able to see her anymore, and she might not be in the kitchen when we wake up in the morning, but she's there. And guess what?"

"What?"

The boy was searching the sky as if hoping she might be watching over them as they spoke.

"I know she's smiling."

Jake laughed too. Not a lot, but enough to let Frankie know that the conversation wasn't too deep.

"She was always smiling, Daddy. I'm going to talk to her every day."

"Good. Because I do too."

"And me." Tom took the place on the other side of Jake. He bent to one knee, using the stone to support his body. He spoke to Jake but looked at Frankie. "I talk to her every day. She is always in our hearts. Every one of us. You, your daddy, and me, and Grandma too."

"Do you think she's looking down at us right now?"

"Of course she is."

"How do you know?"

Talking through the medium of the boy, Frankie replied to Tom to let him know he was okay. "Well, you know I went away for a little while?"

"Yes. You said it was work."

"It kind of was and it kind of wasn't. The truth is, Jake, I spent a week looking for Mummy. I thought I'd lost her. I came all the way here to Lincolnshire to find her."

"And did you find her?"

The boy's face was a little panicked as if he was frightened his mother would be gone. He stared at the stone in front of him to hide the wetness in his eyes.

Frankie, looking past Jake to his father-in-law, found Tom's eyes moist and reddening. His lower lip trembled in anticipation of Frankie's response.

"Yes. She was with me all along. I looked in barrows like this one. I searched in forests and fields. I even searched in the hearts of others and I couldn't find her. But then I realised..."

"Realised what, Daddy?"

"I realised that all I have to do is close my eyes and she's there. Wherever I am. Try it. Close your eyes."

Together, the two men and the little boy crouched beside the three-thousand-year-old monument and closed their eyes. Tom reached for their hands and they connected.

There was a silence while Frankie waited for Jake to announce his thoughts. And Jacqui smiled at him, from a market stall in Bombay, from the Grand Mosque in Abu Dhabi, and from beneath her favourite wide-brimmed hat on a beach in the Maldives.

But the boy said nothing.

Holding onto her image for a moment longer, Frankie savoured her smiling face as she looked back at him from a pavement in London. A rock in a river of suits.

Tom squeezed each of their hands to bring the memory to a close and they opened their eyes. He spoke to Jake, his tone excited and happy in contrast to the difficult conversation they had just navigated.

"Did you see her?"

Jake was quiet. He wasn't sad or forlorn but appeared content, musing on a thought.

They stood and headed back to the car park. Tom's blue Jaguar was parked by the entrance. Parked at the far end was an old Vauxhall. A woman stood leaning on the bonnet. She wore a short, dark jacket, jeans, and tan boots. She watched them as they left the fenced-off heritage site.

Tom caught Frankie's gaze with a furrowed brow and flicked his eyes down at the boy, showing a little concern for Jake's silence.

But the boy spoke gently and with a wise maturity that eased their concerns.

"I saw her, I think."

They walked on with Jake in the middle. He reached for both of their hands again and pulled them close.

"And you were right, Dad."

"I was?"

"Yes. She was smiling. Just as I remember her."

Tom was the first to laugh. He ruffled Jake's hair and unlocked the car. Jake opened the rear door and climbed in. As Frankie watched him pull his seatbelt across, and Tom slid into the driver's seat, the woman he'd seen called out to him.

"Frankie Black?"

Frankie hesitated then turned to face her, stepping out of earshot of his son and meeting the woman mid-stride. She approached with caution and took furtive glances over her shoulder, afraid of something.

He said nothing, waiting for the woman to continue. His expression confirmed his name but he offered no further prompt.

The woman appeared to be in her mid-fifties. Age lines were taking root on her face and heavy bags hung beneath her eyes. Frankie recognised the look. The sleepless nights, the dishevelled hair, and the lost eyes that seemed to search for hope.

Her voice reflected her appearance. Frankie softened. He'd been there. He'd worn that same look not so long ago.

"I hear you're a man who knows how to find people."

The End.

Also by J.D. Weston

Award-winning author and creator of Harvey Stone and Frankie Black, J.D.Weston was born in London, England, and after more than a decade in the Middle East, now enjoys a tranquil life in Lincolnshire with his wife.

The Harvey Stone series is the prequel series set ten years before The Stone Cold Thriller series.

With more than twenty novels to J.D. Weston's name, the Harvey Stone series is the result of many years of storytelling, and is his finest work to date. You can find more about J.D. Weston at www.jdweston.com.

Turn the page to see his other books.

Free Novella

The game is death. The winners takes all...

See www.jdweston.com for details.

The Silent Man

To find the killer, he must lose his mind...

See www.jdweston.com for details.

The Spider's Web

To catch the killer, he must become the fly...

See www.jdweston.com for details.

The Mercy Kill

To light the way, he must burn his past...

See www.jdweston.com for details.

The Savage Few

Coming 2021

Join the J.D. Weston Reader Group to stay up to date on new releases, receive discounts, and get three free eBooks.

See www.jdweston.com for details.

THE STONE COLD THRILLER SERIES

The Stone Cold Thriller Series

Stone Cold

Stone Fury

Stone Fall

Stone Rage

Stone Free

Stone Rush

Stone Game

Stone Raid

Stone Deep

Stone Fist

Stone Army

Stone Face

The Stone Cold Box Sets

Boxset One

Boxset Two

Boxset Three

Boxset Four

Visit www.jdweston.com for details.

THE FRANKIE BLACK FILES

The Frankie Black Files

Torn in Two

Her Only Hope

Black Blood

The Frankie Black Files Boxset

Visit www.jdweston.com for details.

www.ingramcontent.com/pod-product-compliance
Lightning Source LLC
Chambersburg PA
CBHW060722190726
48285CB00001B/24